IN THE DARK

Deborah Moggach is the author of many successful novels including, most recently, *These Foolish Things* and *Tulip Fever*. Her screenplays include the film of *Pride and Prejudice*, which was nominated for a BAFTA. She lives in North London.

ALSO BY DEBORAH MOGGACH

DEBORAH MOGGACH

In the Dark

VINTAGE BOOKS
London

Published by Vintage 2008

6 8 10 9 7 5

Copyright © Deborah Moggach, 2007

Deborah Moggach had asserted her right under the Copyright, Designs
and Patents Act 1988 to be identified as the authors of this work

First published in Great Britain in 2007 by Chatto & Windus

Vintage
Random House, 20 Vauxhall Bridge Road,
London SW1V 2SA

www.vintage-books.co.uk

Addresses for companies within The Random House Group Limited
can be found at: www.randomhouse.co.uk/offices.htm

The Random House Group Limited Reg. No. 954009

A CIP catalogue record for this book
is available from the British Library

ISBN 9780099507123

The Random House Group Limited supports The Forest
Stewardship Council (FSC), the leading international forest
certification organisation. All our titles that are printed on
Greenpeace approved FSC certified paper carry the FSC logo.
Our paper procurement policy can be found at
www.rbooks.co.uk/environment

Printed in the UK by CPI Bookmarque, Croydon, CR0 4TD

To the memory of my grandmother, Helen, and her first husband Tommy, who was killed in action in 1918.

Prologue

1916

The lights are going out all over Europe; we shall not see them lit again in our lifetime.

Sir Edward Grey, 1914

It was a dank day in March when the telegram came. Ralph, who was fourteen, was sitting in his bedroom looking at the bust enlargement pictures. Such was his absorption that he heard nothing, neither the dog barking nor the doorbell jangling, downstairs in the hall.

He had retrieved the magazine from beneath his mattress, where he kept it hidden from his mother and Winnie, the only people who would possibly come into his room when he wasn't there. Mr Boyce Argyle, who lived on the top floor, had given it to him. Ralph had a deep admiration for Boycie, who was eighteen years old and something of a dandy. By day he was an upholsterer but at night he became a man about town, issuing forth in his canary-yellow waistcoat and returning smelling of cigars. There was nothing about women that Boycie didn't know and he had given Ralph some tips for the future, along with the magazine. Ralph had had it in his possession for some months now. His shame at its

1

possible discovery made him blush at unpredictable moments – a meeting on the stairs with one of the lodgers on their way to the bathroom; a glance from some passer-by in the street. They must know what he had been doing; it must be written on his face.

How I Enlarged My Bust Six Inches in Thirty Days. The advertisement showed a sequence of pictures: the same woman, whose expressionless face gave no sign of the miracle she was experiencing. Her chest, flat in the left-hand picture, swelled as she was repeated across the page. It swelled as if inflated by an invisible pump. *I had tried Pills, Massage, Wooden Cups, and Various Advertised Preparations Without the Slightest Results.* Such was its size in the final image that were she real the woman would surely topple over; her bodice strained at its bulk. *With what pity must every man look at every woman who presents to him a flat chest – a chest like his own. Can such a woman inspire in a man those feelings and emotions which can only be inspired by a real and true woman, a woman with a beautiful well-rounded bust?*

Every few minutes the window panes rattled as a train passed; Ralph's room was at the back of the house, and overshadowed by the massive brick viaduct that carried the railway to London Bridge Station. The sounds of normal life however seemed very far away.

Even the dog seemed to know that Ralph was engaged in a shameful activity. The appearance of the magazine had prompted Brutus to slink out of the room and go downstairs, presumably to join Ralph's mother who was in the parlour. Though something of a relief, this deepened Ralph's sense of mortification; since his father had gone, the dog had attached himself to Ralph, padding around behind him and sleeping beside his bed. Their mutual comfort had been a sustaining bond over the past two years. But the dog knew, as Ralph's mother must surely know. They knew that upstairs in his bedroom, the doors to his mother's room firmly closed, Ralph was experiencing the same warmth in his private parts that he had first felt at the age of ten, when looking at a picture of the sinking *Titanic*.

A beautiful, well-rounded bust. As the woman gazed at Ralph, it dawned on him with dismay that she bore a distinct resemblance to his mother. The same handsome hauteur, the same challenging stare – indeed, she wore a remarkably similar blouse. And though it didn't bear thinking about, his mother too was possessed of an ample chest. Ralph couldn't have helped noticing this; it was not as if he especially looked. Her figure was there for everyone to see. But one night, when he was ill, she had bent over him in her nightdress and he had seen the two globes that by day had been united as a chest; he had glimpsed the mysterious darkness of the valley between them, the most secret place on earth, and the most forbidden.

So Ralph didn't hear the doorbell, or Brutus barking. When the news of his father's death arrived, he was thinking of his mother's bosom.

*

Nor did Winnie, the maid, answer the bell. She was downstairs in the kitchen, mixing suet, and her hands were greasy. Besides, her mistress was upstairs in the parlour, which was nearer the front door. Mrs Clay was labouring over the accounts. Winnie could sense the stillness, the concentration, through the floorboards. They creaked when Mrs Clay rose to collect some papers from the sideboard, and creaked again when she returned to her chair. Winnie could almost hear the dog shifting and sighing as he adjusted his position at his mistress's feet. Winnie's sense was finely tuned; it was the skill she needed to survive in this world. She could tell, before knocking on a door, the mood within. The house, the five floors of it, thrummed with its human cargo.

Mrs Clay had a good head for figures. In fact, even when her husband was at home she had organised the household finances, Mr Clay being something of a dreamer. A dear man, Winnie thought, but disconnected from the realities of life. However, for better or worse he had brought home a wage. Now he was gone to the war and money was short. Over the past months Winnie had grown closer to her mistress – not intimates, Mrs Clay didn't encourage that, but they had established a kind of solidarity. The charwoman had left, to work in the munitions factory in the Gray's Inn Road, and that had meant that Winnie and Mrs Clay had to do all the housework themselves, with the help of the boy. Winnie suspected that her mistress had hoped for better things in life but the war had put paid to that, as it had to so many things. So they cooked and cleaned for the lodgers, trudging up and down the four flights of stairs; they waged their own battle against the soot that, even with the windows closed, fell noiselessly, speckling the surfaces minutes after they had been polished. Winnie was a country girl, she had had no idea of this enemy's stealth.

The trains made it worse. They belched out smoke which fell into every crevice and settled on the curtains like black fur. Though travelling by train was a thrilling thing, the railway did wreak havoc in a neighbourhood. Palmerston Road had been built as a street of terraced houses for the well-to-do. However, a few years later the railway line had been built; it sliced through it, demolishing its middle section, amputating the houses on either side and plunging the street into permanent twilight. Mr Clay, who knew about history, had told Winnie this. Soon after it happened the houses had fallen into disrepair; they had been divided up into lodgings whose inhabitants struggled to retain their respectability. And now conditions were worsening. The war, which they thought would soon be over, showed no signs of coming to an end. In fact news was arriving of U-boats sinking British ships, merchant ships importing food; butter and sugar were already short and people talked of rationing.

Winnie, however, had troubles of her own. Though loyal to Mrs Clay, on that particular afternoon she spared little thought for the housekeeping problems. Nor, indeed, for the vast and incomprehensible momentum of war. Archie was outside, whistling. How could Winnie possibly go to the door with her tormentor loitering in the street?

Winnie's usual view of passers-by was of their nether regions. She saw this through two sets of bars – the stout bars of the kitchen window and beyond them the railings. She didn't have time to be curious and, secure in her cage, seldom speculated about the upper halves of those who passed. The only legs that materialised into human beings belonged to the people with whom she was on familiar terms – the delivery men, who carried their parcels or heaved their goods down the steps and into her domain.

Some of the familiar faces had gone – Gyles, the young lad from the greengrocer's; the faintly threatening man who delivered the fish and whose name Winnie had never caught. They had disappeared, like so many men, and been replaced by younger boys.

One of these new arrivals was Archie, who had taken up a position at Mr Turk's butcher's shop on the Southwark High Road, where Mrs Clay had an account. Archie was seventeen years old but small for his age – a ginger-haired, wiry boy with a grin that lit up his face. He had taken to lingering for a cup of tea and a macaroon. When she asked if Mr Turk would be angry he shrugged; 'He can jump in the lake.' His cheek made Winnie laugh. 'Heard the one about the elephant and the Chinaman?' he asked, with a wink. How lumbering were her slow wits, compared to his battery of jokes! Winnie started to wait for the sounds of his arrival – his faint whistling, the clatter of his bicycle as he flung it against the railings. She darted to the mirror and tidied her hair. As the weeks passed a shy hope flickered in her breast. Surely he couldn't be sitting down in every kitchen he visited? Her heart thumped when she walked to the shop, to place Mrs Clay's order. It thumped in the hope that it might be Archie serving behind the counter, that she might glimpse him in the back room amongst the carcasses.

How could she have been so foolish? After the shock of what happened, the shock that sent her reeling, she realised how stupid she had been even to entertain the idea that somebody could form an attachment to her. Could even find her tolerable. At Sunday School she had learnt the Bible story, how Eve saw she was naked and was ashamed. She too had been blind, before she bit the apple.

So Winnie didn't go upstairs. She went into the scullery and washed her big red hands under the tap. Wiping them on her apron, she returned to the kitchen where the prunes waited to be chopped.

By now she had forgotten about the doorbell. Somewhere in the back of her mind she realised that Archie's whistling had stopped. He would have left, to play football. That was why he was loitering outside in the first place. It was nothing to do with Winnie, of course – it happened to be his half-day and he met his friends in Palmerston Road. They would move off, shuffling and shoving, to kick a ball around in the long dark tunnel of the railway arch.

Winnie, however, didn't feel relieved. The house was too silent. Ralph, who read books, had told her that in some foreign country people hung crickets in cages outside their front doors, to warn them of burglars. Crickets sang all the time, that was why; it was only when a stranger approached that they fell silent.

Winnie stood still, as alert as an animal sensing danger. Then she rushed to the door, drew its bolt, pushed it open and ran up the area steps. The street was empty. At one end, from the cavern of the arch, came the echoing whoops of the football game. At the other end, far in the distance, a telegram woman, on her bicycle, turned the corner and disappeared.

No sunlight penetrated the parlour where Eithne Clay sat, struggling over her accounts. The room faced north, with heavy drapes at the window; a half-lowered blind and gauzy netting veiled its occupants from passers-by. The wallpaper was a pattern of brown upon ochre, darkened by age and the smoke from countless lodgers' cigarettes. The massive mahogany sideboard, inherited from the previous tenants, sucked into its bulk any remaining light. When Eithne and her husband took over the lease he had planned to redecorate the room but when he considered the disruption – where would everybody eat? – a certain lassitude set in. That was Paul, through and through. His head was filled with dreams and schemes that seldom came to anything, because sooner or later something else would take his fancy and they quietly expired.

His latest enthusiasm had been snail-shell-collecting. The summer before war broke out he had taken the train to Box Hill, with Ralph and the dog, and come home with a bag of snail shells. The calcium in a chalk soil, he said, produced shells of the most delicate colours. Eithne had been in a sulk that Sunday, and hadn't accompanied them. She had long since forgotten the reason for her miff – no doubt some task he had left undone. What she did remember was her husband's boyish excitement on his return. The wonder of the shells! However closely you examined them, none was the same. Each a tiny miracle of creation, each so beautiful, with chocolate stripes against palest lemon, with black stripes against terracotta. Eithne should have been charmed but in truth she was exasperated. Where did snails get you? There was something of the amateur about her husband, he should have been born into the gentry which had a long tradition of useless hobbies. The brutal realities of life seemed to evade him.

These papers, spread over the table – they were the brutal realities. Paul, away in France, had no idea of their problems. She gave no hint of them in her letters for he must surely have other matters on his mind. At present his regiment was stationed near the Marne river, which was somewhere in northern France, planning an offensive. His letters, however, were relentlessly cheerful in tone: *We gave Fritz a pretty good bump this time! A rat, rifling through my kitbag, resembled Ralph exploring his Christmas stocking.*

On occasion Eithne felt that the hardships at home were at least equal to those suffered by the men who might be fighting for their country but who were removed from its daily grind. Theirs was a life freed of the responsibilities that beleaguered her as she sat there, her head in her hands, gazing at the papers spread over the tablecloth. Tea had risen to two shillings and twopence and was in short supply; butter was one shilling and tenpence a pound. There were nine mouths to feed and most of her lodgers had hearty appetites – Mrs O'Malley, though eighty years old and crippled with arthritis, always cleaned her plate and even swabbed it with bread like a Continental. There was money owing to the tradespeople and now Mr Boyce Argyle had been given his call-up papers and would soon be gone. How was *his* rent to be paid? Then there was the matter of the Spooners, on the top floor. They already owed three pounds fifteen shillings in arrears but in their

9

circumstances Eithne hardly had the heart to demand it. She wasn't made of stone.

In fact she was a woman of strong emotions and could love with a passion. For her son she felt such a fierce and protective ardour that the very sight of him, his frail neck rising out of his manly suit, his large ears, could bring tears to her eyes. Nobody had warned her of this; it seemed to be one of the many surprises that women had to discover for themselves. Motherhood unravelled a woman. However strong she might seem to the outside world, a son had her in his thrall.

And the feeling was mutual. Ralph loved her deeply and in the absence of his father was doing his best to look after her. They were very close, during this time. The dog followed Ralph around and Ralph followed his mother. When she flung herself in the armchair, exhausted at the end of the day, he sat on the arm and stroked her brow. He was too old now to be put to bed; they found themselves retiring at the same time and, lying in their adjoining rooms, murmured sleepily to each other through the interconnecting doors. He was her solace, and she his.

When they walked down the street and she took his arm they resembled a married couple. Ralph had grown tall enough to be a husband, and when he shouted at some boy whose ball had nearly hit them it was hard to remember that a mere whisper ago he had been that boy himself. This filled Eithne with both pride and sorrow. For Ralph took his responsibilities so seriously that sometimes she had the feeling that it was her son who was growing up too fast whilst her husband was trapped in time – trapped in a perpetual present of advance and retreat, a war game, a boys' adventure, whose rules were as incomprehensible as cricket. Somebody had to win, of course, but it all seemed curiously pointless.

And while the men were away, life had moved on. Two years earlier Ralph had been a boy, with a piping treble voice. He had jumped up and down with excitement and urged his father to go and bash the Hun. He wanted to be proud of him, he wanted to show off to the other boys at school. Though Eithne's feelings were mixed she, too, had been fired with a certain patriotic zeal. Somewhere, deep within her, she longed for her sweet and self-effacing husband to prove himself a man. The thought of him in uniform aroused her. Life was suddenly simple, thrillingly so: he would fight for her and save her from the Germans, he would return a hero, with flags waving and medals glinting on his chest, and she would swoon in his arms. It was as she dreamed a man and woman should be, when she was a girl. Transformed by his bravery, he would whisk her away from this dismal house and forge his way in the world, and they would be happy.

Besides, like everybody else she thought the war would soon be over. Not that the years would pass and her son's voice would break; that he would reach the age of fourteen and a fuzz would appear on his upper lip and there would be no father at home to show him how to shave. That when his father returned, for a brief week's leave, it would be somehow a disappointment. There were no altercations; time was too short for herself and Paul to slip back into their old ways. But for the same reason intimacy seemed to elude them. They seemed to be acting at marriage rather than living in it. He was neither a changed man, whom she had to get

11

used to all over again, nor the old Paul with whom she was so familiar. He was inert, like a photograph of himself – a truthful approximation, but an approximation all the same. Eithne couldn't get a grasp on him. He scarcely seemed to inhabit the house; with him there, it felt like a waiting room.

When Paul departed, at the end of his leave, she had felt a shameful sense of relief, that he could revert to the hero she had fabricated. Of course she was distressed, but not quite about this man. As she kissed him goodbye, she felt stagy. They had stood in the hallway, lost for words.

He turned to Ralph. 'You look after your mother. She's a good woman.' He had never spoken like this in his life.

'I'll do my best, sir.' *Sir?* There was a silence.

Ralph was too old to be hugged. Paul shook his hand. They were the same height now. Eithne noticed the similarity of their profiles – the beaky nose, the prominent Adam's apple.

Only the dog behaved naturally. Scenting, beneath the cleaned and pressed uniform, the beloved human within, he jumped up and mounted his master's leg.

'Goodbye, old pal,' said Paul, easing him off. Brutus gripped tighter. 'Sorry, old chap, wrong gender.' Paul put him down. 'Wrong on all accounts .'

Ralph pulled the dog away and held him by his collar. There was another silence. Eithne suddenly remembered the mutton bones; she had left them boiling in a saucepan, for stock, and Winnie was out. Had they boiled dry? She was sure she could smell burning.

Distracted, she kissed her husband on the cheek and the next moment he was gone.

*

The fire had died down but Eithne didn't have the energy to put on more coal. She sat there gazing at the rent books, the notebook of household accounts, the chits and receipts. They filled her with a panic-stricken torpor. The cat, Flossie, lay asleep on the greengrocer's bills; she didn't give a fig.

Outside, the grey day weighed down; it seemed unnaturally still, as if thunder were threatening. What was Ralph doing, up in his room? The boy spent too much time alone. There was no doubt that he missed his father but he seldom spoke of him. Neither of them did. Eithne, if she were truthful, sometimes forgot about her husband for days. The trouble was, he had been away for so long. Of course she felt guilty, that he was out there fighting for his country and yet he didn't cross her mind for days at a time.

Today, however, Paul was in her thoughts. That was the strange thing. Maybe she had a presentiment that something was about to happen. For as she sat there, the world holding its breath, she heard the creak of a bicycle approaching. It was that quiet. She even heard the sound of it being laid, gently, against the railings.

It was only then that the dog started barking.

*

Ralph found his mother in the back room. She sat very still, as if she were a vessel whose contents would spill with the slightest movement.

'There's been some bad news, I'm afraid,' she said.

Ralph sat down beside her. She took his hand.

'It's about your father,' she said. 'You're going to have to be a very brave young man.'

Chapter One

1918

The mode of slaughtering sheep is perhaps as humane and expeditious a process as could be adopted to attain the objects sought: the animal being laid on its side in a sort of concrete stool, the butcher, while pressing the body with his knee, transfixes the throat near the angle of the jaw, passing his knife between the windpipe and bones of the neck; thus dividing the jugulars, carotids, and large vessels, the death being very rapid from such a haemorrhage.

Mrs Beeton's Book of Household Management

Eithne was boiling potatoes when the kitchen window darkened. A man was descending the steps. He knocked on the basement door. Eithne wiped her brow with the back of her hand and hurried down the passage.

'Goodness!' she said. 'The great man himself.'

Mr Turk, the butcher, filled the doorway. 'Morning, Mrs Clay.' He was in shadow, the great bulk of him. 'Short-staffed today,' he said. 'And seeing I was passing.'

She moved aside to let him in; he seemed to presume it.

'Brought your bit of neck,' he said, putting a package on the table.

14

Eithne's heart thumped. She knew why he had come to her house in person.

'I'm so sorry,' she said.

'And what might you be sorry about?'

'I was coming round tomorrow to settle up.'

Mr Turk leaned against the dresser and looked at her. 'You don't have to bother yourself about that.'

'You've not come for the money?'

He shook his head. 'As I said, I was passing.'

The ceiling felt lower, with Mr Turk in the room. He was a big man, built like a bull, with a florid complexion and thick black hair. It gleamed in the lamplight. Eithne had never seen the butcher out of his shop. It gave her a jolt; the same readjustment she had to make when, as a girl, she had seen her schoolteacher out of the classroom – playing tennis, in fact, in the Stockport Recreation Gardens.

'I've just made a pot of tea,' she said. 'Or are you in a hurry?'

'No hurry.' Mr Turk pulled out a chair.

Eithne was sorry. It was laundry day, the busiest day of the week. She should be going upstairs to help Winnie with the sheets. However, she was in this man's debt to an alarming degree. To the tune of one pound, fourteen shillings and sixpence, to be precise, and it was in her interests to keep him sweet.

Mr Turk stretched out his legs. He wore caramel-coloured trousers and a smart black waistcoat and jacket. His watch-chain winked as he reached for his cup.

'Big place you've got,' he said. 'A lot of work, I dare say.'

Eithne nodded. 'Keeps us busy.'

'But good solid houses, good foundations. Known this street since I was a boy. You own the freehold?'

Startled, Eithne shook her head. The question struck her as impertinent. Still, she felt obliged to answer. 'My husband and I had rooms on the top floor. When the old lady died we took over the lease.'

'Take a tip from me, Mrs Clay.' He took a gulp of tea. 'Get your hands on that freehold. Pawn your soul, if need be. Soon this war'll be over and know what'll happen then?'

Eithne shook her head.

'There'll be a housing famine,' he said: 'and know why?'

She shook her head again.

'Because nothing's been built for these past four years. And know what'll happen then? Property prices'll go through the roof.' He grinned. 'In a manner of speaking. If you need any advice, I could put a good man your way. Believe me, Mrs Clay, you're sitting on a gold mine.'

'Nothing I can do about it,' she blurted out. 'I've got no money! You know that perfectly well. I haven't paid you for two months and I can't come round tomorrow to settle up either.'

Startled, he looked at her. The sudden intimacy shocked them both. Neville Turk drew his hand across his moustache. In the silence they could hear the water bubbling.

Eithne tried to gather her wits. The man was confusing her but she'd had no call for that outburst. She dropped her gaze, and caught sight of his hand. 'You poor thing!' she said. 'How did that happen?'

He looked at the scar. 'Knife slipped. Lucky not to have lost a finger.'

'It must be strange, cutting up dead animals all day.'

'Stranger if they were alive.'

Eithne laughed. The butcher drew in his breath. Some of her hair had come down, she could feel it tickling her neck.

'Must drain those potatoes,' she said, 'or they'll be falling to bits.'

'Can't have that.'

'No.' She stood up. 'You caught me on the hop.'

Eithne lifted the pan off the range. She felt his eyes on her as she walked out of the kitchen. In the scullery she hastily inspected herself in the mirror. She looked distrait, like a child who had lost her parents in a crowd. She tried to pin up her hair but gave up. If only Winnie would come downstairs!

In the kitchen the butcher pushed back his chair. 'I'll be off then,' he said. 'Let you get on.'

'Yes.'

He stood up. 'Your son in good health?'

She nodded.

'Hard for a lad,' he said.

Eithne nodded again. He put on his hat. She was seized by an urge to keep him there a moment longer, to feel again that thrum of intimacy.

'A new lodger's moved in,' she said. 'He's blind.'

'Blind, eh?'

'He was gassed. The poor man. I have to tell him, at dinner, what he's about to eat. Just so he knows.' She laughed, shrilly. 'In fact, with my cooking, they *all* need to know.'

Mr Turk raised his eyebrows. 'That bad, are you?'

She had only meant it as a girlish sort of self-deprecation, to catch his interest. Rallying to her own

17

defence, Eithne said: 'Well, there's nothing in the shops, is there? You queue for hours and when you get there it's gone. And the quality's so poor there's nothing you can do to make it taste of anything. We had some sausages last week and they were so full of bread I didn't know whether to spread them with mustard or marmalade.'

Even as she was speaking Eithne realised what she was saying, but it was too late. Her words had a will of their own. She clapped her hand to her mouth.

'Oh, I'm so sorry!' She felt the blush spreading.

But Mr Turk was grinning. Head on one side, eyebrows raised, he watched her with amusement. 'I knew you were a woman of taste,' he said. 'In fact, I'll let you in on a secret.' He leaned closer; she could smell his hair oil. 'I've got some top quality bangers, sixty per cent pork, for my favourite customers. I'll have them put aside. Tell your girl I said so.'

Eithne tried to be grateful, but she prickled with resentment. It was all his fault that she had made a fool of herself.

The butcher bowed his head and was gone. Eithne sat down at the table. She looked at the blood seeping through the parcel. How could the man have led her along like that? Yes, it was all his fault, for marching into her kitchen as if he owned it, for speaking to her with such presumptuous familiarity. It was no way for a tradesman to behave.

He had a carnation in his buttonhole, too, and stank of brilliantine. No doubt he was off to see some fancy woman, he looked the type. In future she would avoid his shop. In fact she would avoid the street altogether, and take the long way round. Winnie or Ralph could drop in the orders.

Even the thought of those two young people, blameless as they were, filled Eithne with irritation. If they had been here, none of this would have happened. And now her morning tasks were all at sixes and sevens and her poor maid was struggling with the laundry alone.

Eithne sat there, recovering her breath. How could her husband have left her like this? She was all alone, with a houseful of people dependent on her. The responsibility weighed her down. Paul had had his shortcomings, but in his own way he had looked after her. She missed his warm body in her bed, and now two years had passed and his very face was beginning to lose definition. She had to resort to his photograph to remember what he looked like.

Eithne's eyes moistened. This alarmed her; she wasn't one of those frilly creatures who sobbed at the slightest opportunity. In fact she despised women of that sort. But the world was cruel, horribly cruel. Paul himself used to suffer on behalf of its victims. Once she had found a slug in the kitchen – a large black slug. It must have slid in under the door. Disgusted, she had thrown it into the back yard and sprinkled it with salt. Paul had been deeply upset. He had gazed at the slug which was bubbling and dissolving in front of their eyes. 'How could you?' he had cried. 'Look at its suffering. It's dying a horrible death, it's drowning in its own mucus.'

Several of the lads have suffered with the mustard gas, he had written in his last letter. *But we have our trusty respirators, the design is much improved now, and last week they issued us with steel helmets. I had grown attached to my*

19

cap, which has been my companion for two years, but it's not much use of course if things get sticky. So, like the snail, we now wear our 'Battle Bowlers' and it's done a world of good for the old morale. My love to you and our dear boy.

On the floor, a trail of slime glistened in the lamplight. Two trails, in fact; they criss-crossed near the dresser. Those dratted slugs.

*

'Describe them to me,' said the blind lodger.

'Who, sir?'

'The people in this house. What do they look like?'

Winnie was bent over Mr Flyte's bed, pulling off the sheets. He sat by the window, his face in shadow, but he appeared to be looking at her. His face was turned in her direction.

'Well, the room above you belongs to Mr Argyle, but he's not there.'

'I gathered that. Never heard a dicky-bird.'

'He's missing in action.'

'Ah.'

'But Mrs Clay has kept the room for him.'

Winnie pulled off the sheet and bundled it into her arms.

'Then next to him, on the top floor, there's the Spooners. That's Mr and Mrs Spooner and their daughter Lettie. They keep themselves to themselves. Mrs Spooner drives an omnibus but Mr Spooner stays in his room.'

'Why?'

Winnie dumped the sheet by the door. 'He's not too well, sir. Lettie looks after him, she's ten years old, she's a treasure.'

'What do they look like?'

'I don't know really. Mrs Spooner has brownish hair. The little girl takes after her.' Winnie unbuttoned the pillowcase.

'And what about the old lady next to me? In the front room?'

'That's Mrs O'Malley. She's been here for ever.'

'What's she look like?'

Winnie pulled out the pillow. 'I don't know. Old.'

'You're not doing very well.'

'I'm sorry, sir.'

'Don't call me sir.'

'Pardon?'

'Call me Alwyne. I call you Winnie, you should call me Alwyne.'

Winnie's mouth fell open. It was fortunate that he couldn't see her face.

'All right, sir – I mean . . .' She stopped, blushing.

'Does that make you feel awkward?'

A train rattled past. On this floor, the railway line was level with the window. Winnie looked longingly at the flash of faces. How happy they were in their carriages, and now gone in a trice! She wished Mrs Clay would come upstairs and rescue her. What was her mistress doing, down in the kitchen?

Mr Flyte lit a cigarette. The room stank from his smoking but Winnie supposed he had few enough pleasures left. The trouble was, if you opened the windows on this side of the house the smuts blew in.

'And what about our landlady, Mrs Clay?'

'Oh, she's very handsome.' Winnie's voice warmed. 'I think she's beautiful. So does everyone. She's tall, with brown hair –'

'Not brown hair again.'

'But hers has got red in it. You can see it in the lamplight. She turns heads in the street, it's the way she holds herself with her skirt swinging. She's got a lovely green skirt with braid round the bottom.'

'Well done, that's better.'

'And her green hat with the guinea-fowl feathers.'

Mr Flyte blew out a plume of smoke. 'And is she a good employer?'

'Oh yes.' Winnie stifled the *sir*. It felt as if her tongue had been amputated. 'She treats me very well.' Winnie was a loyal young woman; she wasn't going to mention Mrs Clay's moodiness in front of this man even if he was a war hero. Besides, she loved her mistress. Their mutual dependency meant the world to her. 'Of course it's hard for Mrs Clay, with her husband dead.'

'Terrible, isn't it.'

Winnie nodded. 'All those young men being killed for nothing. They're out there fighting and we've stopped believing in it and nobody's told them and they're going on dying.'

'I mean the class system, Winnie. Here you are, an intelligent young woman, why should you wait on people who're perfectly capable of looking after themselves?'

Startled, Winnie considered this. 'Because I get paid for it. If they looked after themselves I wouldn't have a job, would I?'

Mr Flyte laughed – a short, harsh bark. Winnie had never heard him laugh before. She looked at him. It was a funny feeling, looking at a blind person. You could inspect them like a piece of furniture. Come to think of it,

Mr Flyte could do with a good spring-clean himself. His jacket was stained and even in this dim light she could see that his shirt was grubby. This was hardly surprising; she, of all people, knew how seldom he surrendered up any personal items of washing. His skin had the waxy look of somebody who never saw daylight. There was, however, something raffish about him – full lips nestling in his beard, a relaxed looseness to his limbs. She suspected foreign blood. In fact, if he spruced himself up he could be a fine-looking man though much good that could do him now. No wonder he had gone to seed.

Today his face was naked. At meals, and out in the street, Mr Flyte wore black spectacles. In his room, however, he often took them off. Somehow, despite the beard, his face looked more bare than the faces of ordinary men. At times he kept his eyes closed, which could be unnerving – was he dozing? When they were open his pupils fluttered at the top of his eyeballs, as if searching for some truth in the roof of his skull. Winnie's heart melted. He had lost his sight for his country, the mustard gas had done it, and it felt wicked even to notice that his fingernails were dirty. After all, *he* didn't.

Winnie plumped up the pillow, in its fresh pillowcase. The poor man – how could he, of all people, question the need for a helping hand? It must be terrible, being blind, the day dawning for everybody else while you remained in darkness – *blackness* – with no hope of even a glimmer. For *ever*. Until you *died*. The terror of it, being locked into your own thoughts. It must be like being bound in a bandage. The panic, the loneliness . . . The very idea brought Winnie out in goosepimples. It was hardly surprising that Mr Flyte's behaviour was odd.

Winnie wondered what his last sight on earth had been. A German face, contorted with rage? A cloud of gas? Was it yellow, the gas? She had no idea. It didn't bear thinking about. In fact she had only the vaguest idea of that parallel world into which men had been disappearing in such vast numbers for so many years. There were photographs in the paper, of course, but they looked posed, and the men who returned seldom spoke about what had happened to them. There was no way, for example, that she could ask Mr Spooner, upstairs, about his experiences in the trenches. He was in no state for anything of that kind.

Winnie unfolded the clean sheet and shook it out. At least Mr Flyte couldn't see his room. That was a blessing, she supposed. It really was in a shocking state. The gutter outside was broken and damp had crept in. The wallpaper was blistered and peeling; one section had come away from the wall and hung down like a tongue. Chalky patches had bloomed down one side of the window, sprouting a sort of cotton wool. A substance resembling boiled toffee had also erupted beneath the cornice, where the wash-basin upstairs had leaked. The whole house was going to rack and ruin but what could Mrs Clay do, living on her war widow's pension?

Winnie tucked the sheet under the mattress. They sent the bedlinen out to the laundry – it would be impossible to wash it all in the copper – and it returned smelling as fresh, as new-born, as a baby's scalp. It brought a breath of hope into the house. She liked burying her nose in the crisp cotton. The scent made her long for a child of her own, a home of her own, but that was not meant to be. She had realised this some time ago.

24

'And what do *you* look like, Winnie?'

Winnie didn't falter. She laid the eiderdown on the bed. If she didn't make a noise, perhaps Mr Flyte would think she had already gone. Where, oh where, was Mrs Clay?

Mr Flyte stubbed out his cigarette. 'Come on, Winnie. Don't be coy.'

'I can't say, sir.' Winnie bundled up the dirty sheets and blundered out of the room.

*

Ralph stood still on the top landing. No sound came from the Spooners' room. What did the little girl do all day, alone with her father? Sometimes she emerged, pattering down the stairs, to run errands but most of the time she was shut up there with him, the door closed. There was no question of school. What did *he* do all day? Before he went to the Front Mr Spooner had worked as a french polisher, but even then he was a shy, retiring man. He had left the house early in the morning and the little family took their evening meal alone, before the other tenants ate. Occasionally he had played chess with Ralph's father in the back room but the games were played in a concentrated silence. Each man drank a bottle of stout. That was in another life, now. It was hard to believe that a mere four years had passed. Now it was like having a ghost in the house – a presence, a creak of the floorboards. Mrs Spooner collected the supper for the three of them and took it upstairs. Nobody remarked upon her husband or his condition, and Ralph could hardly bring the subject up. Even Winnie just rolled her eyes and busied herself with something else.

Ralph took a breath and turned the knob of Boyce Argyle's door. He stepped in and was flooded in sunlight. Though no fire had been lit for months it felt like the warmest spot in the house. This was because, during winter, it was the only room that caught the sun. The railway bridge blocked the lower floors but Mr Argyle's window was above the gloom; outside was blue sky and a view of rooftops. Only now did Ralph realise that it was a dazzling January day. The windowsill was still encrusted with pigeon droppings; Boyce had liked feeding the birds. How many times had they landed there before giving up?

Down in the yard Winnie was beating carpets. He heard the faint, rhythmic thud, like jungle drums. His mother was out shopping. She had taken the dog, so there was no danger of Brutus padding up to this room to seek his master.

Winnie had made up the bed, as if its occupant had just popped out and would return at any moment. This was a relief; Ralph had dreaded finding a stripped mattress. The room had been tidied – Boyce lived in a state of spectacular disorder – but otherwise everything was as it had always been. The watercolour of Colwyn Bay hung on the wall, its frame stuck around with ticket stubs from variety theatres – the Alhambra, the Tivoli, the London Pavilion. Upholstery held no charms for Boyce; he planned to go on the stage. 'The smell of the greasepaint!' he said, 'the roar of the crowd!' Ralph would sit on the bed while Boyce practised his routines, twirling his cane and singing:

I'm Burlington Bertie, I rise at ten-thirty
And reach Kempton Park around three . . .

He taught Ralph to foxtrot, bundling him around the room like a chest of drawers.

The theatre, of course, was known for its fast women. 'I'm catnip to them,' said Boyce, 'I've got the knack, it's easy when you know how.' Ralph was enthralled by Boyce's amorous conquests. The chap was a sophisticate, through and through. Once he said, with airy insouciance: 'Women are cheap in Rio de Janeiro.' He knew the names of all the soubrettes on the London stage and had pinned their photographs to his wardrobe door – Gladys Cooper, Madie Scott and his latest hot potato Vesta Carr. She was Ralph's favourite too, because her photograph was the most intoxicating – leaning against a pillar, a come-hither smile on her lips, she was draped in strategically placed ostrich feathers that left little to the imagination. Boyce declared himself in love with her and that he would follow her to the ends of the earth. She was a regular fixture at the Tivoli, where Boyce would applaud her from the gallery, and in fact it was after her most thrillingly suggestive number, *If you've got it let me see it* that the lights came up and they carried the recruiting tables on to the stage.

Ralph missed Boycie keenly. Almost as keenly, in fact, as he missed his father, something that caused him a certain amount of guilt. Boycie was the elder brother he had never had. But it was more than that. The fellow made him laugh. His subversive presence had lightened the somewhat oppressive atmosphere of the house. He opened up another life for Ralph, the possibilities of it; he pulled back the curtains to reveal a stage filled with gaiety and illusion. Who was to tell which was the more real – the daily grind at home or a world of wine, women and song? Boyce returned with gifts from this other place – a wilting rose, paper twists of sugar which he stole from West End restaurants and which Ralph hoarded like gold dust. In fact, nowadays it *was* gold dust.

Ralph knew that Boyce wasn't dead. He was too full of life. He couldn't be stopped, at eighteen years, with Ralph growing older and slowly catching him up. In another two years he himself would be eighteen, he would overtake him with Boyce still stopped, it didn't bear thinking about, it made Ralph's stomach turn over. Boyce was playing one of his practical jokes.

That night when the Zeppelin came over – that night, for instance, when they all rushed out into the street, the searchlights criss-crossing the sky and old Mr Crocker, from opposite, standing there in his nightshirt shouting and pointing.

'Where is it?' asked Boyce.

Mr Crocker flung up his arm. His nightshirt rode up. Underneath he was bare, the bits dangling. 'There!'

'Where, Mr Crocker? I can't see it!' said Boyce, and the old man flung up his arm again like a railway signal. Up went the nightshirt.

'There, boy, you blind or something?'

'Where?'

Up went the nightshirt, revealing the turkey giblets. Boyce and Ralph had snorted with laughter.

'Oh yes, sir, I can see it now,' said Boyce. 'It's not as big as people say.'

No, Boyce would turn up. 'Only joking,' he would grin, stepping through the door in his khaki uniform, slinging down his kitbag. He was always leaving things in the hallway for people to trip over.

Ralph fetched the book from the shelf. He should be studying for his exam but his mother would be out for most of the morning, what with all the queuing. He sat down on the bed, the springs creaking. *Thud-thud* went his heart. Down in the yard Winnie thumped the rugs. Had she ever looked inside the book? *The Human Figure in Motion*, its title, gave no hint of what lay within. Boyce had borrowed it from an art student friend of his and never given it back.

Ralph's palms were moist. He turned the pages one by one, searching for his favourite photographs. *Woman walking up incline carrying bucket. Woman standing and ironing. Woman pouring water.* The rows of photographs showed a woman performing these humdrum tasks, *and she was bare. Completely naked.* The sight was deeply, and intoxicatingly, shocking. Somebody called Eadweard Muybridge had taken the photographs but the women – for there were several different ones – seemed unaware of his presence. What sort of women could they be, to expose their bodies like that? Nobody he knew, for sure. They had breasts and buttocks and – most transfixing of all – dense black triangles of hair between their legs. *Woman picking up broom.*

Ralph's heart hammered. He knew, of course, that underneath her clothes Winnie was bare but what made him blush was that she didn't know he knew, that he was trying not to think about it. Not just her – other women too. Women he saw in the street, unaware of his penetrating eyes; the female students at his book-keeping course. His mother was out of bounds; he couldn't even *think* of that.

Ralph thought: if Boyce really is dead, I can keep the book.

This seemed the most shocking thought of all. He snapped the book shut and sat there. Dust danced in the shafts of sunlight. Winnie said that dust was made of human skin, somebody had told her it was made out of tiny particles of the stuff. That was what she swept up, day after day, and beat out of the carpets, just like the woman in *Woman beating carpet*. She was inhaling the inhabitants of the house, alive and dead. Perhaps she was breathing in his *father*.

It was hard to believe his father was dead, with no body sent back to them. A parcel had arrived containing his personal items but that was all. His commanding officer had written a letter: *Corporal Clay was a brave and trustworthy soldier, liked by all who knew him,* but there was nothing about the manner in which he had died, or whether he had suffered, or what there was left of him – if, in fact, anything had been left at all.

Ralph couldn't speak to anyone about this. He certainly couldn't speak to his mother. Any mention of her husband upset her and they avoided mentioning his name. Her sorrows were profound, but grief had closed her off from him. She had grown so pale and thin that his heart ached for her. And yet here he was looking at dirty pictures, just as he had been looking at dirty pictures when the telegram came.

Ralph, up on the top floor of the house, didn't hear the sound of the front door. He was thinking: I shall look after my mother as long as I live. She has only me, in the world.

You're going to have to be a very brave young man.

Ralph got to his feet and put the book back on the shelf. Never again would he indulge himself by gazing at its contents.

It's about your father.

Just then he became aware of a sound. It was Brutus, climbing the stairs. He was looking for his master. The final flight was uncarpeted; Ralph heard the dog's claws scrabbling on the wood.

Brutus pushed open the door and came into the room. He carried a bone in his mouth.

Padding up to Ralph, tail wagging, he dropped it at his feet.

'My word,' said Ralph. 'Where did you get that?'

It was a big bone, a leg bone of some kind, streaked with blood. Brutus gazed at Ralph, his tail waving from side to side.

'I know where you've been,' said Ralph. 'You've been to the butcher's.'

A string of saliva hung from Brutus's jaws; it grew heavier and dropped on to the floor. With his nose, the dog pushed the bone towards Ralph's foot.

'No thank you, kind sir,' said Ralph.

He kicked it away and Brutus pounced on it. The dog lowered himself on to his haunches and tried to gnaw at it, but the thing was too big. He inspected it, his head tilted to one side, then he held it down with his paws and started to lick it tenderly, like a mother licking her new-born baby. He licked off the blood with his pink tongue.

Only then did Ralph become aware of another sound. It floated up from deep within the house, from the back parlour, and for a moment it took him by surprise. A long time had passed – years, in fact – since he had last heard it.

His mother, home from the butcher's shop, was playing the piano.

Chapter Two

Mr Turk's butcher's shop was a thriving emporium that dominated the northernmost end of the high street. It straddled three frontages, having swallowed up the two neighbouring shops to one side. The far shop had belonged to a pork butcher. Like many such establishments it had been run by a German family and when war broke out and patriotic fervour gripped the nation a local mob had smashed its windows, ransacked the place and flung its fitments into the street. The Weissmans had fled back to Düsseldorf and Mr Turk had taken over the lease.

That made the shop in between – a hardware store – a most attractive proposition. Like all good businessmen Neville Turk could sense the vulnerability of a fellow man, just as a lion can sniff out the weakest creature in a herd, and he gambled on the fragile health of the man who ran it, whose only son had gone down with the *Lusitania*. Sure enough the shop rapidly declined, the butcher bought the freehold at an advantageous price and his empire-building could begin.

Workmen arrived to knock down the interconnecting walls and install electric lighting. Where did Mr Turk find them? It was a mystery to the local shopkeepers, for strong, healthy young men were a disappearing species and their own small repairs remained undone. Mr Turk, however, was a powerful man. He had connections. Rumour had it that he was a Freemason, funny hand-shakes, hush-hush, and everyone knew that Freemasons had plenty of fingers in plenty of pies. *You scratch my back and I'll scratch yours*. Within a matter of weeks vast, modern refrigerators had been heaved into the back regions, mahogany counters and display cabinets had been hammered into place, and Turk Quality Butchers was reopened for business.

And it prospered. Neville Turk knew a carcass. He could read its density of muscle, its weight of meat to water, the length of time it had been hung. He knew, by the subtlest tension in its fibres, the extent of the animal's distress at its moment of slaughter and hence the tenderness of its flesh. Down at Smithfield, in the freezing dawn, he prodded and sniffed; he sized up a flayed beast as a man would size up a whore, raising his eyebrows and giving its pimp a nod. He struck a hard bargain but he was respected for it; pressing flesh both alive and dead, closing the deal.

Back at his shop he was a consummate salesman.

Elderly ladies were charmed by his compliments, he made them skittish. The drabbest housewives felt their step quicken as they approached his shop, and even domestics, whom he could treat brusquely, felt themselves blushing as he sized them up while sharpening his knives. Not everybody took to him; he was considered too big for his boots. But like all powerful men he exuded a magnetism, a sense that in his proximity life warmed up.

Besides, he was forty years old and still a bachelor. This gave his presence an added *frisson*, that of a stallion on the loose. It was generally considered his mother's fault that he had never married. Mrs Turk was a tyrannical old biddy who kept her son in order – the man seemed afraid of her! It was comic, the way he kowtowed – he, of all people. Mrs Turk had worked at the cash till. Nothing escaped her as she sat in her glass booth, her eyes swivelling from side to side like a mechanical doll at a fairground, on the lookout for a predatory female who might steal away her son. But she had died a year earlier, during the big freeze of 1917, and now Neville lived alone above the shop. Whether he was courting or not, nobody could tell; he certainly spruced himself up, of an evening, and sallied forth but he had always led a mysterious life. The stamina of the man, and up at four in the morning!

The main reason for the shop's popularity, however, was something more vital. Times were very hard, that winter. The shortages had worsened; rumours of food deliveries – tinned salmon, butter, tea – led to mutinous queues and even riots. Bread and potatoes had doubled in price, coal was scarce, and sugar practically non-existent. There was talk of rationing. Families were struggling to survive, living on bread-and-a-scrape, cabbage leaves picked up from the gutter when the market closed, and thrice-boiled tea.

Despite this, there was plenty on offer at Mr Turk's shop. His lights blazed into the dingy street. People pressed their noses against the glass, gazing into his theatre of meat – shapely legs of mutton, hanging in a row; heaped, glistening necklaces of sausages. And he was its impresario, standing behind the counter in his rust-smudged apron. In that time of hunger a sirloin held more allure than any showgirl. And even when stocks were low he somehow rustled up some choice cuts he had put aside for his special customers. How he managed this was anyone's guess.

Winnie liked going to the butcher's. Archie, her tormentor, the ruination of her hopes, had long since gone. He had enlisted on his eighteenth birthday and hadn't been heard of since. Her relief at his departure filled her with guilt, for she was a kind-hearted girl, but she *was* relieved. She was *glad*. It was terrible but true. No doubt she would be punished for it but then *he* had punished *her* and after all she wasn't hoping for him to be killed, she wasn't that sinful. Down in Kent, where her father lived, she had heard the bombardment across the Channel when she had gone there for a visit; she had felt the earth tremble. At night she had seen the orange glow of the fires. And she had prayed for them all, even for Archie. She wasn't that heartless.

It was a grey, foggy day at the end of February, a real pea-souper, the sort of day that had barely begun before it was time to light the street lamps again. Figures hurried along the high street, their heads bent, they loomed out of the fog and were gone. Trams rattled past, jangling their bells in warning; a motor lorry rumbled by, belching smoke. Winnie, chilled to the bone, hurried towards the butcher's shop. She had been out and about, running some errands, and forgotten to buy the lard.

The shop was busy, as always, the assistants chopping up meat and dumping it on the scales, their heads cocked sideways as they inspected the weight, their hands wiping themselves on their aprons. Winnie stood next in line at the counter. Under the glass lay a huge, goosepimpled ox tongue, its great root wrenched from the throat. The young girl in front of Winnie said: 'Sixpennyworth of pieces, please.'

It was then that Winnie saw Mrs Clay. She hadn't spotted her at first because her mistress's back was turned and she was wearing her velvet jacket with the pinched-in waist. The poor woman must be freezing. She was standing by the counter talking to Mr Turk. Her hat feathers trembled as she shook her head; she appeared to be disagreeing with something Mr Turk said. He tapped his finger against his nose and she burst out laughing.

Mrs Clay twirled around on her heels, like a mare shying. She caught sight of Winnie and stopped.

'What are you doing here?' she snapped.

'I've come for the lard.'

Mrs Clay laughed shrilly. 'And why do we need lard?' Her face looked hectic; there were high spots of colour on her cheeks.

'For the pasties,' said Winnie.

Mrs Clay looked at Winnie as if she had arrived from some foreign country. In the electric light her mistress looked coarser, with her reddened face and the wrinkles showing around her eyes. She said: 'I came here for the chops. It's best to see them first, to see what we're getting.'

Later it all made sense but Winnie was a trusting girl, she believed what she was told. Besides, her mind was elsewhere. She was wondering if Mr Flyte, the blind lodger, would ask her to read to him again that night, and whether she could cope with the long words. When she stumbled, his knee started jiggling up and down. This only made her the more flustered. Besides, who was this Karl Marx? She had asked Mr Flyte to explain but he seemed to think that everybody knew. He really could be very trying.

Winnie walked home with Mrs Clay. It was dark now, and the fog was so thick that they could only sense they were passing under a bridge by the echoing sound of their footsteps. Several bridges loomed above them, carrying the trains from the coast to the Waterloo Station, to London Bridge and Charing Cross. Down below, in the narrow street, buildings reared up on either side. She couldn't see them; just the bleary lights shining in their windows. This neighbourhood had a shifting population, people came and went, it was due to the railway termini nearby. Winnie, a village girl, found it mystifying that people could live yards from each other and never meet. And yet she found it thrilling – the heedlessness, the freedom, the faint scent of decadence like something rotting behind the stove. A girl like herself could arrive from Kent and fall into bad ways. A person could be *murdered* and not found for weeks. She read about such things in her *Penny Pictorial*, the sort of magazine that Mr Flyte would no doubt consider beneath his interest.

She wished she liked him more. There was a bit of the bully about Mr Flyte – *Alwyne*. He bullied her into saying things she didn't believe. And when she helped him across the road he stroked her wrist with his finger. Still, she repeated to herself, the poor man had few enough pleasures in his life. And tragedy was not choosy in those it afflicted; a falling shell didn't care who it blew apart. There had been plenty of evidence of this over the past few years. She avoided walking past the Hop Exchange in the Borough Road, for instance, because an amputee stood in its doorway selling matches. They didn't want to beg, they had their pride, so she always bought a box for a halfpenny but he never said *thank you* and once he had spat at her feet and now her room was stacked with matchboxes, it had cost her a fortune. All for a war veteran with one leg, hopping outside the Hop Exchange.

Winnie wanted to laugh but there was nobody to share the joke. Mrs Clay wasn't the type, and besides, she seemed wrapped up in her own concerns. Winnie's mistress walked in silence, her teeth chattering with the cold. Mr Boyce would have appreciated it but he was missing in action. He had sent her a letter from the Front, describing his nincompoop of a commanding officer and ending with a joke: *If bread is the staff of life, what is the life of the staff? One long loaf.*

She missed Mr Boyce keenly. It was funny – she always thought of him as Boyce, it came naturally. Yet trying to call Mr Flyte *Alwyne* was like clambering over a five-barred gate.

They crossed the road at the Mitre. A roar of laughter came from the saloon bar. Somebody else was telling a joke. Winnie thought: I'll tell the hopping joke to Ralph. He didn't have Boyce's sense of humour, but she loved him. He was like her little brother and she would walk to the ends of the earth for him.

*

'*The modern bourgeois society that had sprouted from the ruins of feudal society has not done away with class antagonisms,*' read Winnie. '*It has but established new classes, new conditions of oppression, new forms of struggle in place of the old ones.*'

Winnie stopped, exhausted. This was more tiring than heaving buckets of coal upstairs. She had no idea what she was reading, of course; the strain was caused by trying to get the words right. 'Bourgeois' had been one of the worst, but she had learnt it now. Alwyne Flyte sat there, his eyes closed. Perhaps he had fallen asleep. It was certainly boring enough.

'Carry on,' he said.

'*With the development of industry*' she said, '*the pro – pro –*'

'Proletariat!'

'Pardon. *The proletariat not only increases in number; it becomes concentrated in greater masses, its strength grows and it feels that strength more.*'

Just then she noticed the mess on the carpet – slivers of bone scattered over the hearthrug. Brutus must have brought in yet another trophy from the butcher's. He had been taken there a lot recently. In fact, she now noticed a larger piece, complete with knuckle, jutting out from under a cushion where the dog had attempted to hide it for later. The place looked like a slaughterhouse.

'Carry on,' said Mr Flyte.

'Improvements in the art of destruction will keep pace with its advance and every year more and more will be devoted to the costly engines of war.'

She should be cleaning it up. In fact she should be washing up the supper dishes but Mr Flyte had insisted she sit with him in the back room.

'You understand, don't you Winnie? Workers of the world unite!' Mr Flyte waved his arms. Ash flew off his cigarette. More mess to brush off the carpet. 'You have nothing to lose but your chains.' He leant forward. 'It's happened in Russia, it'll be happening here, you mark my words. Comrade Lenin is here in our midst!'

'Where?' she asked, alarmed.

'Here!' He tapped his head; more ash fell. 'It's ideas, not guns, that will change the world. We have to seize the moment, Winnie, while the enemy is weak, to sweep the capitalist class system out of existence!'

First I'd better sweep up those bones, thought Winnie. 'Will that be all?' she asked.

'Wars have no use, otherwise. They're utterly self-destructive, don't you understand? You remember what Marx said, about the military process? We read it last week. Whoever wins, the outcome is imposed by the conqueror on the conquered, and thus carries within itself the seeds of future wars.'

Winnie didn't remember, of course. She had far too much on her plate. She watched his eyes fluttering; they reminded her of saints in church, plaster models of them in rapture.

'If we don't break this cycle, that will be the pattern of the twentieth century! You mark my words, Winnie. The only solution is to put power into the hands of people like yourself.'

'Do I have to?' asked Winnie. 'I'm quite happy as I am.'

Mr Flyte sighed. 'Oh, Winnie.'

'But I agree about ending war,' she said. 'It must have been terrible.' She summoned up her courage. 'What was it like, Mr Flyte?'

'*Alwyne!*' He stubbed out his cigarette. 'You don't want to know, my dear.'

Silence fell. She shouldn't have asked, but the question had been burning in the back of her mind. There was nobody else she could approach on the matter – certainly not poor Mr Spooner, upstairs. And nowadays she felt more relaxed with Mr Flyte. His hectoring familiarity was starting to rub off on her and she felt bolder about asking him questions – even, on occasion, teasing him. She was starting to get the measure of the man. Besides, though undoubtedly clever, he was as helpless as a baby. In that department it was *she* who held the power. *Workers of the World Unite!*

'Tickling the ivories again, I hear.' Mr Flyte jerked his head towards the wall. Mrs Clay was playing the piano in the front parlour. 'She's taking that Chopin too fast.'

'I think it's lovely,' said Winnie. 'I love it when she plays.'

'Wonder what she's so happy about?'

Winnie shrugged, and then remembered that he couldn't see. 'I don't know,' she said.

There was no doubt that Mrs Clay's humour had much improved during the past few weeks. She not only played the piano. Sometimes, when there was nobody around, she sang. She spent longer at her toilette and

42

tried on a large number of outfits before deciding what to wear. Her bedroom looked ransacked. Winnie didn't mind clearing it up, however, because she was glad her mistress's spirits had lifted. There was less friction all round. However, she was hardly going to speculate about the cause, even if she knew it, with the grubby old lodger. It was Mrs Clay who paid her wages.

The music stopped, as if her mistress had guessed their thoughts. The door opened and she came into the room. Mr Flyte, as always, remained seated. This was due either to his political convictions or his blindness; Winnie never knew.

'Winnie, could we have a word?' she asked.

Winnie jumped up. 'I'm so sorry about the dishes, I'll be going down directly.'

'It's not that.'

Mr Flyte got to his feet. 'I'll be off,' he said. 'Got an appointment with a pint of mild.'

'I'll help you,' said Winnie. 'Where's your coat?'

He waved her away. 'I can manage.' At the door he turned: 'What exactly was that bit of fish we ate tonight? I've been trying to work it out.'

'Hake,' said Mrs Clay shortly. 'I think.'

Alwyne left the room. He didn't like being helped around in the house. They heard him fumbling for his coat in the hallway, and then the click of the front door.

'He's a strange man, isn't he?' said Mrs Clay. 'Something I can't put my finger on. And so swarthy. Do you think he's an Israelite?'

'But he's from Bolton.'

'That's no reason. They get everywhere.' She looked at Winnie in a vague way. 'You mustn't let him presume on

43

you, Winnie. I heard him trying to bamboozle you on your half-day.'

'That's all right. I'm learning things.'

Mrs Clay's heart wasn't in this conversation. Winnie had turned up the gas jets, for reading, and lit two lamps. She could see her mistress's face quite clearly. Mrs Clay was agitated. Her cheeks were flushed, her eyes bright.

'Tomorrow night you can make the suppers. I've put some beans to soak. You can make some rissoles, mash them up with the barley and that bit of mince.' She added, casually: 'I shall be out.'

'Out?'

The mantel clock chimed the hour. Nine o'clock already! The evening felt all out of kilter.

'I'm meeting a friend.' Mrs Clay went to the door. 'Mind you boil the barley first.'

And she was gone.

*

After the show Neville took her to supper at the Café Royal, in Regent Street. It was lit like a palace, with chandeliers hanging from the ceiling and candles glowing behind fluted pink shades. Columns, topped with naked figures, supported a ceiling painted with frescos. They knew him there. The head waiter shook Neville's hand and showed them to a table next to a potted palm. A band of old men scraped at their violins.

'Champagne?' Neville asked her.

A vase of tuberoses sat on the tablecloth. The scent made her head swim. Neville clicked his fingers and the waiter reappeared. They all seemed powerless to resist him. Eithne sat there, in her watered-silk dress that was too

44

loose on her now and that shamed her in these surroundings. She needed fattening up. *Fattening up for the slaughter*. Eithne felt the laughter bubble up; she clapped her hand across her mouth. Neville was opening his heavy, leather-bound menu. He fished out a pair of spectacles and she was absurdly disarmed. The man had a weakness! She felt as gay as a pit pony released from the underworld; she tossed her mane and galloped round the meadow.

And other people took this for granted! She had no idea there were so many people left in the world to do this sort of thing. The place was filled with men and women who dined out as a matter of course, they were a dazzle of top hats and crimson gowns, they had lives as unimaginable as creatures from Mars, and yet they were here with her tonight, just for tonight, and the moment was thrilling to her.

'What's the joke?' asked Neville.

Eithne couldn't reply *I was picturing the cow-heel stew I cooked, stirring the pan as it grew thicker and thicker until it turned into a grey glue so disgusting that even my boarders couldn't eat it, and they were HUNGRY. Mrs O'Malley's dentures got stuck together, and even the dog wouldn't go near the leftovers. And now it's funny because it doesn't matter, I'm alive, we're all alive, and better still I'm here.*

'Nothing,' she said. 'I'm hungry.'

'Glad to hear it.'

'Hungry as a horse.'

'Can't be doing with wilting violets who peck at their soup.'

How many wilting violets had Neville brought there? None could touch her tonight, none was as powerful as Eithne Clay because she needed this place more than they had ever needed it. Who cared about her ill-fitting gown with its frayed cuffs that Winnie had promised to mend? Tonight she was the queen of the Café Royal and even the waiter sensed it as he stood there waiting for her order.

'I'll have the oysters,' she said, 'and the sole, and the veal escalope.'

He bowed and withdrew, folding the menu gracefully, like a prayer book. She smiled across at Neville. 'You're spoiling me.'

'We only live the once.'

Paul's face flashed in front of her, and was gone. He would want this for her, it was no betrayal that she was sitting here sipping champagne that fizzed in her nostrils. He would want her to be happy.

'Do you believe in heaven and hell?' she asked.

Neville raised his eyebrows. 'Now that's a question for a Thursday night.'

She drained her glass. 'I don't believe in any of it. Not any more.' She eyed him recklessly, challenging him. The wine had gone straight to her head.

'It's a big bad world,' Neville said. 'We must shift for ourselves.'

He passed her the basket of rolls. Eithne took one and broke open the crust. It released the sweetest aroma. Inside, it was white and as fluffy as thistledown. *This* was holy. They could keep their God.

'I'm so tired of eating nasty hard grey bread with lumps of potato in it,' she said. 'Why do they make us eat it? I'm so tired of it all.'

'Baker I know, he bakes bread like this. Give me the nod and I'll get him to deliver you a loaf. Loaves. As much as you want, my dear, sky's the limit.'

My dear. 'You know everybody, don't you?'

He shrugged. Tonight was the second time she had seen Neville in mufti, so to speak. His hair shone with oil, his skin looked scrubbed and pink. Tonight he wore a white carnation; he had given her one too, he had fixed it to her bosom. He wore a tan jacket, a maroon cravat patterned with horseshoes and a matching handkerchief in his breast pocket. There was definitely something vulgar about the man, something of the racecourse. He really wasn't her type at all. Besides, he was a tradesman. She might be temporarily embarrassed, but that arose from circumstance rather than birth. After all, her father had held a respectable position at the Sun Insurance Company, he had been a man of some standing in the community. In fact it was his bequest, after his death, that had paid for the lease at Palmerston Road.

The oysters arrived. Neville leant towards her but she pushed his hand away. 'I know how to do it,' she said. 'I have eaten them before, you know.'

Neville grinned. He had a wolfish grin, white teeth gleaming under his moustache. Eithne's stomach shifted. She busied herself with the lemon and the Tabasco, a few drops here, a squeeze there. Neville busied himself with his. It felt suddenly companionable; it had been a long time since she had eaten alone with a man.

She lifted the shell to her mouth, parted her lips and tipped in the oyster. As a girl she had, of course, believed in God. She had drunk His blood and taken, on her tongue, the flesh He had given the world to redeem its sins.

For a moment Eithne held the oyster between her teeth, as gently as a cat holding a mouse. Then she bit,

47

and her mouth was flooded with salty-sweetness, the ocean made flesh.

Across the table Neville lowered his shell. He wiped his lips with his napkin.

'To be honest,' he said, 'I didn't happen to be short-staffed that day.'

'What day?'

'That day I came to your house. With the meat.'

'No?'

He shook his head. 'I came, wanting to see you.' He held her gaze, across the table. 'I'd been thinking about you, see. Thinking about you a lot.'

Eithne's throat closed up. 'Is that so?'

He nodded. 'I'm glad it wasn't the girl.' There was a silence. The voices of the diners echoed from far away. Neville grinned. 'She's an ugly brute, isn't she?'

Eithne froze. 'Who?'

'Your domestic. Used to have a Staffie that looked like that. You know the Staffie, the bull terrier? Great little fighter but by God the face on him –'

'Stop it!' Eithne cried. 'Don't say that!'

Her lip trembled. She glared at Neville. He lifted his hands. 'Sorry, sorry.'

*

The mood was broken. They carried on eating but Eithne had withdrawn from him like a deer, fled from his outstretched hand back into the woods. She must be fond of the girl.

Neville cursed himself. Women were tricky creatures, you had to tread warily in their vicinity. They blew hot and cold for no reason; all sweetness one moment,

48

snarling virago the next, how could a man please them when they were as unpredictable as the March weather? His mother, God bless her, had given him a thorough education in the combustibility of the female psyche.

Neville, however, was undaunted. It was not for nothing that he was three-times winner of the heavyweight championship, down at the Elephant and Castle. He could handle a challenge.

For the woman had bewitched him. Her low, thrilling voice; the swell of her bosom; the vibrancy of her! There was a distinction to her, the way she held herself, quite hoity-toity, yet beneath he guessed that she was as soft as butter. *She's all woman. She's my woman, and she knows it.*

So they ate their dinner, and made constrained conversation, and around them the great mirrored walls reflected them back to themselves, just another handsome couple out on the town.

*

While his mistress was out, Brutus emptied his bowels on the landing outside her bedroom. It was Ralph who smelt it. He had been cleaning boots in the kitchen. This was one of his tasks, cleaning the lodgers' boots, but nowadays there wasn't much to do. Boyce had possessed the largest assortment of footwear – pairs of brogues and boots, crocodile-skin and calfskin, patent-leather slippers for his evenings out on the town – but Boycie was gone. Mr Spooner had no call for boots, never leaving the house, and though Mr Alwyne Flyte left a pair outside his bedroom door on a regular basis there seemed little point in polishing the boots of a man who couldn't see what he was wearing. Still, Ralph persevered with his diminished clientele, and was walking upstairs with Alwyne's boots when the smell hit him.

Cursing, Ralph dumped the boots and hurried downstairs. The dog was nowhere to be seen – probably skulking underneath some table, in shame. It was half-past ten and the house was quiet. Down in the scullery Ralph lit a lamp and searched for a bucket. It was freezing cold, in this back part of the house.

Winnie had retired for the night; her door was closed. She lived in the small room next to the scullery. Even when he was younger, Ralph had seldom stepped inside her private domain; he sensed, somehow, that it was out of bounds.

Tonight, however, he made a clatter as he heaved the bucket into the sink and, sighing loudly, turned on the tap. It worked. Winnie's door opened and her face peered out.

'What's happened?' she asked.

Ralph told her. Winnie wrapped a shawl about herself and came out. She wore a long nightdress that appeared, in the dim light, to be printed with flowers.

'Here, let me do it,' she said. 'We need some rags, and that Dettol there, in the cupboard. Any hot water left on the stove?'

Upstairs, on the landing, Winnie got down to her customary position on hands and knees and started scrubbing.

'What a naughty boy,' she said.

'Maybe he ate something that disagreed with him,' said Ralph, who was sitting on the stairs. 'Did you give him any of those rissoles?'

'There was none left,' replied Winnie tartly. 'People liked them, so you can mind your tongue.'

Upstairs, on the second floor, Alwyne Flyte's door creaked open. Light leaked out. Ralph wondered why a blind man bothered to illuminate a lamp at all. Perhaps it was a comfort, the glow against his eyelids. Perhaps it kept the nightmares away.

'What's that disgusting smell?' said Mr Flyte. They told him. 'Your mother not back yet?'

'No, she said she'd be late,' replied Ralph. 'She's gone out with a friend.'

Mr Flyte barked with laughter. 'Well, the dog's certainly made his opinion plain about *that*.'

*

Winnie sat back on her heels. Of course, the dog realised that something was up. That was why he was upset. Dogs had a sixth sense. *She* knew something was up, but then she had known for some time. Servants knew things even before their mistresses did. It was one of the things they had in common with animals.

'Animals know what's going to happen,' she said. 'Dulcie knew they were coming for her.'

'Who's Dulcie?'

Winnie paused. She hadn't meant to talk about Dulcie, but she was still groggy from sleep.

'She was a horse,' she replied. 'They've got a sixth sense too.'

Suddenly Winnie was seized with grief. She sat slumped on the stairs, unable to move.

'What happened, Winnie?' asked Mr Flyte. 'Spit it out.'

'They came to take the horses away,' Winnie said. 'We all knew, in the village. Some people tried to hide them in the barns and in the woods, but the horses started whinnying to each other. They knew something was up.' Winnie stopped. She should be removing the evil-smelling bundle of rags, she should be trying to scrape the stuff down the water closet, but the strength seemed to be emptied out of her.

'They took the two big Clydesdales from Mr Bancroft's farm. Captain and Dolly were their names. They left him one, they left him Bismarck so he could do the ploughing.' Winnie spoke in a rush, she couldn't stop. 'They took the carter's mare, Judy, she knew the way to the station by heart, she could walk all the way to the railway station even when Mr Forrest was tipsy. And they took the vicar's horse, and they took all the hunters from Lord Elbourne's stables, they took them for the cavalry, all six of them, big Irish thoroughbreds, sixteen hands high some of them with plenty of bone.' She stopped for breath.

'I didn't know you knew anything about horses,' said Ralph.

'My father's the groom,' she replied. 'Lord Elbourne's groom.'

Ralph looked down at her, from his upper stair.

'I didn't know that,' he said.

'It broke his heart.'

'Who's Dulcie?' asked Mr Flyte.

'She shouldn't have gone, sir!' Winnie burst into tears. 'She was twenty years old, she was too old, they shouldn't have taken her! See, it took her a while to get used to a person, you had to spend time with her but once she trusted you she'd follow you anywhere, I used to feed her treacle, she loved treacle, she'd lick my fingers with her big slimy tongue, she'd lick between my fingers, she used to rub her head against my chest and I know it was only to get rid of the flies but it seemed she loved me, anyway I loved her.' Winnie gazed at them through her tears. 'She's frightened of strange people. She's frightened of bangs. When a motor car backfired she went into the ditch. What's she going to do out there?'

Winnie sat, her shoulders heaving. None of them heard the front door. Suddenly Mrs Clay was standing there, trying to keep her balance.

*

Eithne stared at the little group huddled on the stairs. 'What's happened?' she cried. 'Winnie, are you all right?'

Winnie was weeping. So many tears in the world, thought Eithne. So much terrible news, how can we bear it?

'Winnie! Is it your brother?'

Winnie shook her head, and wiped her nose with the corner of her shawl.

'It's a horse,' said Ralph, his voice thick.

'A horse?' Eithne tried to gather her wits. Her head swam; she hadn't drunk wine for years.

Winnie struggled to her feet. They were as large as a man's. There was something shocking about their nakedness. The three of them watched the plain, raw-boned girl bundling up the rags.

Eithne sniffed the air. 'Has anyone noticed a smell?'

Chapter Three

The best and most humane way of killing all large hogs is to strike them down like a bullock, with the pointed end of a poleaxe, on the forehead, which has the effect of killing the animal at once; all the butcher has then to do, is to open the aorta and great arteries, and laying the animal's neck over a trough, let out the blood as quickly as possible.

Mrs Beeton's *Book of Household Management*

That March the Germans launched a major offensive. During the retreat at Arras, the Allies suffered their greatest defeat of the war, with a devastating loss of men. Hundreds of thousands were slaughtered and some ninety thousand soldiers were taken prisoner. General Haig pronounced, *With our backs to the wall and believing in the justice of our cause each one must fight to the end. The safety of our homes and the freedom of mankind alike depend upon the conduct of each one of us at this critical moment.*

Deep in Southwark, Neville Turk was launching his own offensive. He had to have the woman. For the first time in his life he couldn't sleep. He had moved into his mother's bedroom, above the front of the shop. He told himself that this was due to its larger size. Nothing to do, of course, with the fact that it overlooked the high street, that the very fact that Eithne Clay walked along the pavement outside, when visiting the shops, gave the room a magnetic pull, even at night when there was no possibility of seeing her. He shifted restlessly in his mother's bed, listening to the church bells strike the hour. He pictured Eithne's body beneath her clothes, those swelling breasts, those wide and shapely hips. He imagined doing such things to her that when she came into the shop even he, a man of experience, reddened.

Neville had been on intimate terms with a large number of women. He was a man of vigorous appetites and had never had difficulty in attracting the opposite sex. These trysts had taken place well away from the eyes of his mother, in small hotels around the Victoria Station where rooms could be rented by the hour – even, on occasion, in the vacant apartment belonging to one of the fellows at the Lodge, a chief constable known for his discretion. These had been brief affairs, however; he might have left some broken hearts behind but his had remained whole.

Eithne Clay, however, had quite undone him. The woman touched something deep within him, he had become a man possessed. The more unobtainable she seemed, the more he longed for her. This one-way pursuit seemed all the more perverse, considering the number of opportunities that were presenting themselves.

Neville's mother was dead. So were the husbands of many women of his acquaintance. The Battle of the Somme had widowed seven of his customers, to his knowledge, and this spring there had been heavy losses with the German advance. Grief, in his experience, could have a startling effect on a woman's libido. Little Mrs Holmes, whom he had considered one of the most demure of his clientele, had surprised him by the ferocity of her demands. He had had to explain the scratches, to his staff, as an accident with a skewer. And they were hungry not only for sex. Meat was in short supply and it was astonishing how many women would drop their drawers for a pound of mince.

Mrs Clay, however, had so far proved resistant. Neville's clumsiness at the Café Royal had taught him to tread carefully. She was a woman of deep loyalties and these no doubt extended beyond her maid-of-all-work; she might still be in mourning for her husband. Besides, she held herself aloof, seldom chatting with the other customers. If her situation was desperate – and he suspected it was – she gave no indication and conducted herself as a woman of means. Maybe she considered him beneath her class. Whatever the reason, her resistance inflamed him and he had had to work out a new campaign. Instinct told him not to ask her out again, not yet; instead, he retrenched, and settled in for a war of attrition.

Neville wooed her with the most powerful armament in his possession. And here the government became, unwittingly, his ally. It introduced rationing. Sugar, butter and tea were already rationed, but that spring they extended the coupons to meat: five ounces per person per week.

Neville was a respected tradesman and a prominent figure in the community. There was no way he was going to fall foul of the law. How fortunate, then, that he counted those very agents of enforcement amongst his closest acquaintance!

'Will that be all?' he asked Mrs Clay as she stood at the

counter, her face blanched by the cold. He no longer called her *madam*, there was a certain familiarity between them nowadays. Their mutual understanding of the matter in hand was creating a deeper intimacy than any candlelit dinner at the Café Royal.

'I do so love an Irish stew,' she would say, casually. 'Nothing beats it, does it, on a filthy winter's day?' Or: 'My son's very partial to liver. Plenty of iron, I've heard, for a growing boy.' Neville nodded; a tremor passed between them and then she swung round on her heel and was gone, her footsteps light with anticipation.

*

Each delivery set Eithne's heart pounding. She unwrapped the paper with eager fingers, as if it were a Christmas present. There, next to her original order, nestled another package. Availability was fitful and sometimes her hints could not be followed up by the item in question. Instead, she received a substitute: a pair of kidneys, a pound of sausages. For some reason this moved her deeply. The butcher, too, was finding times hard and was doing his best to accommodate her wishes. Tenderly, she pictured him puzzling as he sought the nearest alternative. She felt close to him at this moment. He did this, she knew, at real personal risk. And – even more movingly – he never charged her a penny.

Eithne understood what was happening, of course. In her own small way she was a businesswoman; she knew that every relationship was a trading transaction. But where was the pressure? Neville seemed to ask for nothing in return; not so far. And this moved her most of all.

Ralph's class was cancelled. A notice to this effect was pinned on the door: *Due to a family bereavement Mrs Brand is unavailable to teach 'Book-Keeping, Typing and Ledger Preparation' in Room 6. Our prayers are with her and her family.*

Ralph's spirits lifted. It was shameful, but they did. He felt the hot, guilty rush of the truant, for suddenly a free afternoon lay ahead of him. He knew he should feel sorry for his teacher – according to his fellow students, her husband had gone down with his ship at Zeebrugge – but he was only sixteen and couldn't help feeling a sense of release. Besides, he didn't like Mrs Brand. She was a testy woman who made him feel flustered. News of death was so commonplace, and had been for so many years, that it was simply part of the background chatter of everyday life. A person only pricked up their ears when it concerned somebody they knew, or somebody more agreeable than a harridan like Mrs Brand.

Then Ralph began to feel sorry for the unknown Mr Brand, that his brief time on earth had been spent married to Mrs Brand, who was not only a harridan but had a moustache. Maybe he had never kissed a hairless woman and now it was too late.

Ralph's vision blurred. It was curious, what started him off. Terrible news could leave him dry-eyed and yet the story of Winnie's horse had filled his eyes with tears. Maybe that was because animals had no choice in the matter. One of his father's letters had described how the cavalry horses were getting so thin that new holes had to be punched in their girths. *They lead them to the saddler*, he wrote, *for a plate and a punch.*

Ralph left the building and started to walk home, along the river. It was a heavy day, threatening rain. St Thomas's Hospital loomed up ahead of him. The wounded were brought here from France. They arrived by train, passing his bedroom window as they travelled up from Kent. He could identify the trains by their lowered blinds.

Outside the hospital, the road was strewn with straw to muffle the traffic. The recent rain had made it muddy; horse droppings were squashed in it. All over London people collected horse droppings, shovelling them into buckets to dig into their vegetable patches. The smallest gardens had long ago been ploughed up, to grow food. Ralph remembered one of Boyce's jokes. *A boy meets his chum who's wheeling a barrow of manure. 'What are you doing with that?' 'Me dad puts it on his rhubarb.' 'Oh,' says the boy, 'we put custard on ours.'*

Ralph hadn't shed a tear for Boyce; if he let the floodgates open, it would be an admission that Boyce was dead. In the matter of his father he had practised the strictest self-control. He didn't cry, not in front of his mother. He didn't want to upset her, he had to be strong for her. He was the man of the family now.

Beside him raced the river – urgent, dun, swollen with the spring tide. Thunder rumbled in the bruised sky above St Paul's. Ralph walked home, unaware of the storm clouds gathering within his own life. He was wondering what his classmates would be doing, now they had the afternoon off. He had seen four of them whispering together on the stairs. Perhaps they had been cooking up a plan, some sort of jaunt, and had been waiting for him to leave. It wasn't his fault that he hadn't made friends; he had always had to hurry off, on the dot of five, to his responsibilities at home.

Ralph left the river and took the short cut back, past the vinegar factory. Outside the gates two boys were punching each other. He moved to the other side of the road. They were a coarse bunch anyway, the fellows at the college, barging around the corridors and sniggering at the female students. He wouldn't have gone on their outing even if they had begged him.

A few raindrops fell. Ralph thought: if Boycie had been with me, if they'd seen Boycie was my friend, they would have changed their tune.

Ralph walked home, through the alleys he knew so well that he could find his way with his eyes closed. Alwyne Flyte, of course, had no such choice. Sometimes Ralph met the man, his tap-tapping stick echoing in the narrow streets as he made his way to the public house by Southwark Bridge. It must be like living in a permanent black-out. People were always stumbling off the pavements and breaking their ankles, but for Alwyne the black-out never lifted. In the early days Ralph would touch his arm, tentatively, but Alwyne shook him off. 'I can manage, young man.' He was determined to stand on his own feet and Ralph had to admire the fellow's pluck.

It started to rain. In the courtyards, women pulled their washing off the lines. The great tenements loomed up on either side, dank and greasy. Ralph walked up Back Lane, past the depots that were roofed by the railway overhead, where people had to shout over the noise of the trains. It was true: his fellow students were an uncouth crowd. Most of them had never read a book in their lives. Ralph's father had slotted letters together all day, and he had given Ralph a love of interesting words. Ralph's mother, too, had a cabinet of books and would certainly read more if she had the time. The trouble was, she was rushed off her feet. But now his class was cancelled he could help her. He pictured her pleasure when he arrived home early.

Ralph was thinking this when he emerged into the high street. To his surprise he saw Winnie sheltering outside the pawnshop. She stood under the awning, with the dog.

'Your mum told me to take him out for a walk,' she said. 'Down to the park.'

'But it's raining.'

Winnie, too, looked mildly bemused. 'We were going to get started on the brass. I'd got the polish out.' She looked down at the dog. 'He's done his business.'

'Let's take him home then.'

'I don't know that I should.'

There was a pause. Outdoors a certain constraint fell upon the two of them. In the privacy of the house they were confidants, they were free with each other, but when they met like this Winnie somehow shrank back into being a servant. This made Ralph feel lonely.

Winnie seemed even more awkward than usual. Ralph had no idea of the reason, then, for her reluctance to return to the house.

'Let's not go back!' she said suddenly. 'Let's go down to the river, there might be a dead body washed up. You used to like that when you were little.'

Ralph shook his head. 'I've just *been* beside the river. Come on.'

Winnie paused. Then she shrugged. They hurried off, bowing their heads against the rain.

By the time they reached Palmerston Road the rain had stopped as abruptly as it had begun. Those people who had been sheltering under the railway bridge moved off. A man remounted his ladder and carried on pasting up an advertisment: DERRY AND TOM'S HALF-PRICE SALE STARTS MONDAY. Ralph's house was the end building, the one sliced off from its long-lost neighbours, and its side was plastered with posters. BOVRIL GIVES STRENGTH TO WIN. When he was young Ralph thought these messages were just for him, renewed by men who had urgent news to impart to himself alone. MAINTAIN REGULARITY WITH FRIAR'S LAXATIVE: AVOID IMITATIONS!

The sun came out and Ralph was flooded with love – a warm, protective love for his home and the souls within it. For all their funny ways, the lodgers were like his family, and it was up to him to take care of them, and his mother. His childish self-absorption seemed laughable now – how foolish he had been about the posters, and how lucky he had told nobody at the time! And how silly to get steamed up about the chaps at the college. He was a man now, and soon he would have a proper man's job, in an office. His father had been a typesetter. Ralph sensed that his mother thought this a lowly occupation, and that his father's ambitions left something to be desired. Ralph would see to that. He would do her proud. He would do his *father* proud. And he would take care of her until she died.

'I'll be off,' said Winnie, and scuttled down the area steps. Ralph opened the front door. Faint music wafted along the hallway.

He recognised the tune. It was *The Massachusetts Foxtrot*.

'Boyce!' yelled Ralph, and hurled himself down the corridor. The dog shot ahead of him.

Boyce was home! Ralph's heart leapt with joy. Boyce *had* been pretending, he had known it all along. This was his best joke ever.

Brutus nosed open the door of the back parlour; music flooded out. Ralph followed the dog into the room and stopped dead.

His mother was dancing with a man. They stopped, startled, and jumped apart.

It wasn't Boyce. It was the butcher, Mr Turk. Ralph stared at him.

'What are you doing here?' gasped his mother. Her face was shiny with perspiration.

'That's Boyce's gramophone record,' said Ralph.

Mr Turk lifted off the needle and sat down heavily. He too was sweating.

'I just borrowed it,' said his mother.

The man was sitting in Ralph's father's armchair. The dog was all over him, wagging his tail, trying to lick his face. Mr Turk lifted him off and sat there, his legs planted apart.

'Why are you home early?' asked his mother breathlessly.

'Mrs Brand's husband was killed.' Ralph looked at Mr Turk's thighs, in his tight trousers. Big thighs, as thick as tree-trunks. He caught sight of the bulge between them and turned away, as if he'd been stung. 'There is a war on, you know.'

'And what exactly do you mean by that?' she snapped.

Ralph's courage failed him. He said, weakly: 'What if the lodgers came in?'

Mr Turk turned to her. 'You let your lodgers come in this room?'

'They can if they want,' she said. 'They hardly ever do.'

Mr Turk raised his eyebrows. 'You don't have a room to yourself?'

Ralph glared at the man. What business was it of his?

'Anyway,' said his mother, 'I don't see what we were doing wrong.'

Mr Turk got to his feet. 'I'll be pushing off.'

'Say hello to Mr Turk,' she told Ralph, flustered.

'Hello and goodbye, young man,' said Mr Turk, extending his hand. Ralph shook it.

The butcher picked up his jacket and left. Brutus followed him. So did Ralph's mother.

Ralph stood there, in the stuffy little room. A fire glowed in the grate; it was very warm. There was a sickly scent in the air – sweat, and perfume, and something else, a glandular smell. He had sniffed it in Flossie's fur, when she was on heat. Ralph's stomach heaved.

His *mother* dancing with the *butcher*. Ralph still couldn't take it in. He felt numb. A vase of roses sat on the mantelpiece. Now that he thought of it, flowers had recently been appearing in the house. Mrs O'Malley had remarked on it only the evening before, how mimosas brightened up a room.

Down the hallway he heard the murmur of voices. The front door closed. Ralph grabbed Boyce's gramophone record, shoved it into its sleeve and ran upstairs.

*

Ralph lay in bed. His mother would come in soon, to kiss him good-night. He knew she must.

The double-doors, however, remained closed. It was late. The procession of footsteps on the stairs, as the lodgers trudged down to visit the bathroom, and queued, and finally trudged upstairs again – those had ceased. Within the wall, the pipes gurgled and were silent. Ralph hadn't extinguished the lamp beside his bed; he lay there, waiting for her.

His mother had been polite all evening, but cool. It was as if *she* were punishing *him*. Not a word of explanation, but then they hadn't had a moment alone together. There was the supper to cook – a flustered business, everything being knocked back by the events of the afternoon – the table to lay, the dishes to clear. Mrs O'Malley's blind had broken, and Ralph had had to fix it with string; Mrs Spooner had been unusually loquacious – he had smelt alcohol on her breath – and when returning her tray had dawdled in the kitchen and told him a lengthy story about how a passenger had run amok on her bus. Even so, had his mother cared to speak to him she could have drawn him aside. She could even have joined him, as she sometimes did, when he took the dog around the block for his final walk before the house was locked up for the night.

Through the doors he heard his mother's clock chime eleven – the silvery chime that punctuated their dreams as the two of them lay sleeping in their adjoining rooms. When he woke in the night Ralph had always found it reassuring. It had chimed the hour, on the hour, since he was born. It was echoed by the deeper strike of the grandfather clock downstairs and the distant sound of the church clock, two streets away, but it chimed first, and reminded him that she was near.

The floorboards creaked. What was his mother doing in there? Flossie lay on his stomach, a warm weight. At least the cat had remained loyal. How could Brutus slobber over that man? Ralph was brooding over this when he heard a tap at the door.

'Are you awake?' whispered his mother.

Ralph hastily sat up and grabbed the letter. The door opened and she came in. With her hair down, she looked like a young girl.

'May I sit here?' She removed the cat and sat down on his bed. The eiderdown sighed.

'I was just reading Father's letter,' said Ralph.

'Oh. Which one?'

'With the poem in it.' Ralph held the letter near the lamp. He cleared his throat and read:

'*When the War is over and the Kaiser's out of print*
I'm going to buy some tortoises and watch the beggars
sprint;
When the War is over and the sword at last we sheathe
I'm going to keep a jellyfish and listen to it breathe.'

She took the letter from him and, tossing her hair back, inspected it. She couldn't read the words, she was too far away from the lamp, but no doubt she knew it by heart. She was sitting on his feet but Ralph didn't mind.

He said: 'He was clever, wasn't he?'

His mother gave him back the letter. She stood up and wrapped the shawl around herself, crossing her arms in front of her bosom. It was her silk shawl with birds on it;

the sheen caught the light. Ralph cleared his throat again.
He read:

> '*When the War is over and the battle has been won*
> *I'm going to buy a barnacle and take it for a run;*
> *When the War is over and the German fleet we sink*
> *I'm going to keep a silkworm's egg and listen to it*
> *think.*'

His mother, hunched up, was pacing round the room.
Her shadow loomed on the wallpaper.

'It's very nice,' she said.

'It's not just very nice. It's extremely clever.' His voice
rose. 'Listen to this!

> '*When the War is over and we've done the Belgians*
> *proud*
> *I'm going to keep a chrysalis and read to it aloud.*'

His voice rose higher. He almost shouted:

> '*When the War is over and we've finished up the show*
> *I'm going to plant a lemon-pip and listen to it grow!*'

Ralph folded the letter and replaced it on the table. His
hand was trembling.

His mother stood at the window, her back to him. Her
hair fell down to her waist. She addressed the curtains.
'I'm thirty-eight years old, Ralph.'

Exactly, thought her son. You're far too old to be
behaving in this manner.

'I'm only thirty-eight,' she said. She still didn't turn

round. 'There's been precious little dancing in this house.'

'I could have danced with you if you wanted,' said Ralph. 'Boycie taught me. He was the woman, too, so I know the man's steps. That's the sort of person he was.'

His mother's shoulders twitched irritably, as if an insect had bitten her. She moved restlessly around the room, and stopped at the mantelpiece.

She said: 'You've no idea how kind he's been.'

'Who?'

'Mr Turk. He's been helping us. He's been so kind.'

'Nobody's as kind as Father. He wouldn't even kill slugs. He was the kindest man in the world! You can tell it in his poem! He listened to jellyfish!'

'Stop it!'

'He didn't kill things like Mr Turk –'

'Stop it!'

'He liked them alive!'

His mother swung round, her hair swinging like whips. 'Your father didn't write the poem, Ralph!' she cried. 'He copied it out of a magazine! It was one of his favourite poems, that's why he sent it to you! Oh God, Ralph!'

She rushed out of the room and slammed the door.

*

Winnie couldn't sleep. The house reverberated with misery. She could feel it through the floorboards, through the pipes and ducts and the chimney flue that led down to her own little fireplace. Upstairs, the grandfather clock struck two. In four hours she had to get up and start work – riddle the stove and shovel in what remained of the coal, boil the water for tea and porridge and heat up the kettle for the three front bedrooms that had no wash-basins. The tasks ahead felt foreign to her, as if she were working in a hotel. Now Ralph knew the truth, a shift had taken place, nothing would be the same again. Mr Turk was a presence in the rooms now, she sensed him like a gas.

Her mistress was in his thrall. She had danced with him, as bold as anything. Winnie didn't like the man, but it was not her place to have an opinion. It was for Ralph that she grieved; she felt his shock in the very fabric of the house. The poor love.

It was April, and still her feet hadn't warmed up. Winnie lay on her side, curled up, her nightdress pulled down over her toes. The only way to avoid the clammy sheets was to remain in one position and cook up some body heat. Despite its damp, she loved her room. It was the only room she had ever had to herself. The back yard felt like her domain, too, and every morning Mr Boyce's pigeons arrived and sat in a row on the wall, waiting for her to throw them crumbs.

What would happen if Mrs Clay married Mr Turk? Would he throw Winnie out? He probably thought she was a poor worker, the house being in such a deplorable state. He had no idea how hard it was to clean a place that had fallen into such disrepair, and her mistress so lovesick nowadays she was no help. *Mr and Mrs Turk.* They would move out; they would start a new life without her! Winnie squeezed her eyes shut. It was only in the small hours, alone in her bed, that she had the time to think about herself, and now she was frightening herself so much that she couldn't get to sleep.

Besides, how could she clean the rooms when their inmates refused to budge? This was a long-standing problem. Winnie was fond of the lodgers but they had a barnacle-like determination to remain stuck where they were. For years now a thorough spring-clean had been out of the question. The rooms should be scrubbed and fumigated, the curtains washed, the walls repapered. How could she do that when the boarders remained doggedly in their rooms, only moving their feet when she brushed under them? If Mr Turk poked around the house he would have a fit.

The clock struck three. What would Mr Clay have made of it all, his wife cavorting with the butcher as if she hadn't a care in the world? Such a sweet man, so kind and gentle; would he recognise his wife now? The past years had coarsened Mrs Clay, there was something hard and reckless about her now. And scheming. What hurt Winnie most was how she had tricked her into taking out the dog; she had suspected something was up. And ordering her to lay a fire, too, when coal was so short. There was scarcely enough in the cellar to keep the range alight, let alone a fire in a room that was hardly used.

And yet her mistress looked magnificent! She glowed; her eyes blazed, she radiated such life that she crackled. Winnie could feel the heat off her, when she passed. How she envied her! She herself would never inspire passion, she had known that for a long time, ever since Archie had done that thing in the street. And yet it lay within her, folded up, like petals packed together inside a bud. At night, in bed, when she had herself to herself, she cupped her breasts in her hands. She drew up her legs to her chin,

70

she pulled the neck of her nightdress over her nose and breathed in her warm, animal smell.

*

Winnie was woken by a frantic knocking. 'Winnie!' Mrs Clay opened the door. 'It's half-past eight!'

The two women stared at each other. Winnie stumbled out of bed.

Hastily tying her apron, she joined her mistress in the kitchen. Mrs Clay looked haggard; her hair still hung down her back. 'I couldn't sleep,' she said. 'And then I must have dropped off.'

'So did I,' said Winnie. 'Where's Ralph?'

'Still asleep.' Mrs Clay avoided Winnie's eye. 'I didn't like to disturb him.'

The stove was dead. Usually it stayed in, overnight, but not until this hour in the morning. Now it was cold and Mrs Clay was standing there, doing nothing

'Oh Lord, Winnie,' she said. 'What am I going to do?'

'Get the kindling,' said Winnie. The house was stirring; she could hear footsteps on the floors above, the hiss of the pipes. Mrs Spooner must have left for work without any breakfast. The other lodgers would soon be gathering in the parlour, and Lettie would be down for her father's tray. Winnie's head spun as she tried to catch up with herself. Her bladder was bursting.

'He's so dear,' said Mrs Clay. She was kneeling at the stove, scrunching up newspaper. Who did she mean, the boy or Mr Turk?

Winnie sniffed the milk and poured it into a jug. At this rate, the porridge wouldn't be ready for at least half an hour. Should she run up to the parlour and tell Mrs

O'Malley and Mr Flyte that breakfast would be late? She was still wearing her nightdress but Mrs O'Malley was too ga-ga to notice and Mr Flyte couldn't see it anyway.

'Don't you agree?' asked Mrs Clay, looking up at her.

Winnie was about to reply when she heard a noise outside the window. Both women paused, cocking their heads. It was a rumbling noise. Men shouted to each other, out in the street.

Winnie went to the window. She could see the legs of the dray horse, standing outside. Men were heaving sacks and emptying them down the coal-hole.

Astonished, the two women looked at each other. 'Did you order any coal?' asked Winnie.

Mrs Clay shook her head. The thunder echoed as the loads hit the empty floor of the coal cellar.

'They must have come to the wrong house,' said Winnie.

Mrs Clay didn't reply. The thunder grew muffled as the cellar started filling up. Mrs Clay turned back to the stove. She sat there, gazing at the grate.

'I told him we were short,' she said. 'I didn't mean him to do this.' She pushed the hair off her face, but still she didn't move.

The thunder continued. Sack after sack was being emptied; the cellar was filling up. Winnie, too, was filled by a warm and unfamiliar sensation. Somebody was looking after them. So what if there was rationing? Mr Turk had sorted that out, and it was not her place to enquire even if she understood the first thing about it. And she was included in his generosity, for now she could heat up the copper with solid lumps of coal, not half-slack, she could work up a good boil for the washing

72

and then she could dry the clothes in the warm-as-toast kitchen, she could light all the fires in the bedrooms all through the summer if the lodgers fancied it, she could even light a fire in her own bedroom because Mrs Clay wouldn't mind, she minded nothing nowadays, she didn't even notice, and they were all going to live a fine and careless life like the people in *Penny Pictorial* magazine.

Mrs Clay swung round. Her face was streaked with soot. 'You do like him, Winnie?' she asked urgently. 'Tell me you like him!'

*

Mrs Clay was as skittish as a filly all morning. It was funny, thought Winnie: the woman was filled with energy and yet she never actually did anything. She moved restlessly about the house, picking things up and putting them down. She stood, transfixed by her own reflection in the hall mirror. A long period was spent in the bathroom; three times Mr Spooner crept down the stairs, and up again.

Ralph kept to his bedroom. If Winnie had the time she would have worried about him but she was run off her feet. With neither of them helping, Winnie had to clean the rooms on her own. She didn't mind – her heart went out to the boy – but it would be a scramble to get it all done before the laundry arrived.

In his room, Mr Flyte sensed something was up.

'*What strange and foreign presence stirs in the House of Usher?*' he said.

'Pardon?' Winnie tipped his cigarette butts into her bucket.

'What's afoot, Winnie? I rely on you to keep me informed.'

'I can't say, sir.'

'Oh, don't be loyal. Would *she* be loyal to *you*?'

Winnie stared at him. 'Of course she would.' In fact, now she thought of it, she wasn't so sure.

'Routine's shot to pieces,' he chuckled. 'Everything's arse over tit. Actually, I'm rather enjoying it.' Alwyne lit another cigarette, and she had just emptied his ashtray. 'We're slaves to routine, and know why we have it? To keep women like you in your place. But where does it get you? A room gets dusted, but then you have to do it all over again the next day. And who really cares?'

Not you, she thought. You couldn't tell anyway. She looked at Mr Flyte as he sat in his armchair. *He* certainly had a routine. The daily explosion of coughing in the bathroom at eight o'clock. The daily trip to the Albion saloon bar after supper, on the dot of nine. It was warmer today, he wore no socks with his bedroom slippers. She could see the veins on his ankles.

'What are you thinking, Winnie?'

Wouldn't you like to know, she thought.

'There are advantages to being blind,' he said. 'I'm learning every day. There's the *before* and there's the *after*. The before is to do with memory, but the after is learning everything afresh. Not just this room, the stairs, things with which I was unfamiliar. You, Winnie. Your face that I'll never see.'

Winnie turned away and busied herself with the dusting.

'People I knew before, of course, I'll remember. But they've stopped in time. It's as if they've died. But with you it's different. I don't know what you look like. What's interesting, Winnie, is without that distraction I can see into your heart. For faces can be distracting – my goodness yes, I've certainly come a cropper in *that* department. But with all that nonsense stripped away, I can see into the heart of things. Into *your* heart, Winnie.'

Winnie paused. Outside, a train rattled past.

'So what am I thinking then?' she asked.

He smiled. 'You tell me.'

'I'll tell you what I'm thinking,' she said. 'I'm thinking that before the laundry comes I should've turned the sheets sides to middle.'

He raised his eyebrows. 'What on earth's that?'

'You cut them down the middle and you sew them up again the other way round.'

'Why would you want to do that?'

Because people like you wear them out, she thought. Really, he wasn't that clever. 'With the not-so-worn bit in the middle,' she said patiently. Mrs Clay should be helping her but Mrs Clay had disappeared on a mysterious errand, ten guesses where. 'I haven't finished them yet.' At least she might come back with a nice bit of meat for supper. 'And I've got to fix the tulle on Lettie's dress. I promised Mrs Spooner. See, Lettie's being taken to Kennington this afternoon, to dance for the limbless men.'

'The limbless men?'

'There's a rest home there. By the gasworks.'

Alwyne Flyte leaned forward. The smoke wreathed up between his fingers. 'Is that what you're really thinking, Winnie?'

She blushed. There was something soft and insistent in

75

his voice. Today he wore his black spectacles. She preferred not to see his eyes. Now they were hidden, Mr Flyte seemed as mysterious as she must be to him. Could he really see into her heart? He sat there, his back to the window, his face in shadow.

Suddenly, Winnie felt a surge of rebellion. It was such an unfamiliar feeling that it took her by surprise. Why should Mrs Clay have the only claims to passion, drifting around the house with that dreamy smile and never helping with the work? Mr Flyte was right: Mrs Clay had no interest in her maid, Winnie was just a useful pair of hands. But Winnie, too, had powerful feelings. She, too, was a woman, if anyone could be bothered to find out. Which they never would, unless they were blind.

The laughter welled up. Winnie clamped her mouth tight.

'Come on, Winnie.' His voice was coaxing. 'There's more to life than sewing, isn't there? Tell me your secrets, I've got bugger all else to think about.'

'But you said you knew.'

'I want to hear *you* tell them to me.'

All right, thought Winnie. Let's see how clever you are.

The heat rose up in her face. Her heart thumped. Later she couldn't believe she had done it – what had seized her? Later, when she thought about it, her knees went weak and she had to lean against the wall.

For she put down her bucket and cloth. Right there, in the middle of the room, she slid her hand down the front of her apron. Her eyes remained fixed on the bearded man sitting in the armchair. *I'll show you*, she thought. She slid her hand down, behind the shield of her apron, and cupped her breast. With her finger, she felt the nipple through the cloth. She stroked it. The warmth spread through her body. And all the time she watched him. *This is what I do in the dark*, she told him soundlessly. He was there in the dark with her, it was his domain. They were in it together.

Mr Flyte didn't move. His blindness excited her. He had no idea what she was doing and just for once, for this short moment in her life, Winnie had a man in her power. A sharp, animal scent rose from her armpits.

Winnie pulled out her hand. She picked up her bucket and cloths, her broom, her dustpan and brush – she fumbled with them, the brush fell on the floor, the broom keeled over – but she finally collected them together and bolted from the room.

*

The meat arrived on a daily basis now – plump lamb chops, nestling together like married couples; a moist crimson topside, marbled with fat; a leg of veal. Eithne Clay no longer bothered to send an order. She waited for the butcher's boy to deliver the parcel, the blood seeping through the paper, the string no doubt tied by Neville Turk's own hands. She unpicked the knot with a shiver of intimacy. The dog was not forgotten. Each delivery was accompanied by a package of bones, which Brutus took away one by one and ate under the parlour table, cracking them like masonry and leaving a scattering of splinters. The dog had long since surrendered to the butcher; he needed no wooing now and pulled at the lead when passing the shop.

If the lodgers were surprised by their good fortune they kept quiet about it. Theirs was not to reason why, and instinct told them to keep their silence. They too had gone hungry, and if others suffered it was Mr Asquith's fault for getting them into the war in the first place. Patriotic fervour had long since evaporated; nowadays it was every man for himself. All day they looked forward to supper and sniffed the air as the hour approached. Gone were the days of glutinous barley stews, of pease-pudding pasties that weighed like lead, of boiled tripe whose rubbery fibres got caught in Mrs O'Malley's dentures. Each night they ate meat fit for Buckingham Palace. If Mrs Clay's cooking left something to be desired they were in no position to complain. There was even bacon for breakfast.

The change in their landlady's spirits also lifted the atmosphere. It had been a gruelling spring, with chronic shortages and terrible news from the Front. At Palmerston Road, however, piano music wafted up the stairwell and jugs of roses exhaled a scent that made their heads swim. Mrs Clay hummed under her breath; she leapt up the stairs like a girl. Her room, always slovenly, could be glimpsed through the doorway in a state of more spectacular chaos. She set forth on her errands dressed up in her best, her maroon hat nodding with feathers. If romance was in the air, there were no clues as to who might be the cause of this transformation. No gentleman callers came to the house; in fact, apart from tradesmen, few visitors ever came to the house at all. Nor were the lodgers, by and large, overly burdened with curiosity. They were content to reap the benefits.

And then, one day in late April, they were told a startling piece of news. Mr Turk, the local butcher, was coming to cook them dinner.

Winnie nearly dropped the eggs. 'He's *what*?'

'He asked me how I cooked the meat and I told him,' said Mrs Clay casually. 'He nearly had a fit when I told him I boiled the chops. So he said he'd come round and show me how to do it. Show you too, Winnie. Isn't he kind?'

'He's going to cook for everybody?'

Eithne nodded. In fact Neville had suggested a dinner *à deux*, taken in the back parlour, but she had told him she always ate with her son and the lodgers in the front room.

'Where's your privacy?' he had asked.

'It would be a shame to leave them out of it. They've little enough in their lives.'

He had smiled at her – a smile that melted her bone marrow. 'You're a real softie, you are.'

In fact, she had simply wanted to include her son. Ralph hadn't met the butcher, to her knowledge, since that incident in the back room. Since then, Mr Turk's name had not been mentioned between them. Two months had passed, long enough for that painful scene to be buried and forgotten. During this time she had been particularly tender with her son, spending time with him, helping him collate his stamp collection and even accompanying him to his book-keeping class in Vauxhall. It was time that he met Neville again, and under more favourable circumstances. How could Ralph fail to be charmed by a man who cooked him dinner? And they would have time to talk, in the civilised surroundings of a meal. He could get to know Neville and see what an admirable man he was, and realise how much they were in his debt.

Besides, she wanted Neville in her home, sitting at her table. She ached with longing for it. She wanted to see him amongst her familiar objects, the shock of him sitting there, eating off her china. She wanted him to move into her world and alter the room with his presence. How would he behave with the lodgers? What would they think of him? What would *she* think of him?

*

'Leave it to me,' Neville said. 'You don't do a dicky-bird.'

He had arrived on the dot of six. Winnie had spent all afternoon cleaning the kitchen and scrubbing the pans, as if for a royal visit. There was indeed something of the potentate about Neville; he was accompanied by one of the boys from the shop who, like a page, carried the supplies for his master. Neville stood, surveying the kitchen. Eithne lowered her eyes in confusion; he seemed both strange to her, and intensely familiar. His thick black hair shone in the lamplight; he wore a tweed suit and yellow cravat. His presence filled the room; he made her feel fragile and diminished, her arms hanging uselessly.

'Can't I do anything to help?' she asked.

But Neville was gazing at the range. He shook his head wonderingly, as if gazing at an ancient monument. 'Can't believe you still cook on one of those.'

'It does us all right,' she said. 'And thank you again for the coal.'

Winnie's presence constrained her. This man – she had sat beside him in the hansom cab, their thighs touching; she had felt his body pressing against hers as they danced the foxtrot. His breath had brushed her face.

But today Neville was brisk, a man with a job to do. He took off his jacket, donned his apron and rolled up his sleeves. Eithne glanced at his arms. They were packed with muscle and matted with hair. She looked at his strong hands. He could strangle me she thought: he could strangle me like a rag doll.

'Aberdeen Angus,' he said, pulling out a bloodstained package, wrapped in cloth. 'These are your rump steaks, tastier than fillet, cut from a five-year-old steer from the best pasture in Craigievar, you won't find anything finer. Supplier's a good friend of mine, kept it for me. Secret's in the hanging.' He unwrapped the cloth. Just for a moment, standing there in his apron, Neville resembled a small boy – boastful, yet strangely defenceless. Eithne, moved, wanted to put her arms around him and say *You don't have to impress me, my dearest. I'd go to the ends of the earth for you.*

She smothered her mouth. For a mad moment, she thought she had spoken out loud.

'I've soaked it in a marinade.' Neville tapped the side of his nose. 'My secret recipe. Juniper berries, vinegar, mixed herbs, port wine.'

'Not so secret now,' she said.

He grinned. 'Aha, but it's *our* secret.'

Her heart lurched. She swung round to Winnie, who was standing there like a dolt. 'Winnie, have you checked the chairs? You might need some more.' She turned to Neville. 'It's a full house tonight. You should be honoured. Even the Spooners are joining us.'

'Not Mr Spooner,' said Winnie.

'What's up with Mr Spooner?' asked Neville.

'God knows!' Eithne laughed, heartlessly. Winnie shot

her a look but she ignored it. 'Run up, Winnie, and check the table.'

Winnie didn't move. Eithne thought: what's the matter with the girl?

*

Winnie stood still. She felt the warmth seeping between her legs. She should have realised, what with having stomach pains all morning. And now a trail of blood was trickling down the inside of her thigh.

The problem was that her pile of rags lay on the dresser. They had been drying on the clotheshorse, in front of the stove, but she had hastily moved them aside before Mr Turk's arrival. How could she fetch them without Mrs Clay realising the reason? Yet if she carried away the whole pile of washing, the butcher might notice that it included six pairs of Mrs Clay's drawers. Either way, there was the possibility of embarrassment. Though Winnie was a plain-spoken girl in many respects, in this matter she was painfully shy. It stemmed from having no mother, and growing up in a houseful of boys.

'Winnie!'

Mrs Clay glared at her. Winnie darted to the dresser. Grabbing the pile of washing, she hurried out.

*

Ralph arrived late, and took his seat without a word. The parlour had a festive air. Outside it was still light, but the candles had been lit in the candelabra, eight of them and all brand new. The table had been spread with a clean cloth and even the napkins had been washed and ironed – *ironed* – before being rolled up again in their holders.

The cooking smells were intoxicating; Brutus stood in the doorway, strings of saliva hanging from his mouth.

Romance was in the air. Even Mrs O'Malley, confused at the best of times, was starting to suspect a connection between the presence of the butcher and her landlady's high spirits. 'Spring's arrived!' cried Mrs Clay, when asked the reason for the meal. 'Isn't it time we had something to celebrate?'

An attempt had been made to dress up for the occasion. Mrs O'Malley wore her hat, as if she were just about to catch a tram. Lettie's hair was tied with ribbons and her mother, normally a mousy creature, wore a turquoise blouse whose tiny pleats had taken Winnie three-quarters of an hour to iron that morning. Only Ralph and Alwyne had made no attempt to smarten themselves up. Mrs Clay advanced on her son with a hair-comb but he ducked away, scowling. 'Come here!' she hissed, but then they had heard Mr Turk's step on the stair and she sat down again.

Mr Turk and Winnie carried in the dinner: a platter of rump steaks swimming in rich, brown gravy; boiled peas and carrots, a dish of new potatoes gleaming with butter – *soaked* in butter, *drowning* in butter.

'Something smells good,' said Alwyne, leaning forward in his chair. He had tucked his napkin under his chin, the cotton a snowy white against the dense blackness of his beard.

'I'll let you in on a secret,' said Mr Turk. He turned and winked at Mrs Clay. 'And casting no nasturtiums on the good lady's cooking . . .'

'Nasturtiums!' Mrs O'Malley tittered.

'With your meat, you have to seal in the juices,' he said. 'Hot pan, hot fat. Brown it on both sides till it's piping hot. So damn piping hot that when you pour on the liquid the stuff bubbles and reduces.'

Nobody was listening. All the eyes were fixed on the food. Winnie started serving it out.

'And you'll do me the honour of drinking a glass of first-rate burgundy,' said Mr Turk, 'supplied for me by Messrs Berry Brothers and Rudd, of St James's Street in Mayfair.' He fetched a bottle off the sideboard where, already uncorked, it had been set to breathe. 'Glasses, Ralph?' He was in high good humour.

Eithne gazed at him, transfixed. All this – he was doing all this for her. And he was a wonderful cook, who would have thought it? Juniper berries, indeed! Marinades! No man she had ever met had known what a marinade was. Neither in fact did she. Nor could she imagine any man of her acquaintance, especially a man as impressive, as *manly*, as Neville Turk, donning an apron and rustling up a meal for the motley bunch of souls who dwelt under her roof. Eithne felt a wave of desire so powerful that it stopped her breath. And look, everyone liked him! Even her son was getting up from his chair and doing what he was told; everything was going to be all right.

Ralph opened the wall cupboard and took out the glasses. Winnie set down the plates in front of each person. When she got to his place Ralph said: 'No meat for me, please, Winnie.'

'What?' She paused, the plate in her hand.

'No meat for me. I'm a vegetarian.'

Silence fell.

'You're *what*?' demanded Eithne.

'The human digestive system is not designed for meat-eating,' Ralph said, laying out the glasses. 'Carnivorous animals – lions, cats – have a short intestine, only three times the length of their bodies. This happens because meat decays rapidly, and the products of this decay poison the bloodstream if they remain for a long time in the body.'

Mrs O'Malley leant towards Lettie. 'What's he talking about, pet?'

'This ensures the rapid expulsion of putrefactive bacteria from decomposing flesh,' said Ralph.

'Don't be so disgusting!' snapped Eithne.

Mrs Spooner picked up a plate and headed for the door. 'I'll just take up Mr Spooner his supper,' she said.

'Human beings, however, have intestines like the herbivores – cows, zebras, horses,' continued Ralph, sitting down. 'Their intestines are twelve times the length of their bodies. This is for the slow digestion of vegetable matter, which doesn't decay and putrefy.'

Mrs O'Malley put down her fork. 'I don't feel very well,' she said.

'Where did you hear all this nonsense?' demanded Eithne.

'Alwyne told me.'

'It doesn't seem to have put *him* off,' she replied, looking at Alwyne Flyte who was calmly eating.

'He asked me and I told him.' Alwyne spoke with his mouth full. 'Several of my more progressive friends in Bolton have forsworn meat.'

'Well, you haven't and neither have we. Stop being so foolish, Ralph, and eat up your dinner. Mr Turk has gone to a lot of trouble.' She turned to the butcher. 'I'm so sorry, Neville.'

Neville. A ripple went round the table. Ralph calmly forked up a potato and put it into his mouth.

Winnie's heart went out to Ralph, whom she pitied more than she could bear, whom she wanted to protect. But how infuriating the boy was! How could he spoil the meal like that? He sat there eating primly, like a curate.

'Glad they're not all like you, my boy,' said Mr Turk. 'Or I'd be out of a job.'

Eithne laughed, shrilly.

'Doesn't explain these though, does it?' Alwyne turned to Ralph and bared his teeth. A piece of meat was stuck between them. He tapped the pointed tooth beneath his moustache. 'Doesn't explain the canines.'

'How do you answer that, young man?' asked Mr Turk. His jovial spirits seemed undiminished.

'It's a terrible thing, to slaughter living creatures,' said Ralph.

'Ralph!' hissed his mother.

Mrs O'Malley belched, and carried on shovelling in peas with her spoon. Mrs Spooner reappeared, shadowy as always, and slipped into her place at the table.

'My husband says thank you very much,' she said to Mr Turk.

'What's the matter with the man?' asked the butcher. 'He ill or something?'

Nobody spoke. Lettie's eyes darted to her mother.

'He's not quite himself, Mr Turk,' said Mrs Spooner. 'Not quite the ticket.'

'Who's for more potatoes?' asked Eithne brightly.

Mrs O'Malley patted her lips with her napkin. 'May I enquire if anybody is going to eat that extra steak?'

'Good God, you can pack it away!' said Mr Turk. 'I like that in a woman.'

Mrs O'Malley giggled and held out her plate. The

butcher slid the meat on to it. The dog sat watching her every move, his tail thumping the carpet. Even the cat had appeared; she jumped on to the sideboard and sat there, her eyes fixed on their plates.

'I do hope you'll come again,' Mrs O'Malley said. 'I'm particularly partial to a broiled chicken, if you could see your way to that. Haven't eaten a piece of chicken since last November.'

'It will be my pleasure, Mrs O'Malley,' said Mr Turk. 'Nothing beats a nice piece of chicken, I'm with you on that one.'

Alwyne turned to the butcher. 'And which do you prefer, old boy? The leg or the breast?'

Ralph's head whipped round. Wide-eyed, he stared at Alwyne.

Mr Turk seemed unperturbed. He grinned at the blind man. 'If she's a good juicy bird, plenty of flesh on her, I'd plump for the breast.'

The word hung in the air. Winnie stared at Alwyne. How could he have said that? His spectacles flashed in the candlelight as he cocked his head, listening to the reaction. The man was enjoying himself!

Outside, the daylight was fading. Mr Turk was engaging Mrs O'Malley in conversation, flirting with her and making her simper. Lettie slipped a piece of meat to the dog. Winnie couldn't finish her food. *Breast*. Was Alwyne looking at her, with his sightless eyes, when he said that word? Thank goodness he couldn't see her blushes. He looked so *knowing*, somehow. As if he knew that she had done that thing in front of him.

And yet it was exciting! Winnie wanted to do it again, she wanted to goad him. Alwyne was sitting opposite her. She had a strong desire to slide down her chair and stretch out her foot – stretch it out and press her toe between his legs. Watch his face then! Watch his lenses flash as he turned his head to and fro, seeking the culprit! Winnie felt, again, that throb of power. See who was the servant and who the master! *Workers of the world unite* – and she just a skivvy.

Winnie stiffened. The blood was seeping out of her, she could feel the dampness underneath her bottom. And she was sitting on the best chair, the chair that had belonged to Mr Clay's mother. Winnie had brought it in from the back room, to make up the numbers.

Winnie's blushes deepened. Silently, she urged them to finish eating. Mrs O'Malley was still working her way through the second steak. Mrs Spooner was taking tiny sips of her wine, eking it out. The poor woman had few enough pleasures but her niminy-piminy manner made Winnie impatient. *Hurry up!* Alwyne was moving his fork around the plate, chasing the last errant carrot, but nobody was coming to his rescue. And now Mrs O'Malley was having trouble with her dentures. Only Lettie was restless, twisting round in her chair and making faces at the dog who was sitting beside her, his eyes fixed on her face.

Finally they finished eating. Winnie readied herself to get up.

Mrs Clay turned to her son. 'Ralph, clear the table.'

Winnie pushed back her chair.

'No, Winnie!' said Mrs Clay. 'Let him do it.'

'But madam –'

'You stay there. I'll help him.' With a grim look at her son, Mrs Clay got to her feet and started stacking the plates. Winnie knew why she was doing this, of course. She wanted to give Ralph a ticking-off in the kitchen.

'This is your treat too,' she said, smiling at Winnie. No doubt she also wanted to show Mr Turk how kindly she treated her domestic. Winnie sat there in a torment. The blood was seeping through to the chair, she could feel it. The seat was upholstered in yellow velvet! She had to hurry down to her room and stuff in a new rag, didn't Mrs Clay understand? She couldn't sit there a moment longer.

Winnie stood up.

'No!' said Mrs Clay, wagging her finger. 'You're off duty now, my dear.' *My dear?* 'Stay here and keep Mr Turk happy.'

'Oh, I'm as happy as Larry,' he said, flashing a smile at Mrs Clay. She was standing in the doorway, radiant in the candlelight. She smiled at him, a smile so dazzling that Winnie flinched, as if she were staring at the sun.

*

The dog was doing his business in the middle of the flowerbed.

'I'm going to marry Mr Turk,' Eithne told her son. They were standing in the little park by the river. 'I'm going to marry Neville. He asked me last night, after you'd gone to sleep, and I said yes.'

Brutus squatted, hunched, amongst the daffodils. The turd emerged and dropped to the ground in a coil. It was followed by a second. The stench wafted up to Ralph's nostrils. He had forgotten to tell them, the evening before, about the impactive effect of meat in the gut. A dog's digestive tract could deal with it but in humans this led to chronic constipation.

'Say something, my love.'

The park had been largely dug up for the growing of vegetables. A fence had been erected to separate the flowerbeds from the patriotic cabbages but in truth there was little to distinguish between the two. They all struggled to survive. Besides, in several places the fence had been flattened. Dogs and children had trampled all over the place. The gardener had long since disappeared; the cabbages had stood there all winter and the ones that hadn't been stolen were rotting.

'He'll never take the place of your father,' she said, 'he wouldn't want to do that. But he's a wonderful man, Ralph, he wants to take care of us.'

'Brutus!' Ralph yelled. The dog had disappeared towards the river. Ralph inserted two fingers into his mouth and whistled. His mother jumped. 'Boyce taught me how to do that,' he said.

Suddenly, he longed to be with his friend. It didn't matter where Boycie was – Ralph wasn't stupid, he knew something terrible might have happened to him. But wherever he was, Ralph wanted to be with him. Boyce would have got him out of this. They could be together. He thought: I love you so much I haven't eaten your little packets of sugar.

'He wants to love you,' said his mother, 'if you'll give him the chance.'

Brutus came bounding up. Ralph sank to his knees. 'Who's my best boy?' He closed his eyes and felt the dog's tongue slobber over his face.

*

Winnie was making her second attempt to remove the

90

stain. She was scrubbing it with carbolic soap, and hot water containing a few drops of bleach. This was risky, of course. There was the danger that the faint, rusty patch would be replaced by a pale, bleached patch, but Winnie aimed to overcome this by scrubbing the entire chair-seat. If this resulted in a paler yellow throughout, with any luck nobody would be the wiser.

Mrs Clay was out, with Ralph. The atmosphere at breakfast had been tense. As Winnie knelt at the chair, scrubbing, she pondered the nature of love. Why, for instance, had she loved Dulcie more than the other horses? What singled out the old grey mare as an object of her devotion? Winnie was fond of all horses, she had grown up with them, but it was Dulcie who touched her heart. When Dulcie lifted her head from the bucket, her muzzle dusted with bran – when she swung her head round and gazed at Winnie, her ears pricked, her eyes deep and moist with recognition – then Winnie's heart shifted in her breast, she could scarcely breathe for love.

Where was Dulcie now? How was she managing, away from home, away from everything that was familiar to her? Four years had passed since they had taken her away. They had tied the horses together with rope, in a line, and led them out of the village. Some of the thoroughbreds had played up, thinking they were going hunting. All through the village people had closed their doors; they couldn't watch.

The clattering had faded away. Dulcie hadn't even been shod, she had long since been retired from work. The sound of their hoofs faded and the village was silent. The doors remained closed. Nobody had spoken of the horses again.

Winnie wiped her eyes with her apron. The thought of Dulcie always brought on the waterworks. She sat back on her haunches. The seat was sodden; the velvet stood up in matted tufts. Only time would tell if the stain had gone.

The front door opened. Winnie scrambled to her feet and moved to the other side of the room. Sinking to her knees, she began to scrub at an imaginary stain on the carpet.

She heard Ralph's footsteps climbing the stairs to his room. The dog followed him. Mrs Clay came in and pulled off her hat.

'Oh, Winnie,' she said. 'Oh dear me.'

With a sigh, she sat down heavily on the chair.

Winnie froze. The seat was wet. Mrs Clay, however, was too distracted to notice.

'He must like him,' she said. 'He *will* like him, it's only a matter of time. *You* like him, don't you, Winnie? Have you ever met anybody so generous? Weren't those violet creams delicious last night? He had them sent from Paris. He wants to take care of us all, you too. Oh I love him so much I can hardly bear it, oh Winnie you have no idea. It feels – it feels – like my heavy fetters have become daisy chains. Oh I can't describe it. I'm so happy I want to die!'

Mrs Clay got up from the chair and fled from the room. Winnie glimpsed a damp patch on the back of her skirt.

Chapter Four

The cow goes with young for nine months, and the affection and solicitude she evinces for her offspring is more human in its tenderness and intensity than is displayed by any other animal, and her distress, when she hears it bleating, and is not allowed to reach it with her distended udders, is often painful to witness, and when the calf has died, or been accidentally killed, her grief frequently makes her refuse to give down any milk. At such times, the breeder has adopted the expedient of flaying the dead carcass, and, distending the skin with hay, lays the effigy before her, and then taking advantage of her solicitude, milks her while she is caressing the skin with her tongue.

Mrs Beeton's Book of Household Management

The wedding took place in mid-May. Once decided, there seemed no sense in delaying things. Besides, Neville was mad to possess her. The thought of Eithne's naked body, under her skirts, obsessed him. Throughout the day, as he sawed and chopped, he pictured her thighs parting, the sweet moistness between them waiting for his finger. He would slide it in and feel her breath quicken. Slowly, oh so slowly, he would take out his finger and put it into his mouth, sucking the juice of her as she pressed herself against him, whimpering, rubbing her face against him, her hair tangled in his nose, his teeth. As he dismembered a chicken he pictured Eithne spread on the slab beneath him, her head flung back, her legs open. Under his bloody apron, his member stiffened. And meanwhile he joked with his customers, he called out the orders. All day, and throughout his long sleepless nights, her face was in front of him – her sweet, neat mouth; her fine eyes and high cheekbones; her soft brown hair released from its pins, all disordered about her shoulders. Eithne Clay carried herself with refinement but this didn't fool him. *I know you better, woman, than you know yourself.*

But first, before he got his hands on her, there had to be a wedding. As a gesture of respect, this was a quiet event. After all, she was a widow, and many would consider her to be still in mourning. And it was wartime; a lavish celebration would be deemed inappropriate. Most weddings were hasty affairs, carried out when the groom had a few days' leave; then he was gone, leaving his sweetheart a respectable woman. Chances were that was the last she saw of him. All she had left was the photograph of a young man in uniform, whom she had hardly known.

For Neville, of course, such circumstances didn't apply but one still had to acknowledge that there was a war on – a war that had become such a way of life it seemed impossible to imagine that it would ever end. It permeated every home; nobody was immune. Even the Prime Minister had lost his son.

So there was a simple ceremony, and afterwards a modest wedding breakfast in Palmerston Road. Neville had laid on cold cuts, a crate of champagne and two sulky waitresses. Winnie had made sandwiches. Tuberoses filled the air with their heavy, corrupt scent.

Strangers stood jammed into the back room. The dog worked his way through them, sniffing, searching for a pair of familiar legs. Few neighbours had been invited, for Eithne was not on intimate terms with them. The guests were Neville's – stout, affable men and their lady wives, men whose watch-chains stretched over their stomachs, men of some position in the community.

'They're Masons,' Winnie whispered to Ralph, grabbing his hand. 'Watch them when they shake hands. They do *this* with their finger.'

Ralph pulled his hand away. 'Stop it!' Her finger, moving in his palm, felt curiously naked, like something squirming under a stone.

Winnie giggled. She was off duty and had already drunk two glasses of champagne.

'That's a high-up policeman,' she whispered, 'and that's Mr Something who's ever so important, he's got that factory down at Woolwich where the girls go yellow from the explosives, my friend Elsie works there, her face is yellow as custard. And that's another bigwig. He's got a wholesale business down at the Borough Market. His daughter's got a club foot.'

Ralph gazed at Winnie with awe. Servants knew more than anybody else, yet he never saw Winnie gossiping in the street. It seeped into them by a sort of osmosis, the thing that plants did. His father had told him about it.

'And they say the Mayor's coming.' Winnie lowered her voice, as if they were in church. 'He's coming to drink their health.'

'The Lord Mayor of London?'

'One of them. It might be the Southwark one. Mr Thingy.'

'Oh yes,' said a voice, 'Mr Turk's got his finger in a lot of pies.'

They swung round. Alwyne Flyte was standing beside them. He must have felt his way through the crowd. They could smell the mildew on his jacket.

'But who cares?' he said, gesturing around. 'This lot will soon be extinct.'

'Ssh!' hissed Winnie. 'They'll hear.'

'They don't look very extinct to me,' said Ralph.

'Oh yes, when the time comes they'll be first for the chop. You mark my words.'

Ralph was pressed against Winnie's side. The room was too crowded for them to move. Just for a moment they felt like a huddle of conspirators, hemmed in by the stiff, rustling bustles of the lady wives. The hats, loaded with feathers, were a menace; the brims kept bumping into their faces. It was very hot.

Alwyne said: 'Tell me what Mrs Clay's wearing – beg pardon, *Mrs Turk*. I'll wager she's the best-looking woman here.'

Winnie nodded. 'And the tallest.'

Eithne had taken off her hat. They could glimpse her on the other side of the room. She was pressed against the wall, smiling and nodding but somehow not in residence.

'She looks ever so lovely,' said Winnie. 'She's wearing her cream tea-gown, it's trimmed with lace and there's a thin blue stripe in it.'

Its inhabitant, however, had the look of a sleepwalker. Winnie had noticed this before, with brides. She felt a stab of envy. How wonderful it must be to love, and be loved in return! Her mistress had moved into a charmed country whose borders were closed. She had slipped away from Winnie, she had slipped away from them all and was already living in the future where they would feature in a more marginal, less necessary role. Her attention would now be devoted to her husband. The newlyweds were going to Brighton for a week's honeymoon and then Mr Turk would move in as master of the house. Mr Clay's suits had already been removed from the wardrobe and given to some distant relative. Winnie was filled with trepidation.

'There's going to be trouble ahead,' said Alwyne.

Winnie jumped. Maybe the blind had a sixth sense. They could certainly hear better, their ears growing sharper in compensation for their loss of sight. Alwyne was always picking up on things which had passed Winnie by.

'Mark my words,' said Alwyne.

Ralph didn't reply. He had been very quiet, the past few weeks. There had been no repetition of his outburst at dinner but he had continued to refuse meat, which had caused some difficulties in the kitchen. Mrs Clay, however – *Mrs Turk* – had not remarked on this but had used her cheese ration to prepare him lumpy yellow sauces which she poured over the vegetables. Motherly love was a wonderful thing.

Winnie drained her glass. It felt odd, not to be helping. Lettie was worming her way through the bodies, searching for food. Winnie felt a rush of affection for the lodgers. For a week they would have the house to themselves, and she would have the responsibility of looking after them. Mrs Turk had given her full instructions.

Just then they became aware of a stir in the room.

'Mr Harbottle's arrived,' whispered Winnie. 'He owns the jewellery shop, he's a friend of the Mayor.'

The guests fell silent in expectation. Men stood to attention; ladies brushed crumbs off their busts.

But the great man didn't appear. Mr Harbottle leaned towards Mr Turk and whispered in his ear. Mr Turk's face reddened with annoyance; he turned, and muttered something to his bride.

The word spread in an instant. The Mayor wasn't attending because his brother-in-law had shot himself. Mr Harbottle, with the sorrowful relish of those imparting bad news, was acquainting guests with the details in a sonorous voice. The man had been wounded at Gallipoli, it appeared. That very morning he had blown out his brains with his service revolver.

In the shocked silence Mr Turk's voice came across loud and clear. He was speaking to the nearby guests, attempting a joke.

'Didn't he know it was my wedding day?' he boomed. 'Really, the fellow had no consideration. He could have waited till tomorrow!'

Eithne stared at her husband. Somebody tittered. There was an uncomfortable silence and then people started talking again in the stagy manner that follows an unfortunate moment.

Alwyne Flyte bent his head. His shoulders were shaking.

'Oh Alwyne!' said Winnie. Her heart ached for him. The poor man; did nobody in the room realise what he had been through? How could Mr Turk talk like that? It was shameful.

Lettie was squeezing past, carrying a plate of

sandwiches. Winnie grabbed one. She took Alwyne's hand, opened the fingers, and placed the sandwich in it.

'It's egg and pickle,' she said. Tenderly she closed his fingers over it. 'I'm so sorry. Mr Turk shouldn't have said that.'

Alwyne raised his head. Winnie realised, then, that he was shaking with laughter. She was taken aback. With his spare hand he wiped his eyes, dislodging his spectacles.

'The man should get a medal,' he chuckled. 'Crassness on that scale is positively heroic.'

'Mrs Clay doesn't look best pleased,' said Winnie.

Alwyne bit into his sandwich. 'I don't expect she married him for his soul.'

Winnie froze. How could he say that, in front of the boy? Such a crude, suggestive remark, he should be ashamed of himself! She looked anxiously at Ralph.

Ralph, however, nodded in agreement. 'I believe he's really quite rich. How can a man have all that money when he's just a butcher?'

The danger had passed. Winnie relaxed. She realised, however, that she was wet with sweat – under her armpits, trickling down between her breasts. Life was much simpler when she was working – just being a maid, doing her job.

Alwyne turned to her. He spoke with his mouth full. 'Any chance of getting your hands on more of that champagne?'

*

Winnie didn't know how it happened. For the rest of her life, when she remembered that evening, she blushed with shame and a sort of dumb incomprehension.

She was drunk, of course. So was Alwyne. The guests had long since gone and the surly waitresses had cleared the glasses and even, it seemed, washed them up in the kitchen. They had gone too. Everybody had gone. Ralph had gone to bed. The lodgers had gone to bed.

All the lodgers but Alwyne.

She and Alwyne had remained in the back room, like two pieces of driftwood when the tide had retreated. They sat on either side of the fireplace, which Winnie had sealed off for the summer with a piece of corrugated card. The room rocked gently around them.

'They'll be in the Ship Hotel now,' she said.

Alwyne nodded.

'In Brighton.'

The clock struck eleven. They sat there in silence, no doubt imagining the same thing: a big double bed; clothes strewn about the floor. It was very close; Winnie had opened the window but the room was stifling.

'You been to Brighton?' she asked.

'No.'

'Nor me.' She felt a lurch of self-pity, then a deeper wave of sorrow for Alwyne. He would never see Brighton now. There were two piers, she had seen photographs, and a promenade. Alwyne would live in darkness for the rest of his life. War was so cruel. And its casualties were not just physical. Only she knew what went on in the Spooners' room upstairs.

'There'll be plenty of canoodling when they come home,' said Alwyne. He stretched out his hand for the bottle; Winnie pushed it in his direction.

'Have you ever been married?' she asked.

He shook his head. 'Never found the right girl.'

'Would she have to be a communist?'

'That's purely theoretical now.'

'What do you mean?'

'Let's be honest, Winnie. Who would want a man like me?'

'Oh I don't know. There's so few boys left that girls are desperate for anybody.'

Winnie blushed. Alwyne burst out laughing.

'I'm so sorry, sir –'

'Don't call me sir!'

'I'm a little bit tiddly.'

'I do love you, Winnie. Know something? You're the only person who keeps me sane.'

Winnie was startled. Yet he spoke so naturally that she wasn't embarrassed. Alwyne had always treated her with familiarity. Just now she liked it. In fact, she was starting to like him.

Alwyne pushed the bottle across the table. 'Go on, have another one. It's Sunday tomorrow.' He grinned. 'Besides, while the cat's away . . .'

Winnie gazed at his ripe red lips, nestling in the tangle of his beard. She poured herself another glass; some of the champagne slopped on to the table. Who cared? She didn't, and Alwyne couldn't see anyway. She felt reckless laughter bubbling up.

'And what about you, Winnie? Have you got a sweetheart?'

'Oh no.' The laughter drained away. 'Nobody will ever marry me.'

Alwyne raised his head. 'And why would that be?'

Winnie took a breath. 'Remember when you asked me what I looked like?'

He nodded.

'Do you really want to know?'

'Yes.'

'I look like a horse. Worse than a horse. I love horses. What I mean is . . .' She stopped. She knew it was going to come out in a rush but there was no stopping it. Like the moment when you knew you were about to vomit.

'Archie was the butcher's boy and I was soft on him,' she blurted out. 'I thought he liked me too. He used to stop by in the kitchen and talk to me. He had ginger hair and such a smile it lit up the place, it made me feel special. I thought he was the one for me.' Winnie stopped.

'So what happened?' he asked softly. 'What happened with this Archie?'

'One day I was walking out, I was walking under the bridge where they played football and there he was, my heart turned over. And he stopped, they all stopped.'

'Go on.'

'I thought he was going to say something like *hello Winnie* but he looked at the other boys and they looked at him and then they started making this noise.' Winnie paused.

'What noise?'

'A sort of whickering noise, like a horse makes when it recognises another horse. A whinnying noise. *Winnie, Winnie* he said, he was making fun of me, he was egging the other boys on.' Winnie started to cry. 'And then the penny dropped. I felt my legs give out, it was the shock of it, and when I got back to my room I looked in the mirror and I knew he was right. I'd never really looked at myself. I know that sounds funny but I hadn't. It was like in the

Bible story when Eve saw she didn't have any clothes on. The scales fell from my eyes. He was right and nobody would ever love me because I'm ugly. I've got this big long face, it's not like a horse, horses are beautiful, it's just a big long face and I've got a great big jaw like a spade, I look like a *man*, and I know there's terrible things in the world but this is *my* thing and I've got it for ever.'

She sat there, sobbing. Alwyne stubbed out his cigarette.

'Don't cry.' He stood up and felt his way round the table. He was a little unsteady on his feet. 'Please don't cry.' He fumbled for her, feeling her shoulder, and reached down for her hand. 'Come and sit next to me.'

He raised her to her feet. Winnie, too, could hardly stand. Her head swam. They moved across the room, supporting each other like invalids, and sat down heavily on the settee.

'You have a beautiful voice,' he said. 'I love it when you read to me. You have a beautiful voice and a beautiful soul, and that means you're a beautiful person, in all the ways that matter. Can I touch your hair?'

'Wait a moment.' Winnie fumbled with her pins. Her hands weren't working as they should. Finally she got the pins out and dropped them on the floor. Her hair fell down over her shoulders.

'Actually, my hair is quite nice,' she said. 'It's brown, but pale brown.'

His face came close to her. She could smell the tobacco on his breath. It thrilled her – the maleness of him, the foreignness. He pressed his nose into her hair and breathed in its scent. When he let out his breath, the warmth spread through her body. She started trembling.

'You smell so young,' he murmured. Could he smell her sweat? She could. His hand was stroking her hair. His thigh was pressed against hers.

'I shouldn't,' she whispered.

'Oh yes you should.' His voice was low and coaxing. 'You know that, Winnie, don't you?' He mesmerised her – his hands, his breath, the press of his body.

'I bet you've done this a lot,' she said.

He smiled. 'I expect I have.' He shrugged. 'But not for quite some time.'

'It's a shame,' she said. 'If you cleaned yourself up a bit you'd be quite handsome.'

Alwyne burst out laughing. He flung his head back and shook, helplessly.

'I didn't mean –'

'You're a caution, Winnie.'

Winnie laughed, shakily. She must be drunk, to say a thing like that. But Alwyne didn't seem to mind. And in fact it was true. He was quite old, of course – he must be nearly forty. But somewhere, under the wild black hair and wiry beard, he looked as noble as a sheikh. And he was hers! This full-grown man was hers. It was her body that was causing him to breathe hoarsely, for now he was pressed against her, his hands moving over her shoulders and down her arms. His hands were trembling too. He took off his spectacles and dropped them on the floor. His eyes were closed, and with his hands he was bringing her alive, like ripples spreading when she dipped her finger in a pond.

'Wait,' she whispered. Disentangling herself, Winnie stumbled to the door. She shut it, and jammed a chair under the handle. As she did so she had a moment of clarity. She thought: I'll show Mrs Clay that I can do it too. She's not the only one, her and her Ship Hotel.

She thought: I'm going to do it because the Germans might bomb us to smithereens tomorrow and I'll never know what it feels like. That silly runty Archie can go hang.

She thought: this man might be blind but only a blind man would have me anyway, and I can give him pleasure, it's the least I can do after all he's sacrificed for my country. Don't I owe him that? In fact, it's my *duty*.

All this was jumbled in her head; it made her dizzy. Winnie made her way back to the settee, knocking over the table but she didn't care because Alwyne was waiting for her, his arms outstretched. She knelt between his legs, which spread open for her. He pulled her towards him. She felt herself passing over a threshold; beyond lay empty space. She could feel herself falling, and he was taking her with him.

They kissed. His lips were soft and ripe; it was like finding a berry in a hawthorn hedge. Winnie kept her lips closed but then his tongue was in her mouth and she surrendered, pressing herself against him, feeling his fingers struggling with the buttons down the front of her dress.

He's blind! He can't see how plain I am. But she didn't feel plain, she felt beautiful, his hands were making her beautiful, and now they were growing more urgent, his breath was quickening and she couldn't be bothered to help him with the buttons. They keeled over, on to the floor, and Alwyne was pulling up her skirt and her petticoat in a workmanlike manner, oh yes he'd done this before often enough, and his fingers were probing inside her drawers. Winnie gasped. She squeezed her eyes shut, joining him in his blindness She knew how it was done, of course, she had seen Lord Elbourne's stallion servicing the mares, but still it was a shock, the big thing nudging between her legs, as solid as a rolling pin. Such an old man, his body soft from sitting around all day, and the thing so solid.

'Oh Winnie, Winnie my love,' he gasped, and pushed it in.

Winnie yelped.

The dog must have heard. Far away, in the other world she had left behind, Winnie heard him scratching at the door, trying to get in.

*

Their room overlooked the sea. The manager was a friend of Neville's and had reserved them the finest apartment in the hotel. It had two windows, swathed with glazed, striped curtains held back with tassels the size of pineapples. Everything smelt new. It smelt of somebody else's responsibility. It had a bathroom all to itself which Eithne could walk in and out of whenever she chose – she, who had spent a lifetime on freezing stairs, waiting for the click of the door. She could walk in and out of it naked, if she fancied, and after a day or so she lost her shyness. It had a rosy-marbled wash-basin, mottled like meat. Thick white towels hung over a radiator which pumped out heat day and night, and in May too. The bath was so large they could sit in it together, which they did, soaping each other and drinking tea from cups balanced on the rim. Inch by inch they became acquainted with each other's bodies. She combed the hairs on Neville's legs with the nail-brush, first parallel lines then cross-hatching them like an etching.

Neville was her husband. She had to get used to the word all over again, to the new taste of it in her mouth, to this powerful, urgent body that possessed her. Sometimes, in the midst of their lovemaking, they drew back and gazed at each other in wonderment.

'You are the woman of my life,' he said. 'You're the woman I've been waiting for.' He stroked her breasts. 'Know something? Thinking about these kept me awake at night.'

'Are they worth the wait?' she asked. 'You don't want your money back?'

Outside it was raining; the sea and sky merged into one grey blur, but they didn't care. They seldom roused themselves to go out. Stupefied, the mere thought of dressing exhausted them.

'I want to show you off,' he said. 'I want to show them what I've got. I want to take you down the Palace Pier and see their faces,' he said, and fell back on the pillows, pulling her with him. They ordered meals to be sent up to their room, it was their own little world, becalmed in time, cut adrift from the past.

When Eithne tried to remember her first marriage it slipped through her fingers, like snatching at minnows. How had it been with Paul, in the early days? Oh she had loved him, she remembered the tenderness but there had been no greed like this, no passion that stopped her breath. She had loved him in a motherly, protective way, he was such a sensitive soul. Too good for this world, she now thought, for she had long ago forgotten the fractiousness and disappointments.

Far away, outside the windows, far away through that inpenetrable mist the war had claimed Paul and he was becoming as unknowable as if they had never met. He had already left her, some time before he died. During his brief leave he was already absent. Now this great bull of a man, her lover, her *lover*, her husband, had blocked the view. Eithne had no energy to look beyond him; Neville sucked her into him and she was lost.

They talked during the afternoons as they lay naked on the bed, sweating in the heat. Later, she could remember little of what they said. She told him about her Irish mother, who loved poetry and died young, and her father who sold insurance. Neville gazed at her as she spoke, smoothing her eyebrows with his thumb, tracing the veins in her wrist, inspecting her. She loved it when he sized her up. She remembered that first day in her kitchen, his head cocked sideways as he watched her make a fool of herself over the sausages.

'I couldn't stand you,' she said, 'I told myself I'd never go near your shop.'

'You did, did you?'

'Lording it over me.'

'How long did it take, eh? Two days, if I remember.'

She jabbed him with her elbow. He rolled her over and bit her shoulder.

It was mainly Neville who talked. He told her about his vision for the future. When the war was over, he said, life would never return to how it had been. The world had changed for ever. Though stirred by his words Eithne couldn't quite envisage this. For a start, she couldn't believe the war would ever end. It was like chronic bronchitis; how could one imagine being well again? Nor could she imagine anything changing. Her life, bounded by the four walls of her house, was so focused on the struggle for survival, its daily grind and petty decisions, that there seemed no possibility of other possibilities, she simply had no energy for them. But Neville flung open the door; fresh air rushed in.

'Mark my words,' he said. 'There's big opportunities out there, for those that want to grab them.'

Eithne had no idea about his plans, not then. She simply gazed at him as he lay propped against the pillows – a magnificent beast who had come to her rescue. He was hers, he was here. Gratitude flooded through her. *My heavy fetters have become daisy chains.* Her mother had read her that, in a poem.

On the fourth day they bathed and dressed and made their way downstairs for dinner. Eithne, her legs like jelly, had to steady herself on the banister. In the lobby men caught her eye. They knew. She gave off a scent like an animal. With a spasm of guilt she realised: I haven't thought about Ralph since Saturday.

In the saloon bar Neville ordered champagne. Eithne was discovering that she had a strong head; yet another thing that Neville admired about her. 'I like a woman who can take her drink,' he said. 'There's nothing mimsy-pimsy about you, my love.'

At the next table sat three young men drinking beer. They gazed at Eithne with a frank appreciation that was as foreign as their uniform. Neville struck up a conversation with them. It turned out that they were American servicemen, just arrived and *en route* to France. America had recently shipped over a large number of reinforcements. These boys were blond and fresh-faced;

big fellows packed with muscle. Bouncing with confidence, they looked a different species to the British soldiers returning from the Front.

'Now we've arrived we'll get that Hun licked,' said Clarence, the tallest of them. He had sloping shoulders, like Ralph, and a prominent Adam's apple. 'General Pershing has their number, so you guys don't have to worry any more.'

Neville ordered them a bottle of champagne and drank their health. Clarence was studying to be an architect. When he returned, he said, he was going to work in New York City, the greatest city on earth, the city of the future. 'There's buildings being put up fifteen, twenty storeys high, beautiful buildings framed in steel. Now they've covered the railroad in Park Avenue you should see the stuff coming up there.' He said there were apartment hotels where people lived all the time, with dining rooms, and bachelor apartment buildings with no kitchens because everybody ate in restaurants. They had doormen who took in the parcels. There were great hotels that had lobbies filled with shops.

Neville lit a cigar. He was not to be outdone by these Yankee whippersnappers. 'There's buildings like that in London.'

'Where?' asked Eithne.

'There's blocks of flats,' he said. 'Victoria, St John's Wood. They got a porter. That's what we'll be building when this war's over. The servants, they're not going to be coming back, not now they've seen what life's like. People are going to have to look after themselves, my love, the war's broken it up like Humpty Dumpty and it won't be put back together again.'

'That's what Alwyne says.' Eithne turned to the Americans. 'He's my lodger, he's a communist, or an anarchist, or something of that kind. He's been filling my maid's head with all sorts of nonsense.'

'It's every man for himself now,' said Neville, blowing out smoke. 'It's not what you're born, it's what you do with yourself. There's money to be made, big money for those who're prepared to stick their neck out. It's not just you –' he poked his cigar in their direction – 'who live in a land of bleeding opportunity, if you'll pardon my French.'

Nibbling a cheese straw, Eithne gazed at her husband. How mature he looked, how experienced and manly, compared to these scrubbed young boys who were going out to face God knew what! Simply sitting with him in company thrilled her, that they had emerged from their rumpled bed, from their secret life, to sit in public with these fellows, the smell of roasting meat wafting in from the dining room. Neville was bragging a little, trying to be cock of the roost but Eithne didn't mind, she would indulge him anything because she knew that after dinner he would take her upstairs and hoist up her skirts and give her such pleasure she thought she would die.

'This is my fiancée,' said Clarence.

Eithne jumped; she had been miles away. The American passed her a photograph.

'Her name is Emily,' he said. 'This is her and me standing outside the Astoria Hotel, New York City. We'd just celebrated our engagement.'

Eithne inspected the photograph. Emily was a plain little creature. She clung to Clarence's arm, proud to have got him. Their eager faces touched Eithne's heart. 'She

111

lives in Brooklyn Heights, her father's in the fur trade,'
said Clarence.

Many months later Eithne would remember these
words. At the time, however, she just felt a comradely
bond with the couple. They too had found love. She was
pleased for them, of course, but with a certain careless
condescension she felt its glow must be a timid thing
compared to her own fierce furnace.

It never crossed her mind that the boy might not return
to claim his bride. Nor that the buildings he dreamed of
designing might never be erected in his beloved city.
Other buildings would rise up, floor after floor of them,
piling into the sky, but none of them Clarence's.

*

While the cat's away. It was the strangest week of Winnie's
life. For it didn't happen just the once, with Alwyne Flyte.
At night he crept down to her room. In his bedroom
slippers he was as quiet as a cat – no blunderings, no
bumping into the furniture. For a year now he had felt his
way about the house, his blind-man's fingers knew every
inch. And there was no need of a candle, of course, to
arouse suspicion; for him it was always the middle of the
night.

Winnie had him in her thrall. She didn't actually enjoy
what he did, huffing and puffing on top of her; he was
surprisingly heavy and there really wasn't room for the
two of them in her bed. But Alwyne wanted to do it and
she was happy to oblige. Besides, it wasn't unpleasant
and sometimes, when he closed his lips over her nipple,
when he sucked at her like a baby and his beard rasped
her skin, she felt a spreading warmth that mildly

resembled the sensation she could produce herself when she was alone.

Her deepest pleasure, however, came from the pleasure she gave him. Such a simple thing it was, to open her legs, and look what happened: a grown man – an *intellectual* – was reduced to helplessness! She knew she should feel wicked. It was a sin, she had been told that in church often enough, but the poor man was mutilated. The real sin, the big sin, was what had caused it. Even as they lay in bed, men and horses were being blown to pieces – innocent horses that should be cropping the grass. How could it matter, with the world turned upside down, that she was bringing a moment's happiness to one of its victims?

Besides, with her mistress out of the house, Winnie felt a heady sense of freedom. It was harder work, of course – the cooking, the cleaning – but she didn't mind. It was a relief doing it on her own, with no suspicious looks. She was a practical young woman: *what the eye doesn't see, the heart doesn't grieve over*. Oddly enough, she felt only a mild sense of guilt. This week was already so curious, a gap between one life and the next, that Alwyne's nightly visits seemed hardly stranger than everything else. Sometimes she even felt a bond with Mrs Turk, that they were both having a honeymoon, of sorts – a thought so funny that she had to stop in the middle of her scrubbing.

It was Ralph who made her feel uncomfortable. Until now there had been no secrets between them. Ralph was a serious, quaint boy, and young for his age. If he found out, he would be shocked to the core. It *did* seem shocking, when Winnie thought of it. But it was so rum that during the daylight hours she found it hard to believe that it happened at all. Alwyne's manner hadn't changed; he remained stubbornly himself: over-familiar, bullying, teasing her about the suppers which in the absence of Mr Turk's supplies had reverted to their old meagre stodginess. Nobody noticed a change between herself and Alwyne, but then why would they? The lodgers lived in their own little worlds and Winnie was grateful for their self-absorption.

Ralph, however, was a different matter and she found herself avoiding him. She set him tasks that he could do on his own – scouring the front steps, mending breakages, running errands. Nor did she ask for his help in spring-cleaning Mrs Turk's bedroom, a major operation which she undertook on her own, washing the woodwork, beating the carpets, turning the mattress on the big brass bed, in preparation for the newlyweds. It was exhausting work and she had no time to speculate on the imminent arrival of Mr Turk, and how their lives were going to change when he was installed. Her only concern was to impress him with the thoroughness of her cleaning. Her future depended on it. If he got rid of her, where would she go?

So when Alwyne pushed open the door with his stick she barely paused. 'What do you want?' she asked.

Alwyne tapped his way into the room, feeling for the bed. He sat down on Mrs Turk's mattress. For a mad moment Winnie thought he was going to ask her to join him.

'When are they coming back?' he asked.

'Friday. The day after tomorrow.'

'While we've still got the place to ourselves, would you do me the honour of stepping out with me?'

Winnie nearly dropped her tin of polish. 'Where?'

114

'Accompany me to the Albion. Let me buy you a drink.'

*

The next morning, the Thursday, the sun shone. It was one of those fresh summer days that felt like the dawn of the world. Outside, the sea shifted like silk.

Eithne and Neville, roused from their days of stupor, bathed and dressed. Their marriage seemed a wonderful thing to them that morning, a gift given to them as freely as the sunshine. She knelt at his feet, lacing his boots. Already missing his skin, she lifted his trouser and pressed her lips against his calf.

'I'm daft about you,' she said. 'I'm as batty as a brush.'

'A brush?' Neville laughed, pulling her to her feet. 'What's batty about a brush?'

She didn't know, she didn't care.

He suggested a tram ride along the front, to Hove. It was their last day, and they were seized with high spirits. He hoisted her on to his back and gave her a piggyback ride across the room.

'Fancy a tub of winkles?' he asked 'Want to see the Floral Clock?'

There was a tap at the door. Eithne slithered to the floor and smoothed her skirts. One of the bellboys came into the room. He had an envelope in his hand.

'What's that?' Eithne's heart stood still. Something had happened to Ralph! Her house had burned down! It was all her fault, for being so happy.

The boy gave the envelope to Neville. 'We found this in the bar, sir,' he said. 'Somebody at your table left it behind, last night.'

Neville opened the envelope and took out the photograph of Clarence and Emily.

'It's not ours,' he said. 'It belonged to that American soldier.'

But the soldiers had left. They would be on their way to France by now.

'He's left his sweetheart behind!' cried Eithne. 'He can't go to war without her.'

'Well, he has,' said Neville.

'We must find him.'

'How?' They didn't know his surname. They didn't know his regiment.

'What can we do?' she asked.

'Nothing.' Neville shrugged.

'How would *you* feel?'

'It's not our concern.'

Eithne glared at her husband. 'It's not your concern because you're not out there, are you? *You're* not fighting.'

There was a silence. Down on the front a tram passed, ringing its bell.

Eithne thought: how could I have said that? She turned away. 'The poor boy,' she murmured.

The mood was broken. Eithne thought: a moment ago I was kissing this man's leg. She gave the photograph back to the bellboy, telling him to leave it at the desk, in case Clarence returned.

'Keep it safe,' she told him. 'Promise you'll keep it safe.'

The boy left, closing the door with a click.

Eithne didn't look at her husband. The energy had drained from her. Suddenly she wanted to go home. She walked to the window and gazed out.

'There's a storm coming,' she said.

'What storm?'

'Listen,' she said. 'I can hear the thunder.'

'That's not thunder, my love,' said Neville. 'That's the guns.'

*

Ralph and Winnie washed up the dishes in silence. After a while he asked: 'When are they coming back?'

'Tomorrow,' said Winnie. 'You'll be at your class.'

'What about his luggage?'

'That's coming tomorrow too.'

'Will he have furniture and things?'

'I don't know.' She turned to him. 'Listen, dear, I'll finish this. Go upstairs and lay the cloth for breakfast, then you're done. Night-night, sleep tight.'

She waited for Ralph to reply *Don't let the bedbugs bite* but he left without a word. She heard him ascending the stairs slowly, like an old man. Oh Lord, and now it was *her* turn to betray him.

Winnie pulled off her apron and inspected herself in the mirror. It was still daylight outside, but the scullery existed in a state of permanent dusk. She peered closer, pinching her cheeks. It seemed silly, smartening herself up for a man who couldn't see her, but there were other people to consider. She looped her beads around her neck and put on her hat.

Upstairs the clock struck nine and, prompt as ever, she heard the front door close as Alwyne went out. They had arranged to meet under the railway arch, the only acknowledgement they had made of the illicit nature of the past week. Winnie paused. There was no sound

117

except the *tink-tink* of the dripping tap. She shouldn't feel guilty; after all, she was off duty now. She had told Ralph that she was popping out to meet a friend. Even if he happened to take the dog out, and spotted her with Alwyne, that wouldn't be so odd.

Winnie let herself out of the door. She climbed the area steps and emerged into the street. The sky was streaked with mares' tails. It had been a beautiful summer's day, though she had seen little of it. The air was balmy; scent drifted from the bush that struggled out of a crack in the basement next door.

Alwyne was ahead of her. She heard the *tap-tap* of his stick; it echoed as he entered the railway tunnel. Silently he waited for her. He stood in front of the goalpost that Archie had chalked on the brickwork all those years ago, his head cocked sideways as if at any moment a ball would come whizzing through the air, kicked by the phantom foot of a boy long gone. *Whinny-whinny* . . . Remembering Archie, her tormentor, Winnie felt a spasm of self-pity. She thought: this is as good as I can expect – a glass of port with a blind man, who can't see how ugly I am.

Winnie was a sensible girl, however. She rallied, and took Alwyne's arm. Just for tonight they were a couple, out on the town. To onlookers, no doubt, she was a kindly young woman supporting a tragic war victim. She knew differently. She knew something they didn't know, something that would raise a few eyebrows.

'Tell me what you're seeing,' said Alwyne.

'We're walking past the shops,' she said. 'They've got their shutters down because they're closed now.' She lowered her voice. 'They say that Mr Bunting the greengrocer's a German spy, they say he's got a wireless station on his roof but he hasn't, it's just his pigeons he's got up there.' They walked past Mr Turk's emporium where the pavement gleamed from where it had been swabbed down; they cut through the backstreets, past the courtyards with the sheets hanging like ghosts and the babies that cried day and night. Women watched them from the doorways; they squatted on their haunches as if they were relieving themselves but Winnie didn't tell Alwyne that, it would sound rude.

'We're walking down Dock Lane,' she said. 'There's a man lives here called Mr Purse. He's got some shrapnel in his leg and every few weeks a bit of it moves down and comes out near his foot. He charges the children a halfpenny to look at it.'

Alwyne barked with laughter. 'I love you, Winnie,' he said, squeezing her arm. 'You're unique, do you know that?'

'I'm nobody,' she said.

'Don't you dare say that! Know what's to blame? Our miserable society that tells you you're nobody, you're invisible. But you're not invisible to me. I'm blind, I have no preconceptions. And know what I see? A singular young woman of kindness and wit, who's brought me back to life.'

For a moment Winnie was too overcome to speak. They had reached the river. She took Alwyne's hand and led him to the embankment.

'Can you smell that?' she asked. 'Can you smell the sea?'

The water gleamed in the setting sun. This was just as good as Brighton. The light was fading, and clouds building up. They heard a rumble of thunder.

'When I was little,' she said, 'I used to think thunder was the sound of God moving furniture around in heaven.'

Alwyne turned to her. 'My darling girl,' he said, and kissed her. He had never done this in public before, but then there was nobody in the vicinity to see them. Winnie tasted his familiar scent of tobacco and beard, but on their skin she smelt the tang of the sea.

'I wonder if *they're* doing this,' she whispered, 'in Brighton.'

'I don't trust that man,' said Alwyne abruptly, and moved off.

'What do you mean?'

'Believe me.'

Alwyne wouldn't say anything else. Winnie wished he would turn back and kiss her again, so bold it had given her a jolt, but he was tap-tapping across the cobbles. She caught him up and they walked towards the public house, the sound of its pianola drifting through the air. A barge passed, making the water rock. The tide was out; little waves lapped the shore, shifting the rubbish – orange peel, bones, bits and pieces. They slopped back and forth, laced with foam, in the fading light.

The saloon bar was thick with smoke. Alwyne ordered her a glass of port, and a pint of mild for himself. He fumbled for the coins in his pocket-book but Winnie didn't help him, he had his pride. Besides, by that time somebody else had paid. Alwyne, with his white stick, was treated with respect. A group of drunken young soldiers cleared a path for them, and found them a seat.

One of the lads pulled up a chair and sat down. He said he was a gunner in the Leicesters and was back on a week's leave. His eyes had the blank look Winnie had come to recognise. She had seen it in Mr Clay's face.

'When are you going home?' she asked.

He shook his head. 'I'm staying put. I'm having a fine old time of it here.'

'What about your mother?' she asked. The port had gone straight to her head. 'What about your sweetheart?'

He shrugged. 'Last time I went home me mum said *look at the state of you. You're crawling with bugs*.' He lit two cigarettes and put one between Alwyne's fingers. 'They can go hang.'

Alwyne started talking about the war. He said it was an act of mass insanity that was waking up the working class from their long enslavement. When it was over, a brave new world would dawn. Winnie of course had heard it all before. One had to make allowances; war had unhinged thousands of men like Alwyne, poor things. Her thoughts were far more pressing, for she had just remembered her earlier worry. What was she going to do about Ralph's sugar?

St Jude's was striking eleven as they walked up to the house, Alwyne a dead weight on her arm. The windows were dark. Winnie was suddenly so exhausted she could hardly open the door. That declaration of love beside the river seemed meaningless now, so much flim-flammery. Tomorrow Mr Turk was arriving and he would be needing his cup of tea.

He was a man who expected his demands to be met. It was her job to look after him and if she couldn't manage that she would be out on her ear. There would be little support from Mrs Clay – *Mrs Turk*. It was quite clear where *her* loyalties lay. Winnie had worn herself out preparing the house for its new master, but the whole effort could be undone by the little business of the sugar. The problem was, their ration had run out four days earlier and there was not a grain of the stuff in the house. Not a grain, except for Ralph's hoard.

Winnie knew where it was hidden; she knew every inch of his room. She also knew that the little twists of sugar were a gift from Boyce. The places where Boyce had got them – the Criterion, the Zanzibar – summoned up Boyce's cocky farewells so vividly that Winnie could almost hear his voice. *Night-night, Winnipeg, don't do anything I wouldn't do.* It would be easy, when Ralph was out during the afternoon, to take just a few of them.

And where was the harm in that? In fact, now she thought of it, Ralph would *want* her to take them. They loved each other, they would do anything for each other, and Ralph surely would hate her job to be jeopardised for the sake of a bit of sugar.

Winnie paused at the bottom of the stairs. The cat pressed itself against her skirt.

'Are you still open for visitors?' whispered Alwyne into her ear.

Winnie didn't reply. Whether he went upstairs to his bed or downstairs to hers seemed of little importance. The real betrayal had nothing to do with Alwyne, and her heart ached.

*

Ralph let himself into the house. It was half past five, his usual arrival time. Brutus bounded up to him, tail wagging, as he always did. You could rely on dogs; they never changed, that was one of the best things about them.

122

Ralph stood still, listening. The faint clatter of pans came from the kitchen. Upstairs, he could hear the murmur of voices. He strained to hear. It sounded like his mother, talking to Mrs O'Malley. '. . . *orchestra* . . .' he heard. '. . . *West Pier* . . .' Mrs O'Malley would have crept down from her room to hear the news from the great wide world. His mother would have emerged from her bedroom, from her unpacking, to chat to the old lady on the landing. Most of the conversations in the house took place on the stairs.

Ralph looked at the hall-stand. No alien topcoat hung there. He glanced into the parlour. The table, the sideboard, the piano, the pictures . . . everything was as it always had been. For a wild moment Ralph thought: it's all been a dream. His mother was home from a well-deserved holiday, and life would carry on as it had before.

Then he thought: they've quarrelled! They went to Brighton and she came to her senses, and it was over as soon as it was begun. It was an infatuation, the sort of madness Boyce had felt for the red-headed daughter of the upholsterer he had worked for, who had turned out to be a minx. *The scales fell from my eyes*, he said. *What a chump I've been! What a top-hole, first-rate noodle!*

'Ralph, my pet!' His mother was hurrying down the stairs. She threw her arms around him. 'I've missed you.'

'What's that smell?'

'Isn't it nice?' She flung back her head, so he could sniff her neck. 'Attar of Roses.'

'Where's Mr Turk?'

'*Neville*, dear. He's at the shop.' She gave him something wrapped in paper. 'It's rock.' Ralph pulled out a long, pink stick. 'It's got writing all the way through,' she said.

She led him into the back room and collapsed into a chair. 'Tell me how you've been and what you've been doing.'

'I've been all right,' he said. 'What's happened to your nose?'

Her nose was bright red. A little bit was peeling. 'I caught the sun,' she laughed. 'It was a lovely day yesterday, was it here? I even paddled. Brighton's so pretty, I shall take you there one day.'

But Ralph wasn't listening. He was staring at the wall. 'What's that doing here?'

'What?'

'That.'

A glass-fronted cabinet hung on the wall above the occasional table. It hung in the place where the picture of *A Stag at Bay* used to be. Inside the cabinet was a collection of silver cups.

'Oh. They're Neville's. He was a champion boxer, you know. This was the only place we could find.'

A little heap of plaster dust lay on the floor, where somebody had drilled into the wall. Ralph turned away, to check the rest of the room. His father's photograph still stood on the mantelpiece. But the room didn't feel the same. Not with that thing there, its powdery excreta dropped on their carpet.

His mother patted the chair next to her. 'Sit down and tell me your news. Shall we have some tea? I'll call Winnie. She even seems to have found us some sugar.'

'Have you taken out Brutus?' Ralph asked.

She shook her head.

'I will then.' Ralph went into the hallway and picked up the lead from the table. 'He must be bursting.'

*

Ralph couldn't sleep. It was very close; he had opened the window but still his room felt stifling. He kicked off the blankets and lay under the sheet, spreadeagled like a starfish. In the next room he heard the silvery chime of his mother's clock. Midnight. The muffled thumps and murmurs had ceased, but he could feel the two of them lying there, on the other side of the double doors. It was the first night that Mr Turk had shared his mother's bed. Ralph could almost hear them breathe.

Brutus was having a nightmare. Down on the carpet he whimpered and jerked. It made Ralph feel very alone, when his dog disappeared into his own secret world. A bone lay on the floor. Mr Turk had given it to Brutus, along with a whole box of provisions he had brought home and given to Winnie to store in the larder. Tins of pineapples, pears, sardines – where did he get all those things? Bottles of stout had been produced at supper. Ralph hadn't drunk any but he had been perfectly polite. He had even asked Mr Turk if he had had a pleasant train journey.

The curtains were open. Outside, a full moon shone; Ralph could glimpse, above the black cliff of the viaduct, the milky glow. Why did the moon come up at different places each night? Why did it sometimes hang low in the sky, and then the next night, at the very same time, shine right overhead? There was nobody Ralph could ask. His mother and Winnie would have no idea. His father would have known the answer, but his father was dead.

Ralph's mother said he was in heaven but Ralph had a suspicion that it didn't exist. In fact he was nearly certain of it. Scientific proof would be only a matter of time. In twenty years, thirty years at the most, people would have solid evidence that God was just dreamed up to make people feel better. *Deliver us from evil*. Well He hadn't, had He?

No, God wasn't in people; He was only in nature. God was in those snail shells Ralph had collected with his father – their delicate whorls, the miracle of them. God painted each a different colour, out of love. Ralph had arranged the shells in his cabinet of curiosities. It hung on the wall, a glass-fronted case filled with birds' nests, skulls and clay pipes he found beside the river. The shells had a shelf to themselves. How beautiful they were, compared to big sweaty humans, all red faces and beery breath!

The dog growled. Ralph became aware of a noise. It came from the next room.

He froze. The noise was soft at first, so soft that only the dog had sensed it. Ralph put his hands over his ears. He lay there, rigid, willing it to stop. He opened and closed his legs like a pair of scissors, frantic to distract himself, as he used to do when he was about to be sick. He pressed the pillow to his face, trying to blot it out, but he could still hear it, the rhythmic creak of the bedsprings next door.

The blood rushed to his face. He got out of bed and crept to the door. He had to escape. He would go up to Boycie's room, where the bed was made up. It was two storeys up, at the top of the house. He wouldn't hear anything there.

Ralph tiptoed up the stairs, up past the first landing. A light glowed under Alwyne's door; he heard bronchial coughing within. Up he climbed, up the last flight of stairs to the landing. Moonlight flooded through the window, bathing the floorboards. He turned the knob of Boyce's door and went in.

Ralph stared. For a moment he thought he had walked into a lumber room. From floor to ceiling Boycie's bedroom was filled with furniture – tables, chairs, a wardrobe, a chest of drawers. There was not an inch of space. Moonlight bathed the furniture in ghostly light; it shone on the polished mahogany. On Boycie's bed somebody had dumped a wooden blanket-chest, as big as a coffin.

*

'But it's Boycie's room!'

'Neville had to put his things somewhere –'

'You kept the room for Boyce.'

'– he put another tenant in his rooms, he had to clear out his belongings. Besides, this is his home now.'

'You said you were keeping it for Boyce.'

They were sitting on Ralph's bed. Eithne took Ralph's hand in hers. She said to him, very seriously: 'Boyce isn't coming back.'

'He might. He's probably lost, and wandering about somewhere. He might have been taken prisoner.'

Eithne gazed at her son. From the stairs came the *swish-swish* of Winnie's broom. 'Ralph, he's dead. I've had a letter from his mother.'

'When?'

'Four months ago.'

Ralph stared at her. 'Why didn't you tell me?'

'It was never the right moment. I thought you had enough on your plate. I thought it would put you off your exams.'

Ralph glared at her.'I don't care about my bloody exams!'

'Ralph!'

'I hate them.'

'Don't you want to be a grown-up man, with a man's job?'

'Why?'

'What do you mean, why?'

Ralph's eyes glittered with tears. 'Where did it get my father?'

There was a silence. Outside the door Winnie was humming, either because she wanted to drown out their voices or because she didn't have a care in the world. Either way, Eithne envied her. It was only eleven in the morning and she wanted to crawl back into bed.

'I've got to help Winnie.' She stood up. 'Let's have no more nonsense. There's potatoes downstairs for you to peel. Neville will be home in an hour for his dinner.'

'He's going to have his *dinner* here?'

'What do you mean?'

'Can't he go to a restaurant or something? What does he usually do?'

Eithne looked at her son. 'Ralph, this is his home. I'm his wife. He's up at five, he works all the hours God gives him, he expects a hot meal in the middle of the day. We have a lot to thank him for, you have no idea.' She noticed, for the first time, a crop of boils on Ralph's chin. 'Things are bound to be different now, but it'll be fine if we all pull together. I'm relying on you, my little trooper. I've always relied on you, and nothing will ever change that.' She smiled brightly. 'Let's go to the pictures, just you and me. Let's go there next week, Monday, Tuesday, any day you want! We can have an ice-cream!'

Ralph looked up at her with a wintry smile, like a teacher with an errant pupil. How elderly he looked, sitting there hunched on his bed! Eithne's heart turned over.

'We can go to the penny arcade,' she said. 'I've got lots of money now, we can do anything you want.'

His face lightened, just a little. For a moment, they had a flash of their old closeness.

Eithne left the room, shutting the door behind her. She nearly bumped into Alwyne, who was lurking on the stairs. Everywhere she went, that man seemed to be in the way.

'What do you want?' she snapped.

'Nothing. I was just looking for Winnie.'

'Well, she's there.' Eithne pointed down to the hall, where Winnie was re-winding a bandage around the broom handle. It had split, some time ago. 'Down there,' she said, forgetting the man couldn't see.

Eithne went into her bedroom and closed the door. At last she was alone. Suddenly she could bear it no longer. She dropped to her knees beside the bed and pressed her nose into the disordered sheets. She breathed in deeply, smelling her husband, drinking him in.

Chapter Five

I came across a Cornishman, ripped from shoulder to waist with shrapnel, his stomach on the ground beside him in a pool of blood. As I got to him he said 'Shoot me', he was beyond all human aid. Before we could even draw a revolver he had died. He just said 'Mother'.

Private Harry Patch, Cornwall's Light Infantry

Neville was obsessed with his wife. *With my body I thee worship.* He'd thought that now he possessed her his hunger would be eased, but if anything it had grown keener. He worshipped every inch of the woman – her heavy breasts, her round belly, the coarse bush of her pubic hair in which he rooted like a pig searching for truffles. On his way to Smithfield, in the pearly summer's dawn, he pressed his hand to his nose and sniffed the scent of her on his fingers. Eithne was his miracle, his stroke of astounding good luck. He had no idea how her husband had been killed, she hadn't spoken of it, but Neville couldn't help himself: he blessed that German shell that had delivered this magnificent creature into his arms.

He loved her langour; he even forgave her slovenly ways. She was too high-class for a life of drudgery; she was born to be a princess, to be pampered and adored, and he had come to save her.

130

For Neville had plans. Eithne was sitting on a valuable asset and his job was to help her exploit it. He didn't tell her the scope of his plans, not in those early weeks, for a woman needed to be coaxed. Eithne had a volatile temperament; he hadn't forgotten her outburst at the Café Royal. She was a creature of powerful loyalties, and he admired her for that. Now he was her husband, he presumed she would do the same thing on his behalf. No, he needed to take her one step at a time; he needed to outline the benefits and make her feel that she too would have come to the same decision if only she had thought of it first. After all, it was all to her advantage.

But how soft-hearted she was! When Neville inspected the rent-book he was astonished to see the paltry sums paid by her lodgers.

'Haven't you heard of inflation, my love?' he said. 'The price of bread's doubled.'

'I know it's doubled. I've been buying it.'

Mrs O'Malley, the oldest resident in the house, had been paying the same rent for the past three years. 'She must think all her Christmases have come at once,' said Neville.

'The poor dear. She doesn't know when it *is* Christmas.'

The Spooners were five months in arrears. 'You've let them get away with it all this time?'

'What can I do? Throw them out on the street? His medicine is very expensive, she's supporting two of her sisters and their children. She works nine hours a day, she's doing her best. How can I ask them for money with the state he's in?' She glared at him, pushing back her hair. 'They've stuck with me and I'm sticking with them.'

131

Eithne's stubbornness enchanted him, for he was newly in love. Neville gave up this particular fight; there was time to deal with that later.

Nor would she countenance the employment of a housekeeper.

'I'll pay the wages,' he said. 'You can't carry on like this. I'm not seeing my wife on her hands and knees.'

'Winnie would hate it, taking orders from a stranger. Why don't we make *her* housekeeper and get in a parlourmaid to help her?'

Neville had to tread carefully here. The truth was, Winnie's work left a great deal to be desired. Neville had yet to inspect the lodgers' rooms, for their inhabitants seemed permanently in situ, but the common parts were in a deplorable state. The carpets were filthy, the wallpaper was stained; cobwebs looped the light fixtures. In the bathroom the linoleum was peeling and the lavatory chain had broken and been replaced by a length of string. Even in summer there was a musty smell, as if the windows were never opened. As for the kitchen, the less said the better. Neville, however, kept his mouth shut. Years of living with his mother had instructed him in the arts of diplomacy.

And like all diplomats, Neville possessed a low sense of cunning. He guessed there might be some resistance to his grand plan for the house. So one day in June he had an object delivered. When he returned from work he found Winnie and her mistress standing in the hallway, gazing at it.

'It's a vacuum cleaner,' he said. 'Mr Hoover's Electric Suction Sweeper.'

A motor, with brushes attached, was mounted on a

stick. A limp cloth bag was attached to the engine and hooked to the support. The two women stood well away from it, as if it might explode.

'No more backache!' he said. 'This little fellow will do the job for you. It was invented by an American, and they know what's what.'

Winnie took a step nearer; she touched it with her finger. 'How does it work?'

'By electricity.'

'But we don't have electricity,' said Eithne.

'I've noticed that, my love.' He twinkled at her. 'Unlike some people, I'm not blind. I have a good friend in the building trade who's prepared to install it at a very reasonable price. Very reasonable. He owes me a favour.'

'Install what?'

'Electricity. This is the twentieth century, my dearest love. We can't go on bumping around in the dark.'

Eithne gazed at him, her eyes wide. His eyes fell to her breasts, straining against her blouse. She wore the jet necklace he had bought on their honeymoon.

'What about the mess?' she asked. 'What about the lodgers? Who's going to pay?'

'Don't you bother your pretty head about that.'

'What about the freeholder? What's he going to say?'

Neville smiled. 'You're looking at him.'

There was a silence. Outside in the street, the rag-and-bone man rang his bell.

Eithne whispered: 'What did you say?'

'You'll be getting a letter tomorrow. It's all done and dusted.'

'You've bought the freehold?'

Neville nodded. He felt a warmth in his groin, a surge of power.

'Why didn't you tell me?' she asked.

'Thought I'd give you a surprise.'

The door opened and Mrs Spooner appeared, home from work. She looked at the three of them, standing around the vacuum cleaner. They moved aside and she scuttled past, casting a backward look at the machine as if it might chase her.

Winnie said: 'How am I going to lug that up and down the stairs?'

Eithne was still gazing at her husband. 'Where did you get the money?'

Neville tapped the side of his nose. 'Let's just say he was only too glad to get it off his hands. Riddled with dry rot.'

Her eyes widened. 'Oh no! Is it?'

Neville grinned. 'That's what the surveyor told them.'

'What surveyor?'

Neville's smile widened.

'I haven't seen any surveyor,' Eithne said.

In the silence, the clock struck six. Winnie disappeared down to the kitchen. Husband and wife stood there, in the hallway.

'Ah,' said Eithne.

It was very close; Eithne's face was sheeny with moisture. Neville pictured it trickling between her breasts.

'So it's ours,' she said.

Neville nodded.

At last – at long last – Eithne smiled. Neville felt the voltage of it, like an electric shock. Her eyes glittered.

'Well well,' she said. 'You're quite the man, aren't you?'

He whispered in her hair. 'And when do I get my reward?'

'Later.'

But Neville was pressing against her, pushing her along the corridor. He bundled her into the back room and shut the door. This room was now reserved for their particular use; Neville had declared it out of bounds to the lodgers. Still, the boy might come in. Neville jammed his wife against the door. He rummaged under her skirt and petticoat, flinging them up.

'We can't,' she whispered. But now he was ramming his hand up, between her legs. How moist she was, through the silk of her drawers!

Eithne's legs buckled. Neville had to keep her propped up, to stop her sliding to the floor. Trembling, she stepped out of her knickers, helping him, using one foot to pull them off the other one.

'From now on, I don't want you wearing these,' he whispered hoarsely, into her hair. 'Right?' He kicked the underwear out of the way.

She nodded wordlessly. He fumbled with his trouser buttons, wrenching them open one by one.

'I want to think of you walking around without them, with only me knowing,' he murmured. 'Outdoors too. I want to picture you in the street, with nothing on underneath.' He laughed, softly. 'Besides, I'm a freeholder now. I want access to my property.'

He and she were the same height; trousers round his ankles, he planted himself in position and pushed himself inside her.

Eithne shuddered; she held his bare buttocks, pressing him into her, deeper. Far away, the bell rang for supper. He thrust in and out, hard. Eithne's head bumped against the door. He cradled it with one of his hands, steadying her with the other for her legs were like butter.

Eithne stared past Neville's head. On the mantelpiece stood the photograph of Paul, dressed in the uniform of the Middlesex Regiment. Suddenly she found herself sobbing – fierce, dry sobs. She heaved with them, juddering like an animal, and then she cried out, as the pleasure flooded through her, and Neville had to press his hand across her mouth to keep her quiet.

*

On Monday the workmen arrived, to install the electricity. Winnie had covered the floors with dustsheets, in readiness for the invasion. They were armed with hammers and drills, and carried great spools of wires. Where did Mr Turk recruit them? It was a mystery, that in the middle of a war he could summon up four able-bodied men at the click of a finger.

The lodgers had been warned, of course. 'What happens if it bursts into flames?' wailed Mrs O'Malley. 'We'll be burnt to a crisp.'

Neville assured her that it was perfectly safe. The piped gas, in fact, was far more liable to explode.

When the men arrived, however, Mrs O'Malley thought they were the Germans. She locked herself into her room and sang Schubert *lieder* in her high, cracked voice. '*Aus diesem Felsen starr und wild, Soll mein Gebet zu dir hinwehen,*' she sang. 'Don't shoot! I'm a friend of the Kaiser!'

Nor did the Spooners like it. They cowered in their room like hares hearing the approach of the beaters. Eithne was irritated by their behaviour. Didn't they realise how she had saved them from possible eviction, quite apart from her generosity over the rent? Paul had always been kind to them, and it was in his memory that Eithne indulged them, even though their presence intruded on her privacy now that she was a married woman and liable to be interrupted by a timid tap at the door. Sometimes she longed for the house to be empty. She pictured Neville and herself scampering downstairs, naked and laughing, sharing the bath with the door open, as they had done during those magical days in Brighton.

But now the house was in a state of chaos, with dust everywhere, with hammerings and drillings, with the alarming crack of pipes being pulled from the walls and endless cups of tea to be made. The workmen promised that the disruption to the lodgers would be miminal, that they could wire up each room in a day if they had a clear run at it.

'What shall we do about my husband?' whispered Mrs Spooner. Eithne suggested putting him into the parlour for the day but one look at Mrs Spooner's face told her this was out of the question. Mrs O'Malley came to the rescue.

'We must all pull together in this perilous time,' she said. 'I, for one, will do my duty.' She offered Mr Spooner the use of her room for the duration. After all, he would be back in his own bed by nightfall.

Eithne was touched by this spirit of co-operation. It spoke of the boarders' appreciation of her husband. If they had any sense they would half-way love him by now. Neville filled their bellies with meat every night, he had rescued them just as he had rescued her, and now he was salvaging the dilapidated house, banishing the gloom of the past and bringing light to their lives. In a week they could click a switch and – hey presto! all would be illuminated.

In addition, the workmen had a further task. This was to remove the double-doors that connected the two bedrooms, on the first floor, and replace them with a wall. Ralph had been consulted about this, of course. Mother and son both knew the reason, though neither of them mentioned it. Sealing him off would afford them both some privacy.

Ralph had agreed to it with a shrug. He had hardly spoken to his mother during these past few weeks, there had been too many distractions. Though he stubbornly remained a vegetarian, he had been polite to Mr Turk, and showed no further signs of rebellion. In fact, they seldom met. The butcher was out of the house before anyone awoke and in the evening Ralph took his supper with the lodgers in the parlour, whilst Eithne and her husband ate together, at a later hour, in the back room. This new regime had been suggested by Neville in the first week of their marriage. Ralph had been invited to share this meal with them, but to his mother's relief – yes, she could admit it – he had declined. The arrangement suited everyone.

Despite the dust, Eithne was happy. The workmen whistled, clumping up and down the stairs, carrying bags of lime for the partition wall. What a change it made, to have the house filled with healthy young men!

They seemed a different species to her broken lodgers and pale, solemn son. The workmen flirted with her; they strode around in their great boots and urinated as lustily as horses in the outdoor privy. She hadn't seen young men of that kind for years. They filled her with hope.

Silently she dared them to guess that, under her skirts, she was naked. The sun beat down; London was in the grip of a heatwave, but how free she felt, how unconstricted! Flushed with her secret, she smiled at them as they drank their tea. *I want access to my property*. In the evening she sat in the back room, leafing through a catalogue of light fixtures. As she did so her husband's hand stole up her skirt, feeling upwards like a blind thing, until the catalogue thudded to the floor.

*

Winnie was worked to the bone. Bone-tired she was, trying to create some sort of order in the sweltering heat. The house was a maelstrom of activity. This sort of thing happened when Mr Turk was about: he was like a tank, crashing through everything in his path, leaving debris behind. The world outside, like the war, had long since drifted into a kind of stalemate. Nothing got done because there was nobody to do it. Down the road, a broken window had remained unrepaired for the past four years, ever since somebody had discovered that Henry Tong was a conchy and threw a brick through it. Henry Tong had long since disappeared, like so many familiar faces. But that had been the only change in the neighbourhood. Shops struggled on, with their diminished staff; people struggled on, living from day to day. In the midst of this torpor, Mr Turk was a galvanising force. Winnie remembered him taking over the neighbouring shops, the armies of workmen, the lights blazing into the night.

How did he manage it? Alwyne hinted that Mr Turk had made a fortune out of the war, but how did he know?

She and Alwyne Flyte had continued their relations. With the arrival of the newlyweds they had initially taken more care, but soon discovered that Mr and Mrs Turk's oblivion to anyone but themselves made the risk of discovery remote. Wedged against her in bed, Alwyne said Mr Turk was the sort of man he despised.

'He's a plutocrat disguised as a working man,' he said. 'They're the worst.'

'He treats me well enough,' said Winnie.

'Can't you think about anything beyond your own little world?'

'Look who's talking,' she said. 'You and your niggles. Who got all fussed about the marmalade this morning?' They could talk like this now. After all, Winnie had seen him at his most undignified; she had long ago lost any respect. In this particular way Alwyne had indeed liberated her. All that class stuff could go hang. 'I trust him, even though you don't. I think you're jealous.'

Alwyne laughed. 'Of that great oaf?' He inhaled his cigarette; the red tip glowed in the dark. He had urged her to smoke, to ward off the influenza, but Winnie had tried it once and it was an experience she didn't care to repeat.

The two of them were close during those weeks. Between them lay the unspoken acknowledgement that nobody else would want them. This was the brutal truth. Even the workmen, a breed known for their interest in the opposite sex, treated Winnie with a brotherly jocularity that was as disheartening as it was familiar. The truth was that nobody took a plain person seriously. They didn't give them their full attention, there was always somebody else to catch their eye. And if that person was a servant she had no chance at all.

Alwyne, however, was different, and Winnie would always be grateful to him. He listened to her. Perhaps because nobody listened to him either. Blind people, she had noticed, were treated like mental defectives. And yet Alwyne was more intelligent than the lot of them.

'He's a bully,' said Alwyne.

In the darkness, Winnie turned to him. She wanted to unburden herself at last. She wanted to tell him how even Elsie, her friend who worked in the Woolwich Arsenal, how even Elsie treated her as a confidante rather than a fellow-combatant in the war between the sexes. Elsie presumed, rightly, that Winnie was out of the running. Even Elsie had a sweetheart, and she was as yellow as a canary. They *called* them canaries. And her fringe had turned ginger

'My sergeant-major was a man like him,' said Alwyne. 'A tinpot little tyrant.'

This caught Winnie's attention. Alwyne never talked about the war. 'What did he do?'

'You wouldn't want to know, my dear.'

'Yes I do.'

'Let's just say that war strips a man down to his essentials. For this we can be thankful, for it's the only good thing that might come out of this bloody mess.' Alwyne laughed mirthlessly. 'Who's going to listen to orders from now on, when they've seen how their CO saved his own skin, how he sat eating omelettes in a village they were forbidden to enter when they'd spent two weeks at the Front up to their bloody waists in mud? When they'd seen their comrades blown to pieces? Don't you see, that's the only thing that gives me any hope in this whole bloody blasted business?'

Winnie forgave him the language; warfare coarsened a man. There was a silence. Soon the dawn would break; it was mid-June and the nights were over almost as soon as they had begun. Alwyne should be going back upstairs.

'You can't put the genie back into the bottle,' he said, flicking his cigarette into the fireplace. 'Not now.'

'What did you do in the war?' she asked.

'Stretcher-bearer. I didn't want to enlist, I didn't want to kill anybody.'

'Even the Germans?'

'Even the Germans. We're all indoctrinated, you see. *You're* indoctrinated, it's part of the system.'

He carried on but Winnie stopped listening. His lectures exhausted her. She was dog-tired and, to tell the truth, she didn't give a fig about indoctrination, whatever that was. The simple fact was that she would sell her soul for a lie-in. Whatever Alwyne's sergeant-major did, however bad, *she* would do it, if it meant that at six o'clock in the morning she could turn over and go back to sleep. They could put her in handcuffs and march her off to the court-martial but, in Alwyne's words, she wouldn't give a bloody blasted damn.

*

The work was completed by midsummer. All the rooms, and even the stairs, were wired up for the electricity. Neville organised a gathering in the parlour, at dusk. He

142

turned to Lettie and pointed to the brass switch beside the door.

'You do the honours, little lady,' he said.

Lettie could just reach. She pressed down the switch; the room blazed with light. She clapped her hands in excitement. The grown-ups cowered, blinking. How bright it was! Corners they had never seen were pitilessly exposed.

'Good Lord,' said Eithne. 'Look at those cobwebs.'

Small wooden discs were all that remained of the old gas piping. A new wire, boxed in, ran up the wall and across the ceiling where the light blazed in its new glass dome. Neville switched on two table lamps, with fringed shades. Now it was revealed, how dingy the room looked!

Winnie thought: I'm going to have my work cut out. Until that moment, the parlour had been one of the darkest rooms in the house. Now she could see that the cornice was grey with soot. Like the furniture, she felt exposed; as if she were naked. As if everybody could suddenly see what had been happening with Alwyne.

Alwyne sat in a cloud of cigarette smoke. He looked unmoved, but then that was hardly surprising. Mrs O'Malley blinked, like a rabbit caught by torchlight.

'Are you sure it'll be all right?' she asked.

A spasm of irritation crossed the butcher's face. Eithne noticed this. 'Well I think it's lovely,' she said brightly.

'Glad someone's grateful,' said Mr Turk, running his hand over his moustache.

Eithne moved to the mantelpiece and looked at herself in the mirror. 'Good grief,' she said. 'I'm getting wrinkles.'

Later, in his bedroom, Ralph inspected his face in the harsh light of the mirror. He too had an unwelcome surprise. Boils seemed to have erupted on his chin. He had noticed them before, when he was trying to shave, but never had he seen them so pitilessly exposed. He gazed at them with fascination. The larger ones, pink and protruding, resembled nipples; some had a yellowish blob at their tip.

Boyce had had some boils too, but it hadn't put off the girls. Ralph remembered Boycie, dressed up in his green checquered jacket and yellow waistcoat, patent-leather pumps on his feet, all set to sally forth and conquer. What a swell! He had had no difficulties in that department. He told Ralph his secret.

'Make 'em laugh,' he said. 'Tell 'em a limerick and you're home and dry.

> *'I know a blithe blossom in Blighty*
> *Whom you, I'm afraid, would call flighty,*
> *For when Zeps are about*
> *She always trips out*
> *In a little black crêpe de Chine nightie.'*

That night Ralph had a pollution. He woke up, hot with shame. The sheet was wet and sticky. What would Winnie think, when she came to change it? Worse still, if his *mother* helped her? These unfortunate accidents were happening with increasing regularity – three times, in fact, since the last laundry day. Three plus one meant four stains, a total impossible to ignore. Ralph could feel the stiffer patches, where the stains had dried, with his finger.

Only the top sheet was affected, as Ralph slept on his back. In the next room the clock chimed three. Nowadays the sound was barely audible through the newly constructed wall. However, it galvanised him into activity. He would fetch a clean sheet from the cupboard downstairs, and replace the soiled one. In the morning he could bundle the dirty sheet into the laundry box and nobody would be the wiser.

Ralph got out of bed and crept to the door. As he did so, he remembered his dream. It had been of Winnie. She had been bending over, her skirt hitched up – no, he mustn't think of it. Blushing, he opened the door and felt for the light switch – the brand-new switch that was somewhere on the wall. He ran his hand across the surface and finally found it. He clicked it on.

The stairs were flooded with light – blinding, harsh light. Half-way up them, a figure froze.

It was Alwyne, making his way upstairs. He stared at Ralph; Ralph stared at him. For a split second, it seemed that their eyes met. They didn't, of course; Alwyne's eyeballs flickered, revealing the whites.

'Who's there?' hissed Alwyne.

'It's only me,' whispered Ralph. His heart was hammering. Alwyne, too, seemed startled. It must be due to the unnatural light. Alwyne could sense light through his eyelids; he had told him this when Ralph had asked why he lit his lamp in his room. *I'm afraid of the dark*, he had said. No wonder, thought Ralph, after all the poor man had been through.

'I've just been to the bathroom,' whispered Alwyne.

'I know,' said Ralph. 'I hear you all the time.'

Alwyne paused. Then he said: 'Can I come in?'

Ralph switched on the light in his bedroom. Alwyne closed the door behind them. He felt his way to the bed and sat down.

'What do you mean, you hear me all the time?' Alwyne asked.

'I know why you have to go,' said Ralph.

Alwyne's head reared up. 'Go where?' he snapped.

Ralph flushed. 'You know where I mean.'

'No I don't, young fellow.'

They were whispering, but Ralph lowered his voice further. 'To the lavatory.'

There was a silence.

Ralph said: 'It's because of the constipation, isn't it?'

Alwyne slumped down. He started shaking. The man was chuckling! Ralph wasn't surprised; the question of bathrooms, and what one did in them, was fraught with embarrassment. He noticed that though Alwyne's black, wiry hair had grown long, he was thinning on top. The white flesh showed through. Ralph was filled with compassion. All sorts of things were being revealed, now they had electric light.

'It's you who told me about it,' said Ralph. 'The binding effect of putrefying flesh. That's why I stopped eating meat.'

Alwyne lifted his head. 'My dear boy. I'm very fond of you.' He wiped his wet eyes with his sleeve. 'You know that, don't you?'

Where did that all come from? Ralph gazed at the man, sitting there in his stained dressing gown and slippers. Behind him the new wall had been painted cream; they hadn't been able to find a wallpaper that matched. Ralph planned to hang things on it, when he thought of things to hang.

'It's not been easy for you, has it?' said Alwyne.

Ralph nodded. 'I'm not sure about this electric light.' He thought: Mrs O'Malley thinks it's going to explode, the Spooners don't want to see anything, Alwyne can't see anything anyway and I don't like it because it shows up my boils. 'My mother says it makes her look old.'

'Your mother is a very beautiful woman.'

'How do you know?'

'Winnie –' He stopped. 'People – have described her to me. You must love her very much.'

Ralph nodded. Then he realised, for the hundredth time, that Alwyne couldn't see him. 'I do.'

Alwyne mused: *'To live in the rank sweat of an enseamed bed, stew'd in corruption, honeying and making love over the nasty sty.'*

Ralph froze. 'How do you know?'

'Know what?'

He knew about Ralph's sheet! But how could he? Ralph paused, confused.

Alwyne said: 'Are you familiar with *Hamlet*?'

'A little bit. Not really.'

'Let the bloat king tempt you again to bed; pinch wanton on your cheek; call you his mouse; and let him, for a pair of reechy kisses, or paddling in your neck with his damn'd fingers, make you to ravel all this matter out. Hamlet was a young man in a not dissimilar position to your own.'

'Was he a vegetarian too?'

Alwyne chuckled. 'Well, plenty of blood got spilt. Enough to make anyone forswear the flesh.'

147

Ralph had no idea what Alwyne was talking about. He had had his doubts about the fellow from the start.

'I expect you're unacquainted with the works of Doctor Freud,' said Alwyne. 'He has some interesting things to say about sons and mothers. Quite explosive, in fact, if anyone cares to read him.'

Ralph was suddenly sleepy. He wished the chap would leave him alone and let him fetch the sheet. The trouble with Alwyne was that he talked too much. Ralph couldn't blame him. After all, there was nothing else for him to do.

Ralph stood up. 'I think I'll go to the lavatory,' he said.

That did the trick. Alwyne, too, got to his feet. He touched Ralph's arm. 'Let's keep this to ourselves, eh? The state of my bowels could be of no interest to anybody whatsoever. Understood?'

*

That Mr Turk now owned the house, and had further plans for it, caused the lodgers some unease. They were at his mercy, and who knew what the future might bring? Until recently they had felt secure in the moribund state of their surroundings. There were upheavals enough in the world, one only had to read the newspapers. A major push was taking place on the Somme, which, if memory served them, was exactly the same place the Allies had been fighting in four years earlier, and all those men dead for nothing. The safest thing was to lie low.

Mr Turk, however, had other ideas. The introduction of electricity was unnerving enough. Mrs O'Malley, fearing it would leak out of the socket in her skirting board, had plugged the holes with lumps of suet pudding. The rumble of the vacuum cleaner, mounting the stairs and bumping against their doors, was as alarming as an approaching tank. And why was its bag so swollen? What had it been swallowing, to be so puffed-up?

It was the speed of Mr Turk's plans that took them by surprise. For in the following week a telephone was installed. Winnie was in the basement, doing the weekly wash. This was a laborious undertaking and took from dawn to dusk – laying a fire, filling the copper with water, bringing it to the boil, pounding the clothes, scrubbing them on the washboard, and then wringing them through the mangle and hanging them up to dry on the clotheshorses in the kitchen, because out in the yard they would get covered with smuts. Then there was the ironing to do, which lasted well into the following day. Sometimes the lodgers washed their own intimate items and dried them in front of their fires but there were still armfuls to deal with, despite the welcome discovery that Mr Turk, perhaps suspecting the household's standards of hygiene, sent his own garments to the laundry.

So Winnie was not party to the commotion in the hallway. Besides, she had other things on her mind. Where on earth were Mrs Turk's drawers?

Winnie was on intimate terms with the bodies upstairs. Each week she scrubbed at their most private secretions until her hands were raw. Bloodstains were the most stubborn to deal with; though Mrs Turk wore pads they were far from efficient and her monthlies were as familiar to Winnie, and as regular, as her own. The state of some other undergarments, particularly those of the male members of the household, left a great deal to be desired. Then there were the stains from past meals – gravy, tea, and worst of all beetroot. Even the sheets, which she bundled off to the laundry, bore witness to what had happened between them. Ralph's stains were familiar to Winnie; after all, she had grown up with three brothers. Mr Spooner's sheets, from his permanent occupation of his bed, didn't bear close inspection. And the sheets belonging to her master and mistress bore the all-too-visible proof of their vigorous conjugal relations. Every garment, every item of bedlinen, was known to her. So where were Mrs Turk's drawers?

There should have been seven pairs in the pile, but as far as Winnie remembered she hadn't seen any for weeks. Mr Turk had bought his wife two pairs of fancy silk knickers, edged with lace, but even these seemed to have disappeared. For a mad moment Winnie thought somebody had stolen them from the laundry-box. Her suspicions fell on Alwyne. There was something grubby about the way he crept around the house; he reminded her of Mr Snape, the rat-catcher in her village, who was rumoured to sniff ladies' bicycle seats. Female undergarments had disappeared from washing-lines and when Mr Snape had enlisted in the navy the thefts had ceased.

Winnie dismissed this thought as both disloyal and illogical. Alwyne had no need of perverted sexual practices, with herself available to satisfy his lust. Besides, could a blind man tell whose knickers were whose, just by feeling them?

It was then that Winnie had the obvious idea of checking in Mrs Turk's bedroom. Wiping her hands on her apron, she went upstairs.

In the hallway she found Mrs Turk, Lettie and Mrs O'Malley clustered around the table. An object sat on it.

'Look at our telephone, Winnie,' said Mrs Turk. 'The man's just gone.'

Winnie had heard the sound of a workman but she had been busy out the back. The stairs creaked as Alwyne descended.

'What's all this then?' he asked.

'We've got a telephone,' said Mrs Turk.

'It's called a Candlestick Telephone,' said Lettie.

'How do you know?' asked Mrs Turk.

'The man said so.'

Black and shiny, it had a tall stem with a mouthpiece on top. A trumpet-shaped earpiece hung on its hook. Brown flex snaked across the table. On the wall nearby was fixed its bell, a wooden box with two brass domes on top, nippled like bosoms.

They had of course seen a telephone before; it was just a startling sight, to have one in the house. It sat there like a periscope connecting them to the underworld. Winnie felt that, if she leaned close, she could hear millions upon millions of people whispering secrets to each other.

'I don't know who to telephone,' said Mrs Turk. 'Nobody I know has one.'

There was a silence. She had spoken the truth for all of them. To Winnie's knowledge, only two people in her village possessed a telephone, the doctor and Lord Elbourne.

They gazed at the object, sitting there ready to serve them. That there was nobody to telephone made them feel friendless. This seemed perverse, of course, as the thing had been invented to connect them up.

'You could always use it to place an order,' Alwyne said to Mrs Turk. 'I know! You could telephone the butcher.'

'But he lives here.'

Alwyne chucked. 'It was a joke.'

'Oh.' Mrs Turk pushed back her hair. 'Of course, he has one in the shop. He needs one here as well, he has a lot of important business to attend to. I expect we'll use it too, when we get used to it. Soon everybody will have one, I'm sure.' She smiled brightly. 'I think it's ever so exciting.'

'How close do I put my mouth?' asked Mrs O'Malley. 'Do I have to pay?'

'For calls? I expect so. Ask Mr Turk. He's in charge now.' She moved towards the basement stairs. 'I must get started on the supper.'

Winnie saw her chance. She hurried upstairs. As she did so she thought: it's a funny old to-do. The electric light shows me how ugly I am and the telephone shows me I've got nobody to speak to. And people say that's progress.

She let herself into the bedroom, opened Mrs Turk's cupboard and pulled out the top drawer. It was full to the brim, as usual, with her mistress's underwear.

Winnie straightened up. There was only one answer. Mrs Turk wasn't wearing any knickers. But why? Was it the hot weather?

Down in the hallway, the telephone rang. Winnie froze. It was surprisingly loud – an insistent, jangling double-ring.

Winnie hurried downstairs but Lettie got there first. Casually, as if she did this every day, she put the trumpet to her ear and spoke into the mouthpiece.

'Good afternoon, Letitia Spooner speaking.'

Mrs Turk, who had hurried up from the kitchen, stared at her. 'How do you know what to do?' she whispered.

Lettie turned to her. 'The man showed us. Weren't you watching?'

How fearless the child was! Truly, the world belonged to them now. 'Letitia Spooner of 45, Palmerston Road.' Winnie and her mistress gazed at the little girl as she spoke into the telephone as if she had been doing it all her life. 'May I be of assistance?'

They heard a scratchy voice, like a mouse's scrabbling claws.

'Who is it?' hissed Mrs Turk.

'Very well, I'll tell them.' Lettie replaced the earpiece in its holder and turned to them. 'It's Mr Turk. He says he's coming home at six o'clock and we've got to go to the window. He's got a surprise.'

*

Throughout his life Ralph remembered that day. Two major things happened. The motor car arrived, and he smoked his first cigarette.

Everything was sharply in focus that afternoon, as if the very sunshine knew, before Ralph did, the significance of that particular Wednesday. He walked home along the river. The warehouses on the opposite bank looked close enough to touch. The vinegar factory in Silver Street cast a knife-sharp shadow. He walked up Back Lane, past the dwellings that echoed with voices whose words just escaped him. When he emerged from the tunnel he noticed that a new poster had been stuck on to the side of his house: DOCTOR FAIRBURN'S RUPTURE

TRUSS. SAY GOODBYE TO HERNIAS. What *was* a truss? And a hernia? Everything seemed crystal clear and yet mysterious, as if the grown-ups had something to tell him that he didn't yet understand.

Alwyne was sitting in the parlour listening to a gramophone record. As a sop to the lodgers for their expulsion from the back room, the gramophone had been moved to the front one. The table was laid for supper.

'Haydn's String Quartet in D minor,' said Alwyne. 'His chamber pieces are woefully under-appreciated.'

They are by me, anyway, thought Ralph. He preferred Boyce's songs from the Hippodrome, *A Little of What You Fancy* and *Jolly Good Luck to the Girl Who Loves a Soldier*.

'Did you see the telephone?' said Alwyne. 'At least when we catch the flu we can get hold of the doctor before anyone else does.'

The influenza was raging across Europe, apparently, as if the fellows there didn't have enough to worry about. Now, in London, people were starting to drop like flies.

'Not that I need to worry,' said Alwyne. 'Smoking's the best protection. Kills the germs, you see. You should be taking it up, young man.' He proffered the packet. 'No time like the present.'

'I can't,' said Ralph. 'My mother . . .'

'I think your mother would prefer you to live. Anyway she's in her room, getting dressed up for hubby. Go on, be a devil.'

There was, in fact, something devilish about Alwyne – the black wings of his eyebrows; the coaxing voice. He had a lisp, too, which made his words thicker and somehow more suggestive.

Besides, why not? Ralph felt a rush of rebellion. He took a cigarette, lit it and inhaled.

His throat closed up. A searing pain blocked his lungs. He bent over double, choking. Alwyne chuckled.

'Persevere, my boy. You'll get the hang of it in the end.'

Through his tears Ralph heard the sound of a motor engine. Not many of them were heard outside his house, which was two streets away from the main road and something of a backwater. A horn sounded.

Upstairs his mother screamed.

Ralph stubbed out the cigarette. He was out of the room in a flash. His mother was thundering downstairs, buttoning up her blouse.

'Mother!' he cried.

She grabbed his arm. 'Ralph! Come here!'

'Are you all right?'

'Come and look!'

The dog was barking. She pulled Ralph along the hallway and flung open the door.

She stood still and whispered. 'Oh my goodness.'

A motor car was parked outside their door. In it sat Mr Turk, wearing a leather cap and goggles. He parped the horn again. Along the street, doors opened and people appeared.

Brutus bounded out and started snapping at a tyre. Mr Turk pulled off his goggles and gazed at his wife.

'Well, my dear?'

He leaned over and opened the passenger door. Eithne flew across the pavement in her stockinged feet, jumped into the car and threw her arms around him.

Ralph flinched, as if he'd been struck. How could his

mother do that, in front of the neighbours? She was kissing the man on the lips! *A pair of reechy kisses.*

A hand touched his arm 'What's the commotion?' Alwyne had arrived, and stood at his side.

'Mr Turk is sitting in a motor car,' said Ralph. 'It's sort of purple, with the hood pulled back. He looks awfully pleased with himself.'

The motor car belched clouds of petrol smoke from its nether regions. Through the haze appeared Mrs Spooner, home from work. Her face was grey with exhaustion; she looked like a ghost, in the smoke. She glanced up at the top window, as she always did when she neared the house.

'Mrs Spooner,' called Eithne. 'Look what Mr Turk's bought! He says it's called a Wolseley.'

Mrs Spooner gathered her wits. She turned slowly to gaze at the motor car.

'Go and get your daughter!' called Neville. 'I was expecting a welcoming party.'

His face was pink with triumph. He sat there, one arm draped around his wife's shoulders.

'Hop in, young lad!' he called to Ralph. 'I'll take us for a spin.'

Ralph struggled with his conflicting emotions. On the one hand, it was undeniably exciting. He had never sat in a motor car before. Perhaps Mr Turk would let him sit at the wheel and steer it!

Winnie and Mrs O'Malley came out of the house, edging him aside. They gasped. Lettie pushed through them; with a quick glance at her mother, she ran across to the motor car and jumped in the back seat. Ralph realised, with surprise, how the past two months had transformed the girl. Once she had looked half starved. Now she had fattened up; her face was rosy with health. She even talked more. Mr Turk's food had performed that miracle. And here Ralph was, thinking that *he* could have taken care of them. How deluded he had been, how pitifully babyish, to imagine that *he* could be the man of the house.

'Room for one more inside!' called Mr Turk.

A crowd had gathered by now. Small boys, their feet bare, gazed at the motor car. They gazed at its polished flanks, its shiny chrome. Even Mr Crocker, the man whose nightshirt had risen up when the Zep appeared, came out of his house to stare.

Mrs Spooner looked up. Despite the noise, with her sixth sense she had heard a sound. Ralph glanced up too. On the top floor the sash was pushed up. Mr Spooner's white face appeared at the window. His wife's face broke into a smile. All this for a motor car! Indeed, Ralph's own heart was beating faster. It was simply so beautiful, so *new*. It made the very houses look tired.

Alwyne leaned close. 'Know what the date is?'

Ralph thought for a moment. 'The twenty-eighth of June.'

At that moment the dog jumped into the motor car and sat in the back seat. He waited expectantly, as if he did this sort of thing every day. Lettie put her arm around him.

'Four years ago, on this day, remember what happened?' murmured Alwyne.

Ralph was confused. 'What?'

'A man called Gavrilo Princip shot the Archduke Franz

Ferdinand as he was sitting in his motor car. Shot his wife too. You know about that, don't you?'

'Oh yes,' Ralph lied.

Alwyne chuckled. 'That's what started this whole damn business.'

Chapter Six

The treatment of Servants is of the highest possible moment, as well to the mistress as to the domestics themselves. On the head of the house the latter will natually fix their attention; and if they perceive that the mistress's conduct is regulated by high and correct principles, they will not fail to respect her. If, also, a benevolent desire is shown to promote their comfort, at the same time that a steady performance of their duty is extracted, then their respect will not be unmingled with affection, and they will be still more solicitous to continue to deserve her favour.

Mrs Beeton's Book of Household Management

Over the next weeks a transformation took place. Mrs Turk became a woman of fashion. A dressmaker came to the house and fitted her with new gowns – shot-silk dresses of midnight blue, of deepest green trimmed with ochre braid that picked up the chestnut lights in her hair. Blouses were delivered in boxes tied with ribbon, lace blouses shrouded in layers of tissue paper. Copies of *Weldon's Ladies' Journal* appeared; after she finished with them she gave them to Winnie, who hoarded them in her room. Mr Turk picked her up in his motor car and drove her to the West End, to department stores whose names were as exotic as the stars in the sky – Debenham and

Freebody, Swan and Edgar. She returned bearing hats, and kid gloves as soft as babies' skin.

In the evenings the two of them disappeared to official functions – banquets in the City guildhalls, where they hobnobbed with aldermen; dinners with local notables at the Clarendon Hotel. She brought home the menus – *quails in aspic, lobster thermidor*. 'They'll give you ideas for supper,' she said, swinging round and inspecting herself in the mirror.

Gone were the days when she rolled up her sleeves and helped Winnie with the housework. Their closeness during the dark years of her widowhood was all but gone; she was a married woman now and there was a shuttered look to her as if she were guarding a secret that Winnie could never hope to understand. In fact, mindful of Mr Turk, she sometimes spoke sharply to Winnie, running her fingers along the top of the picture frames and ticking her off. Winnie missed the old days; despite the hardships, she and her mistress had pulled together. During her first marriage there had been a bond between them: a shared, unspoken irritation with her sweet but ineffectual husband whose existence was now the faintest of memories.

And the work had become heavier. Alwyne complained that Winnie had no time to read to him but there were not enough hours in the day. Even the ironing now took up the best part of a morning – the goffering and crimping, the delicate pleats and lace, the rows of tiny, tiny buttons. One night Winnie was so tired that she fell asleep while saying her prayers and woke at dawn, still kneeling at her bed, her head laid on the blanket. All day she had a cricked neck.

She had a mind to blame Jesus for this but to tell the truth He had long since gone from her life and she was only going through the motions. He had disappeared the day they took the horses away. During her previous sorrows – even during her mother's last illness – Jesus had kept company with her, holding her hand. But now He seemed to be gone for good. Winnie told nobody this, not even Alwyne who would no doubt be gratified, what with being an atheist. 'Christianity is a conspiracy,' he said. 'It's created to keep you working classes in your place, in the ludicrous belief that all will be happy in the next life if you knuckle under in this one.'

Maybe his ideas were seeping through. For Winnie was feeling a small stir of dissatisfaction. She was used to the lodgers' demands, however odd, and had always gone out of her way to help them – Mrs Spooner in particular, whose life was very hard. Indeed, their habits were so familiar that Winnie seldom had to be summoned by one of their bells ringing in the kitchen. However, when she saw DRAWING ROOM jangling, she felt a stab of irritation. Mr and Mrs Turk were the largest and healthiest adults in the house. Couldn't they come down and fetch whatever they wanted themselves?

Alwyne said it was like that in the trenches. His unit had rebelled against their cowardly sap of a CO and the barriers had broken down. 'When the war's over, the battle will commence,' he said, wagging his nicotine-stained finger. In fact it had already started. Winnie's friend Lily worked in a stocking factory down the Whitechapel Road. Formerly a timid girl who wouldn't say boo to a goose, she had come out on strike over wages and turned into quite the militant.

This slippage in Winnie's loyalties was alarming. She blamed it on Mr Turk. Despite his jovial spirits, there was something about the man that made her uneasy. *I don't trust him*, Alwyne had said, and Winnie was inclined to agree. That he had further plans for the house was not in any doubt. She had seen him sizing up the rooms with the speculative look she had seen in Lord Elbourne's face when a dealer brought him a new hunter. Something was brewing. It made her uneasy in a way she had never felt when Mr Clay was in charge. Mr Turk could sack her and bring in more staff; he could sell up and kick her out into the street. These four walls were not as safe as they looked and she was utterly in his power. Sometimes she envied Lily, and even Elsie with her canary face. They laboured hard for their twelve shillings a week but at six o'clock they were released, as free as birds.

Winnie was thinking this as she served the three of them dinner, one day towards the end of July. Mr Turk was talking about an American soldier they had met in Brighton.

'He was a bright young lad,' said Mr Turk, his eyes darting to Ralph. 'Know what he had? Plenty of get-up-and-go.'

'I wish he'd remembered his photograph,' said Mrs Turk. 'I hope he's all right.' She turned to Ralph. 'He reminded me of you.'

Mr Turk raised his eyebrows. 'Bit more oomph to him, wouldn't you say?' He spooned the potatoes on to his plate. 'Mark my words, that young man'll go far.'

'If he gets out alive,' said Mrs Turk.

Ralph cleared his throat. He turned to his stepfather.

'Why haven't *you* joined up?' he asked.

There was a silence. Winnie nearly dropped the serving-dish.

'Ralph!' hissed his mother.

Mr Turk's eyes twinkled. 'That's all right, my dear. Perfectly natural question.' He turned to Ralph. 'I've got a Certificate of Exemption, young man. Want to see it?'

Ralph blushed. The spots on his chin glowed livid red.

'Want to see it?' Mr Turk stood up, his chair scraping. 'I'll fetch it right now.'

'Neville!' said Mrs Turk. 'Sit down.'

'The lad doesn't believe me.'

'Of course he does!' She turned to her son. 'What do you think you're doing, asking a thing like that?'

Ralph swallowed. His Adam's apple moved up and down. 'I was just asking,' he muttered.

Neville lowered himself back into his chair. 'No offence taken.' He shot a look at the boy.

Mrs Turk turned to Winnie. 'Lots of people haven't been called up, have they, Winnie? Two of your brothers, for instance.'

Winnie nodded. 'They're in a reserved occupation.'

'Exactly,' she said. 'They work on a farm. And Neville works in a shop. He *runs* a shop.'

Winnie moved to Ralph. She felt sick, as if she had betrayed him. She longed to say *You've asked what nobody else has dared.* Ralph helped himself to some mashed swede. He acted unconcerned but she could see his reddening neck.

Mr Turk tucked his napkin into his collar and started to eat. His eyes darted around the table as he put a piece of pork into his mouth. Winnie thought: he looks like a

163

pig. Pink face, little piggy eyes. Except she was fond of
pigs.

*

It was Sunday afternoon. The house slumbered in the
oppressive heat. Ralph's final exams were the next day:
Advanced Book-keeping Level 3. He tried to concentrate
but the figures danced around on the page. What was the
point of adding things up? None of it made sense
anyway. Mr Turk said Ralph could work in his shop. He
could sit in the cash desk and take the money. Ralph had
no intention of doing this. He wanted to work in an office
for thirty shillings a week and bring home a wage for his
mother. *You're my little trooper*, she would say. He would
sit on the arm of her chair and stroke her hair. At night
they would lie in their beds, the doors ajar. She would
say *Night-night, sleep tight* and he would reply, *Don't let
the bedbugs bite*, the cat a weight on his legs, the dog
beside him on the floor, twitching as he chased rabbits in
his dreams. The next day they would pack sandwiches
and take the train to Box Hill where Brutus would chase
real rabbits and Ralph would pick up snail shells and
show his mother the wonder of them, the wonder she
had never appreciated when his father was alive. All his
father's love for them would come back in a rush.

Suddenly Ralph missed his father so much it stopped
his breath. How could his father have left him to the
mercy of this impostor who sat at the table, his big thighs
planted apart? His father had died for them while this
man stayed safely at home, chopping up defenceless
creatures and totting up the profits with his bloodstained
fingers.

Ralph was glad that he had tackled Mr Turk on this subject. The man had definitely looked shifty. Certificate of Exemption, indeed! Ralph had never heard of such a thing. His only regret was that Alwyne hadn't been there to witness his triumph. Alwyne hated bloated plutocrats and said they would soon become extinct. There was one law for the rich and another for the poor but world events were fast overturning this iniquitous state of affairs. The workers would triumph, as they had done in Russia. Of course, Mr Turk himself could be considered a working man, but Alwyne would have an answer for this. Ralph had full confidence in the fellow.

He had grown closer to Alwyne during the past few weeks. Alwyne, a veteran of one war, understood that another sort of battle was raging in the house – a silent, bloodless battle, that sucked up energy like the vacuum cleaner. It festered in the airless rooms. As for Winnie, Ralph suspected that she, too, was on his side but they had scarcely spoken recently. He hadn't been able to help her as much as he should, due to studying for his finals. When he did speak to her, she seemed distracted. No doubt she hated Mr Turk as much as he did, but anxiety about her job stopped her from confessing such a thing. This made Ralph sad; their old closeness seemed to be another casualty of the hostilities.

Today, however, was Winnie's day off. She had gone to Woolwich, where her friend Elsie was in hospital with the lyddite poisoning. She had got it from packing the shells with explosives. Ralph's mother and Mr Turk had gone boating on the Serpentine.

Ralph put down his pen. He couldn't concentrate on his revision. He knew the reason, of course. The blood had drained away from his brain, it had drained down to the usual place where it throbbed and burned, tormenting him. The heat made it worse. Did every boy his age go through this torture?

Ralph stood up. Now was his chance, with the three of them out of the house. He opened the door. Not a sound; the house was sunk in somnolence. The lodgers were either out or having a snooze.

Ralph went downstairs, down to the basement. He tapped on Winnie's door, for form's sake, but he knew the room was empty. She wouldn't be back until the evening.

He felt like a trespasser but he told himself Winnie wouldn't mind. After all, he was only going to borrow one of her magazines for an hour – *Weldon's Ladies' Journal*, if possible. She would have no idea of the use to which he would put it.

The problem was, he had run out of stimulating material. Apart from an engraving of a lady receiving a letter, the house contained no images of the female form. Boyce's book of photographs had been packed up with his other belongings, when Ralph was out of the house, and sent home to the chap's mother. Ralph cursed himself for not predicting this and retrieving the book – indeed, stealing other mementoes with which to remind himself of his beloved friend. But it was too late now and he could no longer even go near the top room, contaminated as it was by Mr Turk's furniture.

He stepped into Winnie's room. There was something virginal about its narrow bedstead and single chair. The walls were bare; nothing hung on them except a crucifix. Her little sanctuary was so pure that Ralph felt his very thoughts were corrupting it like a lewd smell. It was the room of a woman doomed to celibacy.

Ralph felt sad. Winnie was plain – remarkably plain. There were no two ways about it – her hefty shoulders, her lantern jaw. He loved her, of course, but not in that fashion and it was doubtful that anybody ever would lust after her with the carnal hunger he all too frequently experienced himself. The brutal fact was that after four years of war there were so few young men left that those remaining could pick and choose, and they wouldn't choose Winnie.

This seemed so sad that Ralph sat down on the bed. His lust evaporated. He looked at her fireplace. Even this was tiny, as if Winnie were of too little account to need as much heat as anybody else.

It was then that he noticed the cigarette stubs. They lay scattered in the grate, five or six of them. Ralph was taken aback. What was Winnie doing, smoking cigarettes?

He frowned, trying to puzzle it out. There was something shocking about the stubs; they were so out of keeping with everything else. But then people had their little secrets, as he himself knew only too well. Who knew what they got up to behind their bedroom doors?

His face cleared: of course, Winnie was learning to smoke. Everyone was doing it, to ward off the influenza. Even his mother was trying it, coughing and spluttering and holding out the cigarette as if it would bite. In fact she had urged Ralph to try it too. 'It's horrible to begin with,' she said, 'but I'm sure we'll get used to it.' Ralph's fears about her disapproval were unfounded; Alwyne was right, as he was right about so many things. He said the influenza had arrived with the American troops. They had carried it to the Front, where it had unfortunately started killing the very troops they had been sent out to support. Truly, God had some rum surprises up His sleeve.

Ralph heard a noise. Footsteps were descending the stairs.

He got up and went to the door.

'It's all right, dear,' said Mrs Spooner's voice. 'There's nobody here, I told you.'

Ralph heard the hesitant shuffle of bedroom slippers.

'I'll make us a nice cup of tea,' said Mrs Spooner. 'And would you like some bread and jam?'

She was talking to her husband. Her voice was soft and crooning – a voice Ralph had never heard before.

'See? It's quite safe,' she said. 'Sit down and make yourself comfortable. Help him, Lettie. I'll just put on the kettle.'

Ralph darted back into the bedroom and closed the door. Footsteps approached along the passage and stopped outside, in the scullery. He heard the gush of water as Mrs Spooner filled the kettle.

'Do you remember that day at Frinton Sands?' she called. 'A lovely sunny day like this one! Wasn't it, Lettie?'

She took the kettle back into the kitchen. Ralph heard her speaking to her husband. He caught the words '. . . rolled up your trousers . . . oh we did have a fine day, didn't we love? . . .'

Mr Spooner replied. Ralph couldn't hear the words. His wife's voice brightened. 'That's right!' she said. 'And you and Lettie made a sandcastle.'

Ralph sat down on the bed. He couldn't leave now; the stairs were in full view of the kitchen. They would jump out of their skins. The shock of seeing him would send Mr Spooner straight back to bed, probably for ever.

Ralph lay down. He would have to wait until they left. He lay there, listening to their murmuring voices and the clatter of plates.

Mrs Spooner spoke to her husband, her voice low and loving. He replied. Ralph couldn't hear what he said, but Mrs Spooner laughed. He had seldom heard her laugh. He listened to the little family eating tea in the kitchen. Through her love, Mrs Spooner was bringing her husband back to life – a pale, trembling wreck of a man, but at least he had come home.

Suddenly Ralph burst into tears. It took him quite by surprise. Once he started he couldn't stop. He lay on Winnie's bed, curled in a ball. He cried silently, weeping for his father, who would never come back to him.

*

Ralph woke with a start. Dusk had fallen. He jumped off the bed; Winnie would be back at any moment!

He froze. A sound was coming from the kitchen. He crept to the door and listened.

Somebody was groaning. It sounded like an animal in pain. Mr Spooner was having a heart attack! Ralph opened the door a crack and listened. It was a rhythmic, grunting groan. Somebody was suffering; had anyone called the doctor?

Ralph opened the door and tiptoed out. He peeped into the kitchen.

The room was dim. For a moment he couldn't make out what was happening. Two figures seemed to be jammed against the dresser.

His mother's skirt was bunched around her waist; her white petticoat glimmered. It was she who was making the noise. Mr Turk stood, his legs planted apart, his back to Ralph. His shirt-sleeve was rolled up. His bare arm was shoved up inside her, like a vet calving a cow. His mother's head was flung back; her body shuddered. Yelps came from her as his arm pushed in and out.

Ralph reeled back. He spun round, and stumbled up the stairs.

Chapter Seven

'I say, waiter! Would you mind closing that door – I don't want my meat ration blown away.'

Picture postcard

Eithne tapped on Ralph's door.

'Your breakfast's getting cold,' she said. 'I've boiled you an egg.'

No reply.

'Big day today,' she said.

Ralph mumbled something.

'What was that, dear?'

'I'll be down soon,' he said.

'Don't be long.'

Eithne went downstairs. It was Monday morning; her husband, and Mrs Spooner, had long since gone to work. From the parlour came the clatter of plates as Winnie served breakfast.

Ralph was such a good boy. He had been studying hard for his exams, he wanted to do the best for his mother. Sometimes, however, Eithne wished he would take more part in family life. What larks he had missed, the previous afternoon! Neville had rowed her across the Serpentine; he had rolled up his sleeves and grinned at her, a cigar clamped between his lips, his strong hands gripping the oars as they sliced through the water. Here was a man who could take care of them. Ralph would have admired Neville's prowess. He would – surely he would – have been gratified to see his mother laughing without a care in the world. They had suffered such sorrow together, the two of them. Didn't they deserve some happiness?

Of course it was also a relief, that Ralph hadn't been there. Eithne hated to admit this, but it was true. Brutus, balancing on his haunches as the boat rocked, was an easier companion than her son. Animals were a relief, in this respect. Their baleful looks were simply a matter of whether or not you took them for a walk.

Afterwards Neville had taken her for a drive. *Work hard, play hard* was his philosophy. He drove fast, his foot flat on the floor. The wind rushed through Eithne's hair; she clamped her hat on her head and gripped the door handle. In the back seat, Brutus swayed from side to side. Horses shied as Neville swerved around them, hooting his horn. No more waiting at bus stops, no more clopping along at a snail's pace! No more fumbling for pennies to pay the fare. In a trice they were roaring through the streets of Bayswater, through Notting Hill Gate, through streets she never knew existed. London was both suddenly vast and suddenly intimate. Their beautiful shiny Wolseley ate up the miles. They could drive to Blackpool, to Bognor, to Bungay, wherever that was. They could drive up to Stockport where she grew up, where her father still lived, and see his face as they shuddered to a halt outside the house and honked the horn. The internal combustion engine was going to transform the world, Neville said. He called it *the eternal combustion engine.* Alwyne, back at the house, had muttered *the infernal combustion engine* but what did Alwyne know? He was blind.

'Fellas want their freedom,' said Neville. 'Mark my words, they'll all be driving 'em soon.' He hooted his way through the crowded streets. The motor car bounced over tram-lines; it got stuck in tram-lines – once, good Lord, they nearly got mown down by a tram that sped towards them ringing its bell. They even braved Piccadilly Circus, a chaos of tram-lines like tangled knitting, a stampede of omnibuses and cabs and motor lorries that made Eithne cower, and grab her husband's arm. Ralph was a boy, he would have loved it. This was his world now, if he'd had the sense to join them. Neville would teach him to drive.

Her husband was good to the boy. Oh, he might be sharpish sometimes but Ralph needed gingering up and only a man could give him the nudge he needed. In the long run, he would see the benefit. Neville was good to them all. *Love me, love my lodgers*, she had told him, the night he proposed. That meal he cooked them had won their hearts. Everything was going to be all right. Eithne had had her doubts but speeding along in a Wolseley blew them away. There was nothing to worry about. The sun was sinking as they drove across London Bridge. It was a beautiful sunset, the sky suffused with pink, the blood-red disk slipping behind the dome of St Paul's.

Eithne pulled off her hat and flung back her head. Her hair loosened from its pins and whipped around her face. 'I'm so happy I want to die!' she shouted.

When she climbed out of the motor car her legs were trembling. She felt sick with desire, ill with it. They stumbled down to the kitchen, to brew some tea. Her husband reached for the kettle but she grabbed his hand and pressed it against her breast.

'I love you,' she whispered. 'I love you I love you I love you.'

Leaning against the dresser, she pulled him to her.

Afterwards, when they switched on the light, she saw Ralph's apron hanging on its hook. It was the green calico apron he wore when blacking the boots. Though empty of Ralph, it was so redolent of the boy that she blushed.

Her dearest son. She loved him so much. What *would* he think of her? Eithne felt so weak, she had to sit down.

*

Ralph had packed his bag. It contained a change of underwear, a clean shirt, the striped woollen vest that Winnie had knitted for him, his toothbrush and toothpaste, a packet of digestive biscuits, the photograph of his parents that he had extracted from its frame, and a book – *Fletcher's Guide to British Birds* – that had belonged to his father. No doubt the birds would be different in France but looking at the pictures would remind him of home. He hadn't known what else to pack. They would supply him with a uniform, of course. If only he knew somebody else who was joining up. He didn't want to humiliate himself by carrying a bag that was either too big or too small. If only Boyce or his father were there, to give him advice!

It was eleven o'clock in the morning; a sultry day, threatening thunder. His mother had gone shopping; she had taken the Underground to Whiteleys, to choose material for new curtains. 'Good luck, my darling little man,' she had said, kissing him. 'You'll pass with top marks, I know you will. And we'll have a special supper to celebrate.' She left. He wiped the saliva off his cheek.

It struck him as curious, that at twelve o'clock his fellow students would be sitting down to their final exam. Harry, Roly, the others whose names he had never caught and whose friend he had never become. Maybe they would all go out afterwards to celebrate the end of term and the end of Mrs Brand. They seemed creatures of another world now, a world so irrelevant that it surprised him, in a mild sort of way, that he had ever been a part of it at all.

The house was quiet. Winnie was out at the shops. She had taken the dog. Ralph was thankful for this; the thought of saying goodbye to either of them was something he had been dreading. He loved the two of them more than anything else on earth, they were all that was left to him. Already he missed them.

Ralph put on his jacket. He patted the inside pocket, checking that his money was there. He had one pound five shillings and threepence. This was the sum total of his savings – one pound and threepence – plus the money Mr Turk had paid him for washing his motor car – five washes at a shilling a wash. Once he enlisted, of course, they would give him the King's Shilling and a warrant, and after that there should be no more expenditure. The army would take care of everything.

Ralph carried his bag downstairs. He took one last look around the hallway and was just about to leave when a voice called from the parlour.

'That you, Ralph?'

It was Alwyne. He sat at the table, smoking a cigarette.

'Thought nobody would ever come,' he said irritably. 'Do me a favour and find me a gramophone record. Does nobody realise they all feel exactly the same – Mozart, Haydn, the divine Schubert? Just a piece of bloody shellac.'

'I'm sorry,' said Ralph. The fellow seemed to be in a filthy mood. 'What would you like?'

'Don't think I'm up to Schubert this morning. I presume Winnie's told you about her friend?'

'No.'

'The poor girl, she's in a terrible state.'

'Why?' Ralph looked at his watch. It was fortunate that Alwyne couldn't see him. He really ought to be getting a move on.

'She's dying.'

Ralph froze. 'Winnie's dying?'

'No, her friend. Pay attention. Her friend, Elsie, who made the bombs.' Alwyne stubbed out his cigarette. 'Find me the Rossini. I'm not up to anything profound just now.'

Ralph searched through the gramophone records. This was most inconvenient. Time was ticking on; he had to get out of the house before Winnie or his mother returned.

He found the gramophone record and slipped it out of its sleeve.

'Stay with me, Ralph,' said Alwyne. 'Listen to it with me, there's a good boy.'

'I can't,' said Ralph. 'I'm late already.'

'Ah yes, I'd forgotten.' There was a pause. Alwyne looked at Ralph, his face unreadable behind the black spectacles. 'I want to ask you something. Are you really sure you want to join the drones?'

Ralph stared at him. The blood drained from his face. How on earth did the man know?

There must be a regiment called the Drones. It was probably a nickname. But why did Alwyne presume he wanted to enlist in that particular one?

'The Drones?' he whispered.

'You're a sensitive lad,' said Alwyne. 'I never met your father, of course, but by all accounts you take after him. Do you really think he gave up his life so you can spend the rest of yours stuck on a treadmill counting up other people's money, clocking in and clocking out like a blithering worker bee?'

It took Ralph a moment for this to sink in. He let out his breath. So that was what Alwyne meant!

'I'm very fond of you, Ralph. You're a good boy and I know you want to please your mother. But if one thing can come out of this damned war, surely it's the liberation of lads like you from the tyranny of the whole blasted system.'

It was late. Ralph put out his hand, to shake Alwyne's, but realised the man couldn't see it. 'I've got to do my duty,' he said.

'Duty?' said Alwyne. 'Your duty is to be a happy and fulfilled human being. That's what your father would have wanted for you. That's why we're on this earth, and let me tell you – God has nothing to do with it. Nobody's going to believe in Him after this.'

'I'm sorry,' said Ralph. 'I've got to go. Goodbye.'

He hurried out and slammed the front door. He was half-way to the railway station before he remembered that he hadn't given Alwyne the gramophone record.

Ralph waited on the platform. The next train to Dover was at half-past twelve. He had bought a ticket – a single ticket, of course. It was the first time he had paid an adult fare – eight shillings and sixpence.

He had no intention of enlisting in his own neighbourhood. There was a recruiting office in the Borough Road but there was a strong possibility that he might be recognised. Dover seemed the obvious choice. Nobody would know him there. It was within sight of France; the troops set sail from its port. He would be half-way to the Front already.

London Bridge Station was raised above the street. Beyond the waiting room he could see the brick wall of the Hospital for Incurables. For a moment he wondered about Elsie, Winnie's friend, but dismissed the thought. He couldn't think about that now. He had to be resolute, and concentrate on the matter at hand. At the far end of the platform a group of soldiers stood, smoking. Their bags seemed about the same size as his – kitbags, of course, and accompanied by helmets and other equipment, but approximately the same size.

Ralph summoned up his courage. He walked to the kiosk and bought a packet of five Woodbines – fivepence – and a box of matches. Winnie had given him some matchboxes – she bought them from the amputees, she had a large collection – but he had left them in his room.

Alwyne said that the *crump* of the mortars sounded like a fat man falling through a chair. Ralph remembered his father's letter: *We gave Fritz a pretty good bump this time!* None of it had sounded too alarming. His father's letters had mostly been taken up with describing football games and practical jokes: the time, for instance, that their numskull of a CO had pulled out his respirator, to show them how to use it, and found the box filled with dirty socks. Ralph was looking forward to it; the whole thing sounded like a grand adventure. He would go to the Front and kill a hundred Hun and avenge his father's death. He would stab their guts with a bayonet and become a hero. All this time his mother would be weeping and wailing, wondering where he had gone. She would be inconsolable. She would blame Mr Turk, and throw the man out of the house. Week after week she would sit there berating herself, sobbing for her son. Where had he gone? The first news would be when her brave young hero was mentioned in dispatches. Or when she got a telegram saying he was dead. That would teach her.

He wasn't going to think of his mother. The train arrived, puffing smoke. It panted, like his mother panted – heavy, groaning pants . . . her skirt hoisted up. *He wasn't going to think of her.* He would think of his father, and how proud he would be. Maybe he would meet some of his father's fellow soldiers, and they would talk about him. Maybe Ralph would find himself in the very same dug-out his father had used! Stranger things had happened. By all acounts, the Front didn't seem to have moved much in the last four years.

Ralph got on the train and found an empty carriage. With a jerk, the train pulled out of the station. Ralph pressed his face to the window, waiting to see his house. He had been on the train before, several times in fact, but not of course under these circumstances. This might be his last glimpse ever.

The train rattled along the viaduct. Ralph caught sight of his childhood streets down in the canyon below, unfamiliar from this angle. The people walking there looked so innocent as they went about their business. They moved about in silence; all he could hear was the noise of the train. The smoke dimmed them – billowing clouds of smoke from the engine. If he were a sniper he could pick them off, one by one, and never find out if he knew them or not. Rifles were better than bayonets in this respect. When he joined up he would be given his own rifle; if he was promoted they might give him a revolver too. Some people managed to keep their revolvers afterwards, like that man who shot himself on the day of the wedding.

The train clanked along at a walking pace. Where he sat, Ralph was on a level with the chimneypots. It was odd, seeing his neighbourhood from this perspective. It separated his new life from the past. He had lived in Palmerston Road since he was six but from this angle it took him a moment to get his bearings.

The train jolted past the roof of the Mitre public house, the words along its pediment, TRUMAN AND HANBURY FINE ALES AND STOUT, slap-up close and peeling. It jolted past the back of his street, the soot-blackened rears of the houses that from the front were so familiar. The back yards became smaller as the viaduct curved round, to cut off the terrace at the bridge. Ralph could see his own house at the end, looming through the smoke. There was no sign of life. Boyce's windowsill was still spattered with white, where the pigeons used to wait for their food. Below was Alwyne's window and below that his own. Further below, deep in the depths, was the brick extension that housed the bathroom, its blind down, and below that, out of sight, the yard and Winnie's window. And then it was gone.

The train picked up speed. The sky darkened as it travelled through the suburbs, through Lewisham and Hither Green. It started to rain. Ralph felt strange, to be here on a normal Monday morning while his fellow students were toiling over their exams.

He thought: I should have spent more time playing with Lettie.

*

The train arrived at Dover Priory at a quarter to three. Ralph alighted and stood on the platform. He wished the journey had gone on for ever. Now he was here he felt his courage drain away. If only he had someone with him, who was doing the same thing! He had a stomach ache, a sure sign of nerves.

Ralph walked to the front of the train, past the engine belching smoke, and made his way towards the exit. On the next platform lay a row of soldiers on stretchers. A woman stood there, with a child. She handed the child an orange, to give to one of the injured men, but the little boy hid his face in her skirt. She bent down and gave it to the man herself. Ralph saw a bandaged hand rising from the blanket.

Ralph turned away, quickly. He asked the ticket collector the way to the recruiting office.

'Down the road and turn right, sonny,' said the man. 'Past the post office on Portcullis Street, you can't miss it.' He didn't bat an eyelid.

Ralph walked out into the rain. He wished he had an

umbrella but that would make him look a sissy. Men signing up wouldn't carry an umbrella, would they?

He could still turn round and go home. He had the money for the fare. He could go home and nobody would be the wiser. But then he would have to walk past all the casualties. Some of them had bandages over their eyes.

Ralph walked down the road, ducking under the shop awnings. He suddenly remembered being happy. It was the first winter of the war, in the snow, and he was queueing outside Mr Jones's dairy. Word had got around that some butter had arrived. Ralph's father was still alive, fighting for his country, and Ralph was helping his mother. Other boys were queuing for their mothers too; he knew several of them from school. All at once they scraped up the snow and threw snowballs at each other. The organ grinder had still been around, then. He had been playing *Hello? Hello? Who's Your Lady Friend?*

How simple it had been, in those days! Freezing cold, Ralph had been, and hungry. But happy. One stray shell had shattered that. One shell and his father was gone for ever, Ralph had to grow up without him, *for ever*. One shell, or one shot, or whatever it was, nobody would ever know, and Mr Turk had installed himself with his thick legs and his tight trousers and his disgusting animal practices; no, worse than an animal. Much, much worse.

Don't think about it. Ralph tried to concentrate on the present moment. His father had joined the Middlesex Regiment but there was no chance of himself following in his footsteps, not now he was in Kent. Besides, the whole enlistment business had become something of a free-for-all nowadays; Alwyne said it had all broken down, due to the high turnover. Ralph would have to take pot luck. But whichever regiment he joined, his new life would be waiting for him. Comrades-in-arms! A marching band! There would be basic training, and then they'd be off to France.

Sodden by the rain, Ralph walked past the post office, past the Temperance Hall, and arrived at a brick building. TERRITORIAL ARMY was carved in stone above the door. The steps were scattered with cigarette stubs. A board, propped on a stand, said RECRUITING OFFICE.

Ralph had an urgent need to go to the lavatory. Indoors, it was so dark that he had to pause for a moment, to adjust his eyes to the gloom. He could make out a lady, sitting at a desk. He asked her the way to the recruiting office and she pointed to a door.

If only his mother could see him now! For he was boldly opening the door and walking into a room. His bowels were churning but that was a trifling matter, considering what he would have to face when he was a soldier.

He found himself in a drill-hall, dimly lit by a skylight. There were no queues of young men; in fact there didn't seem to be anybody there at all except a sergeant, sitting at a table. He looked up from his newspaper.

'Good afternoon, young man,' he said. 'And what can I do for you?'

'I've come to join up, sir,' said Ralph.

The man looked at him. 'You have, have you?'

'Yes.' Ralph waited for him to ask for his name.

'And how old might you be, my boy?'

'Eighteen, sir. My name is Ralph John Clay.'

The man cocked his head, inspecting Ralph. 'You brought your birth certificate?'

'No.'

The fellow gazed at him for a moment. He seemed mildly amused. 'Come back in a couple of years, sonny.'

'But I am eighteen!'

'Let's have a dekko at that birth certificate then.'

He wasn't unfriendly. He just smirked, as if he had seen it all before. Ralph stood there for a moment but the interview seemed to be over.

'Can I go to the lavatory?' he asked.

*

Lettie was waiting outside the Mitre. She was sheltering from the rain in the doorway of the public bar. Winnie, returning home with the shopping, saw her before she recognised her – a little girl wearing battered boots, her petticoat drooping below her skirt, her shawl tight around her shoulders. Her father would be inside. Every so often, nowadays, Mr Spooner would slip out of the house, Lettie trotting beside him, and disappear into the Mitre where he drank himself into a stupor and had to be helped home.

'Hello, Brutus.' Lettie patted the sodden dog. Winnie gave her a toffee. She felt sorry for the poor mite. Lettie's two brothers had died, as infants, of the whooping cough. What a burden it was for a girl her age, to take on the sole responsibility for her father, drunk and sober! Lettie had no school, she had no friends. Why didn't her father just pull himself together? Didn't the man have any consideration? It was a welcome sign of recovery, of course, to get out of bed, but did he really have to get drunk in the process?

Winnie's temper was short that day, but she was upset.

Elsie's condition had come as something of a shock. Winnie had been to visit her in the hospital and for a moment she hadn't been able to recognise her friend. She had told Alwyne about it but he had taken the opportunity to give her a lecture on the iniquities of war. All she had wanted was for him to put his arms around her.

Winnie trudged home. There was no dinner to cook that day; both Mr and Mrs Turk were out, and Ralph was at the college doing his exam. She let herself into the kitchen.

Alwyne was fumbling around, searching for something to eat. The lodgers were supposed to make their own arrangements at lunchtime but Alwyne always knew, with some sixth sense, when the coast was clear.

Winnie dumped the shopping basket on the table.

'Did you go into my room yesterday?' she asked, shaking her umbrella.

'No,' said Alwyne, surprised. 'Why would I?'

'My bedspread was all pulled about, as if somebody had been lying on it.'

'My dear girl, I would do no such thing. Why would I lie in your bed without you being in it?'

Winnie was gratified by this sign of his affection. Theirs was such a curious union that she had no idea on whose side the obligation lay, let alone anything resembling love. That it took place under cover of darkness, in conditions of the utmost secrecy, disconnected it from the realities of life. During the day it was hard to believe it had happened at all – indeed, had been happening several times a week for the past two months.

Yet sometimes she felt that the truth lay the other way round. That the only moment she came alive was when Alwyne lay beside her, stroking her arms and murmuring into her hair. She was desirable! She inflamed a grown man's passion! He was starting to learn what pleased her. Even more gratifyingly, she was pleasing him. She was putting this broken man to rights, like a shattered vase.

Not only was she serving him, of course, she was serving her country. War had a heady effect on women; Winnie had seen plenty of evidence of this over the past four years. The gin palaces around the railway stations swarmed with girls only too willing to perform their patriotic duty. Even respectable women melted at the sight of a uniform. Who cared about virtue when in a few days the poor fellow might be dead? When *everyone* might be dead.

'Shall I make you some bread and dripping?' asked Winnie.

'Come here.' Alwyne's arms waved in the air, seeking her. They reminded her of a sea anemone, waving its tentacles for the touch of a passing victim. She had seen them in the rock pools at Ramsgate.

Winnie touched his hand. It closed over hers. Alwyne drew her down to sit beside him.

'I hope Ralph passes his exam,' she said.

'Let's forget Ralph.'

'I wish he had more friends. I don't think Mrs Turk should've kept him apart from the other boys. She thought he was too good for them.'

Alwyne's hand was stealing up her skirt. 'Mrs Turk has always had ideas above her station,' he said.

'Don't you sound the snob! And I thought you were a communist.' Winnie chuckled; his fingers were tickling her. 'I'll bet you come from the gentry, for all your talk.'

'It's irrelevant, my dear. Only this need concern us.' He slid his fingers inside her knickers. 'There's no politics in a pussy, thank God.'

Alwyne was fumbling with his trousers when they heard the sound of footsteps on the stairs. Winnie sprang back and smoothed down her skirt.

Mrs O'Malley came into the kitchen. The old lady looked surprised. 'I had the impression that everybody was out,' she said.

She, too, had been sneaking down for some food. Winnie recovered her breath. 'Shall I make you some bread and dripping, dear?' she asked.

*

Ralph sat in a pub down by the docks. He had drunk two half-pints of Bass; though considered too young to die for his country, it seemed he was old enough to drink its beer. He had also managed to smoke a cigarette without making a spectacle of himself. A pianola sat beside him. It was playing *Burlington Bertie* all by itself, the keys rising and falling.

> *I'm Burlington Bertie, I rise at ten-thirty*
> *And reach Kempton Park around three . . .*

Ralph considered his options. He could join the navy in the time-honoured role of a stowaway, and never be seen again. He could stumble off into the countryside and find Winnie's village – her family lived somewhere in Kent, he wished he had asked her more questions about it. Once there, wherever it was, he could hunker down in Dulcie's abandoned stable and wait it out, whatever *it* happened to be. Or he could go home.

The pub was filled with smoke and noise. He couldn't help noticing that nearly every fellow except himself was wearing uniform. Most of them were sailors. They all looked like full-grown men who shaved every day.

> *I'm Burlington Bertie, I rise at ten-thirty*
> *And saunter along like a toff.*

It was Boyce's favourite song.

> *I walk down the Strand with my gloves on my hand*
> *Then I walk down again with them off.*

The keys rose and fell, played by ghostly fingers. When he was little Ralph had found the pianola a terrifying instrument. He thought it was played by a dead person.

> *The Prince of Wales' brother along with some other*
> *Slaps me on the back and says 'Come and see Mother.'*

Maybe Boyce wasn't dead! Maybe he had been there on the platform, lying on a stretcher and raising his arm to catch Ralph's attention!

'Feeling lonely, love?'

Ralph swung round. A young woman had seated herself next to him.

'Not really,' he said.

'You look like you could do with some company.'

She wasn't much older than him. There was nothing youthful about her face, however.

'You going to buy a girl a drink then?'

Oh heavens, how much would it cost?

'What would you like?' he asked.

'I wouldn't say no to a glass of sherry.' She flashed a smile at him, shifting restlessly in her seat, her eyes flickering around the room. He had to admit that she was quite pretty. She had brown curls and a felt hat covered with badges.

Ralph made his way to the bar. As he waited to be served he sensed the girl's impatience across the room. It reminded him of the lodgers, smelling meat frying in the kitchen. At last the bar-lady noticed him and poured him a glass of sherry. It cost ninepence. He carried it carefully, so it didn't spill, and sat down beside her again.

'What's your name then?' she asked.

'Ralph.' He didn't tell her his surname. Some instinct stopped him.

'I'm Jenny,' she said, 'Jenny Wren.' She giggled. Was it supposed to be some kind of joke? She raised her glass. 'Bottoms up.'

She wore a bright green dress and feather boa. Ralph had a grave suspicion that she was a prostitute. He wasn't stupid. Several of them plied their trade around the pubs in his own neighbourhood. Though alarmed, he also felt a stirring of excitement. What would his mother think of him now?

'You signed up yet, love?' she asked.

Ralph shook his head. 'I'm going there tomorrow,' he lied.

'Good boy.' Not only was her hat covered in badges;

189

more regimental badges and buttons were sewn on the bodice of her dress. When she moved, they winked in the gaslight. Ralph couldn't help noticing, with disappointment, that her chest was as flat as the first picture in the bust enlargement advertisement.

'Army or navy?' she asked, draining her glass. Goodness, was he going to have to buy her another one?

'I'll go where I'm most needed.'

'That's a brave lad,' she said. She put her hand on his knee. The intention was unmistakable. 'Want to spend a little time with me, dear? I have a special arrangement for those what're going to fight.'

Ralph got to his feet. 'Actually, I think I'll get an early night. Big day tomorrow. But thank you very much.'

She shrugged. Thank goodness she wasn't offended. In fact, her eyes were already darting around the room. 'If you change your mind, you know where to find me,' she said, getting to her feet. 'Just ask for Jenny.' She blew him a kiss and, flicking back her boa, made her way across the room, towards a group of soldiers.

Ralph escaped into the street. Darkness had fallen; the wet cobblestones gleamed in the lamplight. It was a quarter to nine. He still had enough money for the fare home, if the last train hadn't already gone.

*

Ralph's carriage was crammed with soldiers, in boisterous spirits. The air was thick with cigarette smoke and alcohol fumes. He sat beside the window, his bag on his knee. One of the soldiers gave him a liquorice bootlace but otherwise they took no notice of him, for which he was grateful. Some of their uniforms were muddy. Ralph had heard about the lice; the question was, could they hop from body to body? He kept himself pressed against the window. The men sang lustily.

> 'Three German officers crossed the line,
> Parlez-vous,
> Three German officers crossed the line,
> Parlez-vous,
> Three German officers crossed the line, fucked the
>   women and drank the wine,
> Inky-pinky parlez vous!'

The rude word gave Ralph a jolt. There were no ladies in the carriage to hear it, and the soldiers obviously thought Ralph man enough to take it in his stride. He knew what it meant, of course. Indeed, that evening he had come perilously close to the prospect itself. He had been propositioned by a female who, despite her childish years, must have performed the thing in question many times – maybe *hundreds* of times.

Ralph nibbled a digestive biscuit. He wasn't hungry, however. He felt feverish; his head felt swimmy. Perhaps he'd caught a cold, from getting soaked in the rain. Perhaps he had caught the influenza! Alwyne said people were falling like skittles. He said it didn't only attack the weakest; it attacked strong young boys too. They got a fever and a pain in their legs and just collapsed. In a few hours they were dead.

That would solve all my problems, though Ralph gloomily. Instead of being angry with him, his mother would be heartbroken. It would be just as tragic as dying in battle. In fact he could picture the deathbed scene, in all its pitiful detail, more easily than his death in action. There were so many different ways to die in a war, that was the problem, and he hadn't chosen which one it would be. But all that was theoretical now.

The songs were becoming ruder. Ralph, blushing, rummaged in his bag and took out *Fletcher's Guide to British Birds*. He opened it and found the page for 'Wren'. Jenny Wren wasn't the prostitute's real name, of course. She would have given herself a false one to put her parents off the scent, in case they came looking for her.

He read: '*Wren (Troglodytes troglodytes). This perky, round little bird is easy to recognise, especially by the upright tilt of its tail. It feeds mainly on insects and spiders. Wrens have many calls, from the "tic tic tic" of alarm to the thin wheezing food-cry of the juveniles just out of the nest. The female sits on five to seven eggs . . .*'

The words swam. They seemed to have nothing in common with the girl at all. Ralph closed his eyes and rested his head against the window.

*

Ralph was struggling through a bramble thicket. The thorns tore at his clothes, they scraped his face, but he couldn't feel a thing. All he knew was that he had to escape.

He pushed through the tangle and opened his eyes. A light blazed. He seemed to be sitting in a carriage filled with bodies.

With a sinking sense of doom, Ralph returned to reality. How peaceful the soldiers looked! They weren't dead at all. They lay slumped against each other amongst their mountains of equipment, snoring and dribbling, their legs, with their muddy puttees and great muddy boots, stretched out in front of them.

Ralph gazed at them with envy. How lucky they were, not to have to face his mother! No battle could be a more terrifying prospect. Ralph's throat was dry. It was only now that the magnitude of what he had done sank in. He had failed in every possible sense – as a soldier, a student, a son.

Ralph tried not to think of Mr Turk's reaction. Then there was Alwyne; he would probably find it all a big joke, which was almost the worst thing of all. What was he going to do? Crawl home and slink into a corner, like the dog did when he'd stolen the sausages?

The train was slowing down. Ralph pulled up the blind. This was forbidden by law; at night, trains had to be blacked out. But there was nobody to see. Perhaps the train had passed his station and was already on its way to Charing Cross.

All Ralph could see was his own reflection in the glass. He opened the window and leaned out.

His cap blew off. He scarcely noticed this: something else caught his attention.

The train was trundling along the viaduct, at a walking pace. Ralph recognised the spire of St Jude's church, near his home. Far below he could see the loading yards. They served the storage vaults built into the arches beneath the railway, which were used by the local traders.

One of the yards was busy with activity. A motor lorry was backed up. Torchlight flashed; a man held up a lamp. In its light, Ralph could see men unloading carcasses from the lorry and carrying them into the vault.

It was then that he spotted Mr Turk. The butcher stood

in the headlights of the vehicle, looking up and down the lane. Beneath the boater his face was in shadow, but it was definitely him. There was nobody about, except for a police constable. He stood nearby, under the gas lamp.

The train trundled on. At the time, Ralph was simply puzzled. What was Mr Turk doing, unloading meat at this hour of the night? It was not just this that seemed odd. There was something strange about the whole business. And why was the policeman there?

A few moments later the train stopped at London Bridge Station. Ralph forgot about the scene. He had more pressing things on his mind.

*

'Where have you *been*?' His mother pulled him into the parlour. The lights were blazing.

'We were celebrating after our exams,' said Ralph.

'I've been worried sick!' His mother pointed to his bag. 'What's this?'

'Some things I'd left at the college. I was bringing them home.'

'Why didn't you telephone us?'

'Telephone?'

'Yes, telephone!'

'I've never used it. Anyway I don't know the number.'

Brutus padded in. He seemed more pleased to see Ralph than his mother.

'Are you drunk? Where's your cap? Goodness, you gave us a fright. Neville's out looking for you.'

No he's not, thought Ralph.

'My own love.' At last his mother hugged him. 'I'm so glad you're back. I thought you were *dead*.'

'I think I'm getting the influenza,' said Ralph. 'I want to go to bed.'

*

The influenza, however, didn't come to Ralph's rescue and release him from life's mortal coil. When he woke the next morning the symptoms had vanished. Perhaps it was due to the linseed tea his mother had made him drink, the night before.

He lay in bed, gazing at the room to which he had thought he would never return. A train rattled by. It was half-past nine; the household was up and about. His mother hadn't woken him for breakfast, either out of consideration for his illness or as a punishment.

Ralph had no idea. He no longer knew her any more. But then, he felt a stranger to himself. His room was a place he had left behind, long ago. Its collections of birds' eggs and cigarette cards belonged to a boy who had vanished years before the disastrous trip to Dover. Ralph realised this now. That boy had gone, the boy whose proud face was reflected in Boyce's patent-leather pumps as he buffed them to a shine; who shared a bottle of lemonade with his father as they sat together on Box Hill.

Ralph climbed out of bed and got dressed. What was he going to do now? He had burned his boats, there was no question about that. If only yesterday had been a hallucination. If only the last few *months* had been a hallucination and he was back with his mother, looking after her, sitting on her eiderdown as she pinned up her hair.

Downstairs the telephone rang.

'Fetch me the sago, there's a dear,' said Winnie.

Ralph was helping her in the kitchen. It was half-past twelve; Mr Turk would be home shortly for his dinner. Ralph had not seen him the night before and dreaded the prospect now. Life was so much simpler, below stairs. All Winnie had to do was to put a plate of food in front of the man and scarper off back to the kitchen. Her day was without complications – no guilt, no warring loyalties. Of course it was sad that she didn't have a sweetheart, and indeed had few prospects of finding one, but the sex urge brought nothing but trouble.

'I think I'll become a butler,' said Ralph.

'Don't be daft,' said Winnie. 'You'll be getting a proper job soon, in an office.'

No I won't, he thought.

'You'll be bringing home a wage and at six o'clock you'll be as free as a bird.' Winnie paused, her hands in the mixing bowl, a dreamy look on her face. 'At nobody's beck and call, won't that be nice? Anyway, Mr Flyte says that when the war's over there won't be any big houses left, so bang go the butlers.'

'You talk to him a lot, don't you?'

Winnie poured the sago into the bowl. 'He's taught me a lot,' she muttered. 'He's ever so clever.'

'I know what he's *against* – people working in offices, and people being servants, and things like that. But what's he *for*? People sitting around on their bottoms talking all the time, like he does?'

'That's not fair!' she snapped. 'He's got nothing else to do, the poor thing.'

Ralph didn't reply. There was something annoying

about Winnie's voice when she spoke about Alwyne Flyte, as if she and the fellow were in cahoots. Didn't she realise the man was only sucking up to her out of class solidarity, or whatever silly term he used?

'Go on,' he goaded her. 'What *does* he believe in?'

'In people like me having a vote.'

'So who would you vote for, then?'

Wide-eyed, Winnie looked at him. '*I* don't know, do I?'

Ralph raised his eyebrows. Neither of them laughed, however. They would have laughed, in the past.

Winnie paused, and gazed at him across the table. A flypaper hung down from the lampshade. It was stuck with black corpses.

'What's the matter, dear?' asked Winnie.

'Nothing.'

'Mr Turk won't be angry with you, I promise. Your mama will have calmed him down. After all, it was only a bit of fun. He probably would've done the same thing himself, if he'd just finished an exam.'

Ralph got to his feet. He couldn't bear to look Winnie in the eye. Betraying her felt the worst thing of all. 'He'll be here soon,' he said. 'I'll take up the plates.'

'Don't worry, love,' said Winnie. 'Your mum's ever so proud of you. She's bought you a present.' Winnie clapped her hand over her mouth. 'Oh, it's a surprise!'

'What do you mean, a present?'

'She wasn't looking at curtains yesterday. That was a fib, to put you off the scent.' She smiled at him conspiratorially. 'My lips are sealed.'

Ralph carried the tray upstairs. He felt sick in his stomach. How could his mother have done such a thing?

Ralph saw a pair of bedroom slippers descending the

stairs. Mr Spooner appeared, accompanied by Lettie. The front door opened and Mrs O'Malley returned, carrying her dinner in a paper bag. She pressed against the wall as Mr Spooner shuffled past, his head bowed. Lettie took her father's hand and led him out of the house.

Ralph felt a wave of loneliness. His home was filled with people yet he was utterly alone with his shame. *Come back in a couple of years, sonny*. Plenty of boys had passed muster at sixteen. The barber's son had joined up; so had another boy from Ralph's class at school. They had lied about their age, no doubt, but in their cases the recruiting sergeant had believed them. They had enlisted and fought – in fact the barber's son, Derek, had promptly been killed. But they had looked man enough to convince.

Ralph started laying the table. As he did so, he heard the sound of the front door. His mother and Mr Turk walked into the parlour.

Something was up. Their faces were grim. His mother's eyes were pink, as if she'd been crying.

'Sit down, sonny,' said Mr Turk. 'You and me got to have a talk.'

Ralph sat down.

'Your mother got a telephone call this morning,' said Mr Turk. 'From the college.'

There was a silence. The dog sniffed Mr Turk's trousers but he kicked him away. 'Eff off!'

'Don't do that,' said Ralph.

His mother sat down heavily and pulled off her hat. 'They said you didn't turn up for your exam.'

The two of them waited for Ralph to speak.

'No,' said Ralph.

'She came straight down to the shop and told me,' said Mr Turk.

Ralph swung round to his mother. 'Why didn't you talk to *me*? Why did you go and see him first?'

'What's got into you, Ralph?' Her eyes glittered with tears. 'Why didn't you do your exam? Know how much that college cost?'

'Look at your mother!' said Mr Turk. 'Look what you've done to her. You ought to be ashamed of yourself.'

'It's none of your business,' said Ralph.

'Ralph!' snapped his mother. 'Don't you dare talk to him like that!'

'But it isn't,' said Ralph.

'Show him some respect.'

'Why?'

'It's all right, love,' said Mr Turk. 'He's just a kid –'

'I'm not a kid! –'

'He's just a spoilt little brat, and if he was my son he'd feel the back of my hand.'

'Go ahead,' said Ralph.

'Stop it!' cried his mother.

'Hit me. I don't care.'

'Ralph!'

'And I'm not your son,' Ralph said. 'I'm nothing to do with you, I didn't want you to come here, none of us did.'

'That's not true!' cried his mother.

Mr Turk turned to her. 'That right?'

'No! They all like you, they're ever so grateful to you.'

'Ah.' Mr Turk turned his red face to Ralph. 'Seems you're outnumbered, little chap.'

'Apologise to Neville,' said his mother. 'Go on, Ralph, say you're sorry.'

Ralph's heart was pounding. He looked at his mother. 'You never even asked me. You said you were going to get married. You never even asked if I minded. You didn't think of anybody else because you were so . . . so . . .'

'So what?'

Ralph couldn't say the word. He looked at Mr Turk's congested face. He looked at his big red hands, sprouting black hair. At his arm that had jerked in and out.

'It's horrible,' he muttered, and pushed back his chair.

Ralph ran upstairs to his bedroom and slammed the door.

He heard his mother following, and the scrabbling feet of the dog. She flung open the door and stood there, trembling.

'What's horrible?' she demanded.

Ralph sat on his bed, looking at the floor.

'Speak to me,' she said. 'I can't help you if you don't speak to me.' She sat down beside him, and regained her breath. When she spoke, her voice was gentle. 'Ralph, my love . . . I was fond of your father but nothing's going to bring him back.' She paused. 'And, to be perfectly truthful, things weren't all that well between us. Not in the last few years.'

'You were happy. We were all happy.'

She sighed. 'You wouldn't understand.'

'What was wrong then?'

She knotted her fingers together. 'Grown-up things. Things between a man and a woman. Oh he was sweet, and gentle, and kind . . . but that doesn't make a marriage. In the fullest sense.'

Ralph's ears roared.

'Perhaps I shouldn't tell you this,' she said, 'but I thought you were old enough to know.'

'*He* loved *us*. He went to war for us. He got *killed* for us!' Ralph started sobbing. 'You didn't even wait till he got to the end of the street.'

'What do you mean?'

'You went down to the kitchen,' he blurted out. 'You didn't even wait till he'd gone round the corner. He might have turned to wave!' Ralph wiped his nose. 'You couldn't even be bothered to wait that long!' Nor, of course, had he. '*Brutus* showed him more love!'

'Brutus?'

'He mated with his leg.'

Her mother laughed, shakily. 'Call that love?'

Ralph glared at her. '*You* seem to think so.'

His mother slapped his face, hard. 'That's disgusting!'

They stared at each other, aghast.

Then his mother jumped up and rushed from the room.

*

The clock chimed three. It was followed by the deeper chime of the grandfather clock downstairs. There had been no sound in the house for some time, not since the muffled bumps against the wall as Mr Spooner was helped up to his room. Ralph had heard Winnie's encouraging murmurs. Winnie was so kind, so full of love. Ralph wondered if his mother had told her about his missed exam, or whether the shame was too deep to be shared with a servant. Sooner or later, however, Winnie would find out. They all would. Even Mrs O'Malley, vague as she was, would join in the chorus of condemnation.

Ralph was seized with recklessness. Blast the lot of them! He didn't give a damn any more. He was a boat, oarless and rudderless, drifting away from a shore that was becoming fainter by the minute. If people shouted at him he no longer heard them. What was the point of it all anyway?

He's just a kid, said Mr Turk. *Just a spoiled little brat*. He was, was he?

Suddenly, Ralph knew what he was going to do. The only question was a financial one. *I have a special arrangement for those what're going to fight*. How much would Jenny Wren charge? He hadn't the faintest idea. He only had two shillings left, not even enough for the train fare.

Just a kid, eh?

Ralph got off the bed. He went to the wash-basin, turned on the tap and spashed water on his face. His eyes were swollen from crying. The boils were as red as ever but when a woman was being paid she was in no position to complain.

His mother and Mr Turk had gone out. Ralph's room was at the back of the house but he knew by the silence that they had left. Perhaps they had gone to his college, to discuss his so-called future.

The coast was clear. Ralph opened the door and stepped into their room. The bed was unmade, the sheets rumpled. It reeked of their activities. *To live in the rank sweat of an enseamed bed*. Intimate items of his mother's lay strewn on the floor.

Ralph averted his eyes. He opened the wardrobe. Mr Turk's clothes hung on the right-hand side. The man always carried wads of money around, not only in his bulging pocket-book but inside his jacket pockets. Ralph looked at the garments hanging in front of him – the frock coats, the evening coats the man wore for his City dinners, the various jackets in their loud and vulgar colours: tweed jackets, chequered jackets, the caramel-coloured one, edged with braid, that he had been wearing the day when he first came to the house. The thought of touching Mr Turk's clothes made Ralph feel queasy. Besides, he had never stolen money before. His parents would be appalled.

Ralph plucked up courage and slid his hand into an inside pocket. But he didn't have parents now. His father was dead and his mother wasn't his mother any more, she was a strange woman smelling of Attar of Roses who slapped his face. And God couldn't see him because God didn't exist. They had all come to this conclusion in Palmerston Road, one way or another. Alwyne had said to him once: *What I like about this house is that absolutely nobody goes to church, except Ada O'Malley, and she's lost her marbles. Now what conclusion can we draw from this, young Ralphy my boy?*

Ralph rummaged in the pockets. Somebody was rewarding him because he soon found some loose change and, finally, in the fourth pocket, a banknote.

It was a five-pound note. With trembling fingers Ralph counted out the coins and coppers. The sum total added up to five pounds, six shillings and tenpence-halfpenny. Ralph stuffed the money in his pocket.

It was then that he saw the typewriter.

It was sitting on the floor of the wardrobe, amongst the shoes. *Remington* was embossed on it, in gold lettering. On top of the typewriter sat a bowler hat; on the hat rim sat a detachable collar and studs. A pink satin ribbon tied them all together.

A card was stuck behind the ribbon.

Ralph leaned down and took it out. It was printed with a nosegay of flowers. HEARTY BIRTHDAY GREETINGS was inscribed in blue lettering, and accompanied by a poem:

> *This Birthday may there be no dearth*
> *To you of Happiness, Luck and Mirth.*

Ralph turned it over. On the other side his mother had written:

> *It's not your birthday yet I know,*
> *But proud of you I am,*
> *Today you might be still sixteen*
> *But for me you are a man.*

For a while Ralph couldn't move. He sat there, gazing at his mother's writing. Finally, he got to his feet. He tucked the card back under the ribbon, closed the wardrobe and left the room.

*

Winnie and Lettie were sitting together on the kitchen stairs. Winnie was pinning up the little girl's hair. As Ralph came down to the hallway they looked up, their faces pale as moons in the dim light.

Winnie removed a pin from her mouth. 'Doesn't she look the lady?' she said.

Ralph nodded. Lettie did indeed look like somebody

else, an unknown young woman, peaky-faced under her burden of hair.

'Where're you off to then?' asked Winnie. Her manner was quite natural. Ralph surmised that she hadn't heard about the exam. She knew about the typewriter, though. He felt weak with misery.

'Just out,' he said.

'Don't you want any dinner? I kept you some.'

Ralph shook his head. 'Can you tell Mother I won't be back until late?'

Winnie raised her eyebrows. Ralph made his escape, tripping over the cat in the hallway.

Outside, he didn't turn right. He needed to make a detour on the way to the station; it had been plaguing his mind all day. Turning left, he hurried down the street, through the dark, echoing tunnel of the railway bridge and out the other side.

He knew where the arches were – two streets away. He made his way down Silver Street, past the garment factory with its buzzing sewing machines, past the rank-smelling warehouse where they stored the seal-skins. He turned right at the Mitre. According to Winnie, the landlord's six children had all died from the consumption. She knew information like that.

How could his mother have bought that typewriter? And a *bowler hat*? His heart ached.

The street led him back under the railway and out into the lane the other side. It ran alongside the arches. Ralph walked along the lane, looking at the doors. Some of them were open. Inside one arch, a man was unloading vegetables on to a handcart. In another, two men were repairing a motor car. The arch in question was three from the end; Ralph could remember it clearly.

He arrived. The gate to the yard was padlocked. Beyond it he could see the door, set into the archway. It was closed and padlocked. There was a moribund look to the place, as if nobody had gone in and out for years. It was hard to believe that only the night before it had been humming with activity. But this was the place. Beside it stood the lamppost where the copper had watched it all happening. And on the cobbles, beside the gate, a patch of dung had been flattened by tyre tracks.

Ralph peered across the yard, to read the words painted on the door. They said W. PEPPIATT AND SONS. BUILDERS MERCHANTS. Nothing about a butcher at all.

*

It was twilight when Ralph reached the Three Tuns. He heard the pianola playing. Mist was rolling in from the English Channel, beyond the buildings. He could smell the sea. Gulls swooped and quarrelled, landing heavily in front of him and fighting over a scrap lying in the street.

He had spent the train journey in a state of suspended animation. It seemed extraordinary to him that only a day had passed since he had last been to Dover. So much had happened that he felt a changed person. And tonight would see the biggest change of all. He would arrive a boy and leave a man. This was his plan and he was going to see it through. There was no turning back.

He pushed open the door and went in. The scene that greeted him looked exactly the same as the evening before. Wreathed in cigarette smoke, soldiers and sailors leaned against the bar and barely registered him as he paused on the threshold. The pianola's keys went up and down.

> *Good bye-ee, good bye-ee*
> *There's a silver lining in the sky-ee . . .*

He looked around. For a moment he couldn't see her. What would he do if she didn't turn up? Maybe she had been murdered by a disgruntled customer. It would be just his luck. There was no denying that it must be an extremely dangerous job. Not all her clients would be as well brought up as himself.

> *Wash the tear, baby dear, from your eye-ee . . .*

Ralph went to the bar and ordered a glass of beer. It was then that he saw Jenny, on the other side of the room. She was standing alone by the parrot's cage, pushing a twig of millet through the bars. She jerked it up and down, trying to get the bird's attention, but her eyes were darting around the room. She wore the same outfit – green dress, feather boa – as the night before. Did she never change her clothes?

Ralph waved but she didn't see him. She stood there restlessly, shifting from foot to foot as if she needed to go to the lavatory. The strange thing was that, though tormented by desire on an almost continual basis, now he was here, with the prospect of it being satisfied, Ralph felt as numb as if he were shopping for a pound of potatoes. In fact, part of him wished she hadn't turned up at all. He took a breath and walked over to her.

'Hello,' he said. 'It's me again.'

She smiled a brief, professional smile but her eyes were blank. She didn't recognise him!

Ralph said: 'Last night, remember?'

Jenny tilted her head and looked at him. 'That's right.' She didn't seem embarrassed that she had forgotten him. Ralph noticed a small sore on her upper lip. Still, he had no intention of kissing her.

'Like to buy a girl a drink then?' she asked.

Ralph fetched her a sherry. He could feel the eyes of people on him, but that might have been all in his head. When he carried back her glass nobody seemed to be taking the slightest notice. Perhaps they thought he was her long-lost brother.

'So what regiment did you join?' she asked.

'The Kents.'

'The Kents what?'

He thought quickly. 'The West Kent Rifles.'

He had made up the name but that seemed to satisfy her. Maybe she knew as little as he did.

'So you got your King's Shilling,' she said. 'What's your name again, love?'

'Ralph.'

'Bottoms up, Ralph.'

She downed half the schooner. He couldn't think of what to say to her but he knew they ought to have some kind of conversation.

Pointing to the badges on her hat, he asked: 'Where do they come from?'

'Everybody asks me that.' She took off her hat. 'Royal Scots Fusiliers . . . London Rifle Brigade . . . 16th Lancers . . .' She pointed to the badges, one by one. 'Royal Artillery . . . Ox and Bucks . . . Tank Corps . . .' Her voice went on and on. Ralph was taken aback. She started on the badges pinned to her flat chest. 'Hood Battalion, Royal Naval Division . . . Monmouthshire Regiment . . . Duke of Cornwall's Light Infantry . . .' She spoke the names like a child reciting her times table. Ralph was impressed. She knew more about the war than he did.

'These were all your friends?' he asked, stupidly.

Jenny nodded. 'Oh yes. They've all been my friends.' She drained her glass.

'Do they talk to you about it all?'

'Talk about what, dear?'

'About the war and everything.'

She looked at him blankly. 'They give me their badges. I got more badges than any of my girl-friends. Buttons too.' She pointed to her chest. 'This one's from a dead German soldier. A very nice young man gave me that.'

Ralph decided to get down to business. He didn't want to buy her another drink. 'Will you charge me your special rate?'

'That depends on what you want, love.'

'Anything, really. I mean, just the usual.'

'Two pounds.'

Ralph gulped. Was that the normal rate, or did she know that he was inexperienced in these matters? Two pounds! It was Winnie's wages for a whole month. He knew that because Winnie had told him. This girl was going to earn that in an hour, or however long it took. It didn't seem fair.

'Okey-dokey,' said Ralph. That was what Boyce would have said, *okey-dokey*. He wished Boyce were with him, to give him courage. *Women are cheap in Rio de Janeiro*. Boyce knew what was what.

She got up. 'Come with me then. It's not far.' Thank goodness they left by the side door, so Ralph didn't have to cross the room with her.

Night had fallen. Jenny took his arm. As they walked down the street Ralph thought: if Mr Turk could see me now! The wind had got up. It blew her feather boa into his face, tickling his nostrils.

'Here we are then,' she said. They had stopped at a tall, dark building squalling with babies. She led him in. 'Follow me,' she said. 'Watch the stairs.'

At each floor he thought she would stop but she carried on, the stairs creaking. It was very dark. Behind every door a new baby started to wail as if they were catching it from each other, like the flu. On the top landing Jenny opened a door.

It was a tiny room, lit by an oil lamp. A brass bed stood against the wall; beneath it a chamber-pot glimmered. There was nothing to distinguish the place from a normal person's room, apart from the smell. It was stuffy up there under the eaves, and a sweet-sour odour hung in the air. It reminded Ralph of his sheets.

'Wash your little soldier, there's a good boy,' said Jenny, indicating a screen.

Behind it stood a wash-stand. Ralph looked at the bowl of water. Had some other man washed in it, before him? And surely it should be *she* who cleaned herself up. After all, it was his body that was pure.

Resentfully, Ralph unfastened his trousers and took out what she called his little soldier. It looked humiliatingly small and soft. He splashed it with water and dried it on a small piece of towel that looked grey in the dim light and that was no doubt crawling with

210

germs. Didn't the girl realise what a privilege it was, to unburden him of his virginity? That this was a turning-point in his life? She was acting as if *he* should feel obliged to *her*.

Ralph emerged from behind the screen. Jenny was sitting on the bed pulling off her stockings. She had also relieved herself of her outer garments and was dressed only in a bodice and petticoat.

'Come and sit down, dear.' She patted the bed. 'You're very young, aren't you?'

I'm probably the same age as you, thought Ralph, but then he had his doubts. Despite her youth, there was something old about her flat voice and hard, unseeing eyes. Her thinness was startling; the knobs of her collarbone stuck out and her arms were like sticks. He tried to summon up some desire. He tried the usual methods – the photograph of the naked woman beating the carpet usually did the trick but tonight nothing stirred.

'Going to take off your trousers then?'

Ralph untied his boots and pulled them off. He pulled off his trousers and underwear. Boyce would know what to do. *Make 'em laugh*, he said, but Ralph couldn't think of any jokes. Besides, he didn't have to do anything like that; after all, the girl was getting paid for it.

They sat for a moment looking at the soft little thing between his legs. 'We'll soon see about that,' she said. She took it in her hand. Her fingernails were bitten down to the quick; they looked sore.

She started rubbing it, looking around the room as if deciding whether the walls needed repainting, which they certainly did. Ralph started to feel a faint sensation.

He was so flooded with relief that he could have kissed her, though he didn't, of course. He wasn't going to make a complete fool of himself.

'That's better,' she said. 'Let's lie down, shall we?'

She was certainly brisk, but then he supposed that time was of the essence. They lay down on her counterpane. He tried not to think of how many men had lain on it before him. Jenny hoisted up her petticoat and put his hand between her legs.

Ralph jumped. The hair felt like the wire pad Winnie used to scour the saucepans. Though his own hair was wiry, he had imagined a female's to be more ladylike. He pushed his hand up beneath the waistband of her petticoat and found her navel. He put his finger in it and started rubbing.

Her body went rigid. 'What're you doing?'

'Finding your love-button.'

'My what?'

'Your love-button.' His finger had indeed found a knobbly bit within it.

She started shaking with laughter. 'Who told you that?'

'Just somebody.' It was Boyce, of course. *Mark my words, it drives a lady to distraction.*

'Your friend knows bugger all about girls,' she said.

'That's a lie!'

'Shouldn't think he's got within ten yards of one. Love-button!' She was helpless with laughter. And Ralph hadn't even told her a joke! 'There is one, dear, but it's somewhere else. Tell your friend that when you see him.'

Suddenly Ralph burst into tears. He couldn't help himself, they just poured out.

Jenny sat up and looked at him.

'You all right?'

Ralph couldn't speak. He sat there shuddering, the stupid tears streaming down his face. He couldn't bear it, about Boycie. He couldn't *bear* it.

'There there,' she said, patting his arm.

Boyce had been pretending, all the time. It was too awful. And now he was dead.

'You're frightened, aren't you?' she said.

Ralph didn't reply. He wiped his nose on the back of his sleeve.

'They all are,' she said. 'Don't worry, you're not the only one.' She gave him a handkerchief. 'They come here so they can forget about it for a bit. A lot of them are like you. They haven't done it before and they want to see what it's like before they go.'

'How can you tell?' he muttered.

'Tell what?'

'That I haven't done it before?'

'It's a bit bleeding obvious, isn't it?'

Ralph blew his nose on the handkerchief. Everything was ruined. *Everything.*

'Come along,' she said. 'You haven't paid to have a cry, have you?'

She laid him down on the bed, more gently this time, and started stroking him. A moment later he felt himself stiffen. There was expertise in her bitten little fingers, he had to admit it.

'There you are,' she murmured. 'Standing to attention, ready for action.'

She heaved him on top as if he were a rag doll. Opening her legs, she put him inside her.

Ralph gasped. Jenny moved her body under his. She put her hands on his hips and showed him how to move with her, and for a few thrusts Ralph was filled with such rapture he thought he would explode. And then the stars were bursting like fireworks and a great white light flooded him, as if he had gone to heaven, and it was over.

Ralph lay there, trembling. 'Don't start crying on me all over again,' she said, but kindly. She stroked his hair.

For a moment neither of them moved. Even the babies downstairs seemed to have stopped wailing. Then Jenny sat up and reached for her clothes.

Ralph roused himself and pulled on his trousers. He found the money and gave her two pound notes. She put them in a box on the little bamboo table next to her bed. He felt such tenderness for her that he wanted to give her something else, something special. Nobody would ever know what she had done for him, and of course he would never see her again.

'Thank you so much,' he said.

She kissed him on the cheek. 'Good luck,' she said. 'We're all proud of you.'

He blushed with pleasure. So he had performed to her satisfaction!

Then he realised what she meant.

'Have a little think of me when you're there,' she said.

Ralph muttered something and made his escape.

*

The train rattled back towards London. Ralph sat there in a stupor of pride. He had done it! He had crossed the threshold; his childhood was now behind him. It was amazing that the other passengers couldn't sense the momentous event that had taken place. Despite the perfunctory nature of the proceedings there had even been a moment of closeness between himself and the bony little prostitute who, in another life, could have been his classmate at school. Better still, he sensed that this was but a foretaste of the deeper raptures to come, in his future dealings with the opposite sex. Now, at least, he knew what it was like, and at sixteen years of age too!

A young infantryman sat dozing in the carriage. Ralph wondered whether, despite the manly uniform, the fellow was still inexperienced in the act of love. His cheeks were as smooth as a baby's; he had certainly never shaved. And yet there he slumped, cradling his rifle, his belt laden with ammunition!

For a while, Ralph could think of nothing else. This seemed to be one of the powers of coitus; like dynamite, it blasted everything else away.

Slowly, however, his worries crept back, like creatures emerging from shattered buildings. What was he going to do about the future? This episode had solved nothing; he might be a changed person but his problems remained the same. In fact, his life seemed even more confusing than ever. So Boyce had been lying about his female conquests. His dearest friend had died *virgo intacta*. This was too painful to contemplate. And what had his mother meant, when she had talked about her marriage to his father? *Things weren't all that well between us . . . grown-up things*. Now Ralph had entered that arena he could suspect what she meant. *Marriage in the fullest sense*. Was his father inadequate in that department? Less adequate, in fact, than Ralph had proved himself to be?

Ralph's brain reeled. He couldn't think about this, it

made him feel ill. Who was betraying whom, in these matters? But whenever he shut them out another image scrabbled at his mind, like a rat scratching behind the wainscoting. It was his mother and Mr Turk, fumbling together in a manner that horribly resembled what he himself had been doing on a soiled coverlet that evening.

Stop it! Stop thinking about it! Ralph tried to concentrate on something else. His growling stomach, for instance. He had eaten nothing but a bun and a packet of digestive biscuits since Monday. It was now Tuesday night. How strange, that only yesterday morning he had packed his bag and set off for the war! Things hadn't turned out quite as he had planned, though a conquest of sorts had taken place.

The two pounds still rankled, however. It might not have been his own money but he still suspected that he had been overcharged. The girl had taken advantage of his innocence. If that was her special rate for departing soldiers, what even more extortionate sum did she charge a normal person? The comparison with Winnie's wages struck him as scandalous. Being a prostitute didn't seem hard work. There was Winnie on her knees all day, scrubbing and polishing, her hands raw. What made it worse was the fact that even should Winnie wish to become a lady of pleasure, it would be highly unlikely that she could find any customers. Nature was indeed cruel.

Ralph was musing over this as the train slowed down. It was eleven o'clock; they must be nearing London Bridge. Idly he wondered whether Mr Turk would be back again under the arch. He hadn't asked him about it, of course. The circumstances the day before had hardly been propitious. Besides, his stepfather frightened him; Ralph was now man enough to admit it. Mr Turk had been a champion boxer in his youth, and had the trophies to prove it. No doubt, if asked an impertinent question, he could still fell a chap with a blow.

After all, there could be a perfectly innocent explanation. Mr Turk could simply need extra storage space. Ralph had no idea how his business worked.

Apart from the sleeping soldier, the carriage was now empty. Ralph pulled up the blind, opened the window and leaned out.

The train was puffing along the viaduct, at walking pace. Everything was exactly as it had been the night before. The smoke cleared; Ralph saw the spire of St Jude's. For a moment he felt dizzy, as if he were caught in a repeating dream. Maybe he had indeed dreamed up the whole thing. For down below there was nothing but darkness. He could see the yard, dimly illuminated by the street lamp. It was empty.

Ralph remained leaning out of the window. The breeze was refreshing. He even liked the acrid smell of the smoke; after all, he had lived with it for as long as he could remember.

He watched his street jolt into view – the black mass of the buildings with their scattering of lit windows. He saw somebody moving around in a room. It was funny how they presumed nobody could see them; he felt this himself, when he was at home.

The train neared his house. He craned out of the window, to look. It drew nearer. The top window – Boyce's – was dark, of course. So was his own. The window in between, however – Alwyne's – blazed with electric light.

Alwyne, the blind man, sat at his table. He was reading a book.

Chapter Eight

'When it's too dark to go on fighting – are you free for the evening, can you get to a cinema?'

Question asked to Lt Bernard Martin,
North Staffordshires, when home on leave

Eithne woke late. It was half-past nine by the time she was dressed. The night before, Neville had taken her to *Chu-Chin-Chow* at His Majesty's, with a spot of supper afterwards. He had done this to cheer her up. They had discussed Ralph, of course, and Neville had come up with a plan. Again her husband had demonstrated his remarkable generosity of spirit. He had proposed that Ralph work for him in the shop on a menial basis. *He can do the deliveries – the boy can ride a bicycle, can't he? Sweep the floor, make himself useful. I'm short-staffed at present and I'm willing to do the lad a favour.*

That he was willing to forgive Ralph for his behaviour, both towards himself and in the matter of his exam, was so overwhelming that Eithne had thrown her arms around her husband and kissed him in front of the other diners. He was a paragon, a prince among men.

Ralph had been in bed by the time they returned, at midnight. She had seen the light under his door. He had been out somewhere – Winnie had said so – but Eithne had no idea where he had gone. She was still smarting from the incident in his bedroom. It was terrible to slap him – Eithne had never done such a thing in her life – but she had been goaded beyond endurance. Now she had simmered down she was filled with remorse. They would hug and make it up. They were everything to each other and would love each other until they died. Their present difficulties would soon be smoothed out. She would take him to the Terminus Hotel, where they had always gone for treats. They would sit in the lounge and order peach melbas in tall glasses. She would tell him Neville's plan, that Ralph would work for him in the shop until January, when he would return to the college and re-take his exams. She had already talked to Mrs Brand about it. Maybe this was even a blessing in disguise. By working alongside Neville her son would get to know him better and see what a fine man he was. Besides, Ralph was bound to be grateful for this opportunity of a second chance.

Eithne tapped at Ralph's door. No answer. She opened it. The room was empty.

Downstairs Winnie had served up breakfast, bless her. The lodgers had come and gone – all but Alwyne, who sat amongst the dirty plates, smoking a cigarette.

'Good morning,' Eithne said. 'Have you seen Ralph?'

She blushed. She was always saying this to Alwyne: *have you seen*? The lodger, however, seemed as unperturbed as usual.

He shook his head. 'I heard him go out with the dog.'

*

Ralph sat beside the river. He had had to get out of the

house. It had been bad enough the night before, hearing Alwyne moving about in the room above. Realising that Alwyne wasn't blind had made every creak sinister, as if Ralph had discovered that the man had committed a murder. The prospect of actually seeing Alwyne in the morning was too much to bear.

The shock was still sinking in. Ralph had gone over and over the image in his mind. Alwyne had been reading a book. Ralph hadn't imagined it. The man had even turned the page as the train trundled past. Why in heaven's name had Alwyne been lying to him – lying to all of them – for the past year?

Ralph remembered the countless times he had taken Alwyne's arm, to guide him down the street. How he had moved Alwyne's fork to his plate. How they had *all* performed the hundreds of small, helpful actions that were second nature to them when Alwyne was in the room. It had been part of the fabric of their lives, of the life of the house – the subtle anticipations, the small accommodations they had made as a matter of instinct, the spoken explanations of things they had presumed Alwyne couldn't see.

Why had Alwyne betrayed them? Why on earth had he done it? Had the mustard gas fuddled his brain? But the man didn't seem confused. On the contrary, his mind seemed as sharp as a razor.

Tell me what you're seeing, Ralphy my boy. Describe it to me. Incidents kept swimming up – the moment, two days ago, when Ralph had forgotten to give Alwyne the gramophone record and had felt so guilty afterwards. The man must have got up, when he had left, and found it himself! Oh, it was horrible.

Brutus nosed along the shoreline, where boys were collecting driftwood for kindling. Ralph himself had done this countless times during the winter, when fuel was short. Even this activity, though nothing to do with Alwyne, seemed tainted in retrospect. The man's betrayal was seeping like poison into every crack of Ralph's life.

Sitting on the wall, Ralph gazed at the dog. Despite his distress he noticed how portly Brutus had grown over the past two months, fattened by the meat that he now consumed on a daily basis. Brutus was a middle-aged mongrel with bowed legs but Ralph loved him dearly. Today he, too, seemed a victim of Alwyne's treachery. Had his animal instincts suspected something was amiss? He treated Alwyne with the same treacle-eyed devotion he treated everybody else. For him there was no distinction between the sighted and the blind, between the innocent and the criminal. Ralph could tell him the truth but Brutus would just wag his tail; he thought the best of everybody.

Ralph heard the clock of St Jude's strike twelve. Even this sonorous chime, the punctuation of his growing years, was no reassurance. It was a heavy, sultry day. He had missed yet another meal and though he wasn't hungry he got to his feet, walked down to the Albion and bought a bag of shrimps from the stall outside the lavatories. He still had two pounds, six shillings and threepence left of Mr Turk's money.

The wind had died down. A hush seemed to have fallen over the river, over the whole city. It was as if the beating heart of the Empire had fallen silent in astonishment. Even the gulls were noiseless as they wheeled above him.

Just then Ralph heard a sound. It was the *tap-tap* of an approaching stick. He swung round. Alwyne appeared around the corner, making his way to the pub.

Ralph stood, rooted to the spot. Alwyne wore his usual rusty black coat; his clothes made no concession to the season. Now Ralph knew the truth, every step the man made looked false, as if he were acting. His spectacles glinted as he turned his head.

Ralph's heart thumped. He stood only twenty yards away from the fellow. Had Alwyne seen him? If he had, of course he couldn't show it. The lunacy of this would have made Ralph laugh if he weren't so frightened. Alwyne paused on the threshold of the pub. He cocked his head, listening. *Watching.*

A barge sounded its horn. Perhaps Alwyne was just admiring the view. But the view had Ralph standing in the middle of it. If Alwyne saw him, he made no reaction.

The dog barked. Alwyne swung round. Brutus ran up to him and nuzzled his hand.

'Hello old boy,' said Alwyne. 'Where's that master of yours?' He looked around. 'Ralph? You there?'

Ralph turned on his heel and fled. He ran up Back Lane, the dog following him. He ran fast, escaping the enemy. As he dodged the children he thought: Alwyne was my friend. I told him things. I told him all sorts of things. He was my *friend*.

A horse had gone down in Mercer Street. It had pulled its cart over; potatoes lay scattered on the ground. It lay there, its legs jerking, its belly exposed to public view. A man was trying to untangle its harness but the horse kicked out.

Ralph pounded up the road towards his house. What

sort of things had he done when Alwyne was in the room? Picked his nose, certainly, and wiped his finger on his trousers. Inspected his pimples in the mirror while Alwyne was lecturing him about Bolshevism. What else? A chap reverted to the animal when he presumed he wasn't being watched. It was too awful to think about.

When Ralph arrived home he didn't go in the front door. He couldn't face his mother, not yet. He ran down the steps into the kitchen.

Winnie was standing by the table, holding a fish by its tail.

'Mrs O'Malley's given me a bloater,' she said. 'Her friend brought it from Whitstable. She wants me to cook it for her dinner but I'm just about to dish up for your mother and Mr Turk. I'm late as it is.' She looked at him. 'What's up with you, love?'

Ralph sat down at the table. A dish of faggots sat steaming on the oilcloth.

He said: 'Alwyne's not blind.'

There was a silence. Winnie put the bloater on the table carefully, as if it would break. 'What was that you said?'

'Alwyne's not blind. He's been pretending. I saw him read a book.' Watching her face, Ralph felt the rush of gratification a person feels when imparting an important piece of news. 'He can see us. He can see everything. He's been pretending, all this time.'

*

For once, Ralph was glad to eat with his mother and Mr Turk. There was safety in numbers. The thought of coming face to face with Alwyne, alone, was too unnerving to contemplate. He didn't tell them the news.

Mr Turk was a powerful man; he might do something violent. Besides, it gave Ralph a pleasant feeling of superiority, to know something they didn't. He felt oddly tender towards the two of them as they sat there in their innocence. In fact, the faggots in gravy smelt so delicious that he almost broke his embargo and joined them in taking one. He resisted the temptation, however; he had his principles.

Winnie served them as if she were sleepwalking. She knocked over Mr Turk's glass of water and barely reacted when he sprang back. Her long slab of a face was ashen. She, too, was in a state of shock. Ralph tried to catch her eye, in complicity, but she was miles away.

As they ate, Mr Turk told Ralph his plan for him to work in the shop. Ralph nodded, dumbly. He couldn't think of anything he would hate more, but no doubt they had planned this as some sort of punishment – a punishment he deserved even more than they imagined, now he had added to his sins by stealing Mr Turk's money. In truth, he scarcely registered what they were saying; he had too many other things on his mind. His mother smiled at him in the bright, glassy way he had come to distrust.

'Neville's very kind, to take you on, and I'm sure you'll do him credit. You'll have to get up early, to help Winnie with the chores, but hard work never hurt anyone.'

Maybe you should do some then, Ralph thought. Suddenly, keenly, he missed the dark days when he, Winnie and his mother toiled together; hungry and cold, but united in their labour.

As Winnie collected the plates, they heard the sound of the front door. Alwyne had returned.

Ralph froze. Winnie, too, stood stock still. As the man made his way past the open doorway, Ralph's mother called: 'Alwyne? Can I ask you a favour?'

Alwyne turned. 'And what might that be?'

'Could I bother you for a cigarette? I'm trying to smoke as much as I can but Mr Turk has left his at the shop.'

'Delighted to oblige,' said Alwyne.

Stick tucked under his arm, he made his way into the room. With his free hand, he felt for the back of a chair. Ralph watched him closely. The fellow was utterly convincing. He'd had enough practice, of course. Besides, a lot of the time, when he kept his eyes closed, he *was* blind. And when he wore his spectacles nobody could tell what his eyes were doing; the lenses were too black. Ralph could swear Alwyne was watching him.

'Sit down and join us,' said Ralph's mother. 'We've finished anyway.'

She moved the chair, to make it easier for Alwyne to sit. He fumbled in his pocket and produced a packet of Players.

'Guess how many people have died of the flu this week,' said Ralph's mother. 'Five hundred, in London alone! I heard it at the greengrocer's.' She turned. 'Winnie, fetch the ashtray.'

Winnie made a small noise. Putting down the dishes, she ran from the room. They heard her footsteps thudding down the stairs. In the cabinet, the glasses shivered.

There was a silence.

'What's got into her?' said Mr Turk.

'She's upset,' said Ralph.

'Why?'

Ralph thought, quickly. 'Her friend Elsie.'

'Who's Elsie?' asked his mother.

'She works at the Woolwich Arsenal,' said Alwyne, passing her the packet of cigarettes. 'She's dying of lyddite poisoning.'

'Maybe she should smoke cigarettes too,' said Ralph's mother. 'It seems to be the cure for everything.'

Alwyne smiled. 'I don't believe that would be wise, in an explosives factory.'

Ralph's mother lost interest in the subject. The mention of dying, however, made Ralph summon up his courage. After all, only two days earlier he had left home to face possible death himself.

It was now or never; he couldn't carry on like this. He had to tackle Alwyne. He would lie in wait for the man and ambush him when he came upstairs.

Ralph made his excuses and left the parlour. He went up to his bedroom. Leaving the door open, he sat down on his bed and waited, like a spider in his web.

It wasn't long before he heard his mother and Mr Turk leave the house. Alwyne's footsteps climbed the stairs.

Ralph's heart thumped. The footsteps drew nearer. Alwyne appeared in the doorway, on the way to his room.

'Alwyne!' hissed Ralph.

The man paused.

Ralph cleared his throat. 'Can you come in a minute?'

'I was just going to have my snooze.'

'You can have it later.'

Alwyne raised his eyebrows. Ralph's tone startled them both.

'Sit down,' said Ralph.

'Pardon?'

'Sit down.' Ralph pointed. 'There's the chair. You can see it, can't you?'

Alwyne stood there, motionless. A moment passed. 'What did you say?'

Ralph got up and closed the door. He turned to face Alwyne. 'You're not blind, are you?'

There was a pause. Alwyne sat down on the chair. He took off his spectacles. For the first time they looked into each other's eyes. It gave Ralph a jolt.

'How did you find out?' asked Alwyne.

'I was on the train. I saw you reading a book.'

Alwyne considered this for a moment. 'Silly me. I should have drawn the curtains.'

Ralph sat down on the bed. His bowels churned, but he had to go through with this. 'Why did you do it?' he demanded.

Alwyne shrugged. It was strange to speak to the man directly, thought Ralph: it was as if shutters had been opened and he was gazing into a room for the first time. 'Why did you do it?'

'Why do you think?'

'*Why?*' demanded Ralph.

'Because I didn't want to join up, of course.'

Alwyne pulled out his packet of cigarettes and offered one to Ralph. He shook his head. Alwyne lit one. Ralph saw with gratification that the man's hand was trembling.

It was taking a while for Alwyne's words to sink in. So he hadn't enlisted at all.

'You weren't gassed?' asked Ralph, finally.

'No.'

'You didn't fight?'

'No. Why should I?'

Ralph stared at him. 'Because everyone else does.'

'They're idiots. This is a fool's war, run for fools by fools.'

'That's no excuse.'

'I can't think of a better one.'

Despite the trembling, Alwyne remained calm. Almost superior, in fact, as if Ralph were asking questions to which the answers were obvious. Ralph felt his grip slipping. There were too many shocks; he needed a moment to catch up with himself.

Alwyne shrugged. 'When they introduced conscription I decided to get out. So I came to London, where nobody knew me, and passed myself off as blind. With remarkable success, as it happens. It's not easy, you know. In fact, the whole thing has been the most enormous strain.'

'What about us?'

'What about you?'

'How could you do this to us? Lying to us all this time?' Ralph heard his voice rise, squeakily. 'We've been ever so kind to you.'

'And I'm ever so grateful, young man.' He blew out a cloud of smoke. 'In fact, it seems to have brought out the best in everybody. I've encountered nothing but kindness, in all directions. It's been quite an eye-opener, if you'll pardon the expression. In some ways I've rather enjoyed the experience.'

'*Enjoyed* it?'

'What harm have I done?'

'You've lied to people. You've avoided fighting.'

Alwyne's eyes twinkled. 'I'm not the only one to have done that, dear boy. Look no further than these four walls.'

'You could have become a conchy.'

'And have some nasty little female shove a feather in my face? A lady who, I dare say, has faced no graver emergency than a ladder in her stocking?' His ash dropped on to the carpet. 'Besides, I've had my work to do.'

'What work?'

'I'm writing a history of the twentieth century.'

Ralph looked at him in surprise. 'But it's hardly started.'

'That's no obstacle for a man of vision.' Alwyne chuckled. 'Blind men are known for their sixth sense.'

'But you're not blind.'

'No. I can see particularly clearly. Which is more than can be said for our so-called leaders.'

Despite himself, Ralph was curious. 'So what's going to happen, then?'

'Ah. You'll have to read my book.'

'How far have you got?'

Alwyne didn't reply.

'How far?'

'Page fifteen.'

'Is that all?'

Alwyne tapped his head. 'It's all in here.'

'You're very slow, considering you've got nothing else to do.'

'Don't be impertinent!' Alwyne snapped.

'Go on then. Tell me.'

Alwyne sighed. 'You wouldn't understand.'

'I'm not a baby!' said Ralph. 'I'm nearly seventeen.'

'Exactly.'

Ralph had a strong desire to tell Alwyne about Jenny Wren but he bit it back. He was supposed to be attacking the man, not confiding in him. Outside, a train rattled past.

'All right then.' Alwyne tossed his cigarette into the fireplace. 'I'll put it in the simplest terms. This war is going to leave Europe in chaos. Reason, beauty and obedience will be obliterated. The ruling classes will be overturned by a series of bloody revolutions, economies will collapse, and what started out as a takeover by the people will succumb to the siren call of the dictator.'

Ralph gazed at him. 'How did you do that thing with your eyes? Did it make them ache?'

'You mean this?' Alwyne's eyeballs flickered, his pupils rolled upwards. 'Bloody agony. That's why I wear spectacles.' He added, with pride, 'I painted them black myself.'

Eyes, Ralph knew, were the windows to the soul. Now Alwyne had opened the shutters, Ralph had to admit that the man looked more twinkling and humorous. More *human*. Ralph, however, refused to succumb to the fellow's charm. He said: 'It's horrible, what you did.'

'Have you told anybody?' asked Alywne.

'Only Winnie.'

Alwyne paused. 'Ah,' he said. 'That's a shame.'

'She's ever so upset.'

'Yes.'

Ralph said: 'I expect she feels the same as me.'

Alwyne didn't reply.

They sat there in silence. Through the wall, the clock chimed three.

Somebody sneezed. Ralph and Alwyne jumped. The sound came from under the bed.

'Who's there?' said Ralph.

There was a pause, then a scuffling sound.

Lettie emerged.

They stared at her. 'What are you doing here?' asked Ralph.

'Looking at your magazines,' she said.

'My magazines?'

'I like the ladies,' said Lettie. 'I like their dresses.' She stood up and dusted down her pinafore.

'Do you do this often?' asked Ralph.

Lettie nodded. 'When you're out.'

Alwyne was gazing at her: 'Have you heard what we've been talking about?'

Lettie nodded. 'I knew anyway.'

'You knew?' said Alwyne.

Lettie looked at him without curiosity. 'Of course. Anyone could tell.'

Flossie had come into the room. Lettie bent down and stroked her.

'Have you told anybody?' asked Alwyne.

Lettie shook her head, her matted pigtails swinging.

'Let's keep it to ourselves, shall we?' he said. 'Mum's the word.'

Lettie nodded, without interest. Alwyne's faked blindness was no odder than everything else in her life. She left; her footsteps pattering up the stairs.

They sat there for a moment. Downstairs the grandfather clock struck three. It was slowing down. Ralph should have wound it two days ago. He always wound it on the Monday, it was one of his jobs.

Everything seemed to be sliding out of control.

Alwyne turned to him. 'The same goes for you, old chap.'

'What?'

'Don't tell anybody, there's a good boy.'

'Why shouldn't I?'

'Why? Because they'll put me in prison. Or send me to the Front.'

'Why shouldn't you go? Why are you so special?'

'We're all special. That's what's so terrible, don't you see?' He shifted, impatiently. 'You have no idea, have you?'

My father was special, thought Ralph. He was special to me. 'Why should there be one law for you and another for everybody else?' he asked.

'Because I've got more brains.'

'You're just a coward.'

Alwyne glared at him. 'Do you really want to know what happens there?'

'How do you know? You haven't been.'

'I know, my friend. Trust me.' He leaned forward in his chair. 'There's young men dying in their thousands, men who had lives to look forward to, and dreams, and unborn babies who'll never be born now; and know how they're dying? With their guts spilling out in the mud and their faces blasted away –'

'Stop it!'

'You really wish that on me?'

'It's not like that! It's noble and brave –'

'Don't be a fool –'

'My father said they played football –'

'Your father lied! And you call *me* a liar?' Alwyne's

233

voice rose. 'It's blood and guts and men drowning in the mud, coughing up their lungs. It's men drowning in excrement, in *shit*, and crying for their mothers with what remains of their mouths –'

'*Stop it!*'

'It's men with their arms blown off taking three days to die in a shell hole filled with the flesh of their friends –'

Ralph leapt up and rushed out of the room.

He pounded down the stairs, two at a time. He needed Winnie. She was the only person who could comfort him now. Winnie was so strong, so solid. He could press his face against her apron and let the tears fall.

Ralph stumbled down the stairs, into the kitchen. It was empty. The bloater lay on the table.

'Winnie?'

Silence.

Ralph hurried along the passage and tapped at Winnie's door. There was no answer.

He opened it. She wasn't there.

Ralph looked around. The crucifix was gone from the wall. Her small, cardboard suitcase had disappeared from the top of the wardrobe.

He opened the door of the wardrobe. It was empty.

Chapter Nine

To The Editor,
Sir, as I was going over the top last week I distinctly heard the call of the cuckoo. I claim to be the first to have heard it this spring, and should like to know if any of your readers can assert that they heard it before me,
I am, sir, yours faithfully, A 'Lover of Nature'.

To The Editor,
Sir, if you will kindly supply me with the name and address of your correspondent signing himself 'A Lover of Nature' I will guarantee that he will not love Nature any more; neither will he hear any more cuckoos. No, sir! Not this spring nor next or any other spring neither. Cuckoo indeed! I'll learn 'im,
Yours faithfully, 'Fed Up'.

The Wipers Times, Ypres, 1917

At first Eithne was upset by Winnie's disappearance. Then she grew angry. After all she had done for the girl. And leaving like that, without a word. It was hurtful, too, after all the years they had worked together, side by side. But then you never really knew, with servants. They lived with you, as close as family, but you could never really tell what went on in their minds. Stories of their cheating ways were two a penny. Eithne had trusted the girl with her life. Neville told her to check the valuables but, to her relief, she found nothing missing. But why hadn't Winnie given in her notice, if she was unhappy? Or, indeed, collected the half-month's wages she was owed? Eithne considered calling the police but the problem was she knew nothing about the girl, not even her surname. Winnie's home village was somewhere in Kent but Eithne knew no more than this. Nor did Ralph, who had been on intimate terms with the maid since he was eleven years old.

And then, three days later, a letter arrived. *I am very sorry to give you trouble,* it said. *I had some bad news and I had to go away. Please forgive me. You have been very good to me and I think of you in my prayers. Please give my best wishes to Ralph for his future happiness. The darning is on the box by the copper. Winifred.*

It was a relief, of course, to know that the girl was unharmed. But what could be the bad news? It must be about her brother, the one who had gone to France.

'That's not the reason,' said Ralph, putting down the letter. 'She's written that to save your feelings.'

'What do you mean?' asked Eithne.

Ralph looked at her. His face reddened. 'I don't think she's been very happy.'

'Why?'

'Ever since . . . things changed here. I don't think she liked it much.'

Eithne's heart sank. 'But Neville's been so kind. I mean, he said her standards left something to be desired but he was right. It was a credit to him that he didn't sack her.'

'She didn't like him.'

'That's not true!'

Ralph's blush deepened. Eithne, eyes narrowed, looked at him. She knew him through and through; he was her *son*. 'You're just saying that to upset me.'

'No, I'm not.'

'I'm sure there's another reason. You know something, I know you do.'

Ralph turned away and switched on the vacuum cleaner. Its roar drowned out any possibility of conversation.

Eithne started clearing the breakfast dishes. Tempers were frayed that morning. Both she and Ralph were exhausted, and the day had hardly begun. First they had discovered that the range had gone out. The supply of kindling had been used up and nobody had thought to replenish it. The butter was finished because nobody had bought any more, and the margarine was scattered with mice droppings because it had been left out. The laundry basket was overflowing with dirty washing. And that was just the start of it. The whole house was gathering soot: it was breeding in the rooms, on the stairs, it was slowly but surely taking the place over. *Winnie, where are you?* wailed Eithne. Only now was she realising just how much work Winnie had done, unseen and unacknowledged; how much she, Eithne, had taken the girl for granted.

And what messy eaters the lodgers were! She should excuse Alwyne, of course. He could hardly help scattering crumbs and ash on the floorcloth, but everything he touched he left sticky with jam – his cup handle, even his chair. The man might be blind, but couldn't he manage to wipe his fingers?

The noise of the vacuum cleaner ceased. Eithne heard Ralph swearing – a rude word too. She had no idea that he even knew it. Hurrying into the hall, she saw him staring at something on the hearthrug. Then the smell hit her.

'I thought you'd taken out the dog,' he said.

'You said you would.'

A stand-off followed this discovery. Eithne was the first to surrender. She went down to the scullery, to find the mop and bucket.

Neville had engaged another maid. The girl was supposed to have started work the morning before but she hadn't turned up. That was typical of servants these days. There was such a shortage that they could behave all high and mighty; a person had to grovel to persuade one to deign to do any work at all. Even charwomen, the lowest of the low, were getting hoity-toity. They were all making bombs at twelve shillings a week. And now it was Saturday, with no hope of any help until next week, at the earliest. As matters stood, there was little possibility of Ralph starting his new job; not for a while. He was needed in the house.

What made Eithne sad, however, was the loss of their old closeness. Her little helper, her little trooper, had changed overnight into a croaky-voiced stranger with pimples on his chin and expletives coming out of his mouth. The reason for this could not entirely be laid at Neville's door. It hadn't been easy for the boy but that was no excuse for the shameful way he had let them all down.

Eithne thought of the typewriter she had bought him, with such pride. A Remington typewriter, two guineas it had cost, the man said it would last a lifetime. It sat there in her wardrobe; she didn't know what to do with it. She couldn't bear to touch it. Or the bowler hat.

Standing at the tap, Eithne remembered the hopes she had had for her dearest boy. Her darling. She slumped against the sink and wept.

*

Ralph sat in Alwyne's room, drinking a bottle of beer. It was late. This was the first time Ralph had sat down all day.

'I'm dog tired,' he said. 'It doesn't seem fair, you sitting about all day getting flabby while I do the work.'

'Well done, boy!' said Alwyne. 'Comrade Lenin would be proud of you.'

'I didn't mind, when I thought you were blind.'

'There's no justice in this world, and the sooner you learn that the better.'

Alwyne was right. There was no justice in a world where his father got killed and Mr Turk stayed alive. Alive and rich.

'I suppose your name isn't Alwyne either.'

Alwyne shook his head. 'I think it's rather distinguished, don't you?'

Ralph thought: We're harbouring a criminal in the house. A flabby revolutionary with no papers, living under an assumed name. He felt a *frisson* of power.

'I could tell the police,' he said. 'I could tell my mother.'

'But you're not going to do that, are you?'

'Why not?'

'Because then you'd have it on your conscience.'

'You're the one who's breaking the law.'

'The law's an ass,' said Alwyne. 'Besides, what good

would my dying in a shell hole do you?' He drained his bottle. 'One less life in the world wouldn't make a jot of difference to the scheme of things, whatever that scheme might be. Its meaning escapes me these days. It would, however, make more than a jot of difference to me.'

'You just think about yourself.'

'And who else is there for me to think about?'

'Some people aren't like that,' said Ralph. 'Winnie wasn't. She thought about other people all the time.' He missed her painfully.

'Poor Winnie,' Alwyne said. 'I'm sorry about her.'

'You're the reason she left, you know.'

'What do you mean?' Alwyne leaned forward in his chair. 'What did she tell you?'

'It must have given her such a shock, that she'd been looking after you and all the time you were pretending.'

'Ah.' Alwyne slumped back. 'Yes, it probably did.'

Ralph drained his bottle. 'After all, she did more for you than anyone else did.'

Alwyne didn't reply. He picked up a bottle. 'Want another?'

Ralph nodded. Alwyne cracked off its cap with the bottle-opener.

Ralph said: 'I told my mother it was because she hated Mr Turk.'

'Wise boy.' Alwyne passed him the bottle. 'A spot of transference there, I believe.'

'What's transference?'

'You're the one who hates him.'

'But you don't like him either, do you?'

Alwyne nodded. 'He's a tinpot little tyrant.'

'I want to kill him,' Ralph blurted out.

'What good would that do? Look what happened to Hamlet.'

'He's changed my mother. She's not the same person any more.'

Alwyne tapped out a cigarette. 'There's one word for that, dear boy, and you don't want to hear it.'

Ralph's mother and Mr Turk had long since gone to bed. Ralph could almost feel them through the floorboards. He put the bottle to his mouth and drank. His head swam.

Ralph wiped his lips. 'I've got a deal,' he said. 'If you kill him, I won't tell anyone that you can see.'

Alwyne paused, the match half-way to his cigarette. 'What did you say?'

Ralph took one of Alwyne's cigarettes, lit it, and inhaled. For a moment he thought he was going to faint. 'You could kill him,' he said. 'Nobody would suspect you.'

Alwyne shrugged his shoulders. 'I think you've gathered by now that I'm not a man of violence.'

'Boyce would have done it. My father would have done it. They weren't cowards.'

'They were fools.'

'They weren't!'

'Poor, misguided fools.'

How could Alwyne say that? Ralph felt the tears well up. Alwyne mustn't see! It had been so much easier when he was blind.

'Killing gets nobody anywhere,' said Alwyne. 'We're seeing that nowadays, are we not? On an epic scale.' He sucked on his cigarette, holding it with his stained fingers. 'What did your father's death do for you? Well, blow me down. It gave you Neville Turk!'

241

Ralph felt his bravado drain away. Alwyne was treating him like a baby. And now he had said it aloud, his plan did indeed sound footling. He hated Alwyne with a fury.

'Steal all his money then,' said Ralph.

'And how shall I do that?'

'He's up to something, I know he is. I saw him on Monday, hiding a lot of meat. Whole carcasses. He hid them under the viaduct.'

Alwyne nodded. He didn't seem surprised. 'Our friend the butcher's making a killing. You should see his investments.'

Ralph stared at him. 'What investments?'

'Munitions, armaments, shipbuilding. Share prices have gone through the roof. Oh yes, our butcher's a canny little chappie.' He chuckled. 'Unlike his meat, there's no flies on Mr Turk.' He dropped his stub into his empty bottle. 'And that's just the legal side.'

Ralph gazed at Alwyne. Behind him, damp had soaked through the wallpaper and hardened into a sort of treacle. 'And what's the other?' he asked.

'Let's just say he's on very close terms with the Meat Allocation Officer. Godfather to his daughter, that sort of thing.'

'What's he doing with him?'

'I think the polite word for it would be profiteering.'

Ralph gaped. 'You mean he's committing a crime?'

Alwyne nodded. 'He'd be looking at six years, at least. More, I suspect, once they saw the sums involved.'

'How do you know the sums?'

'I've seen them.'

'How?' Ralph asked.

242

'I'm blind, aren't I?'

Ralph gazed at him, puzzled. Alwyne gave him a small smile. 'Amazing what a chap will leave on a table, when he's opening his post and needs to pop to the lavatory. And there's just a sightless *mutile de guerre* in the room, listening to Paganini.'

*

Eithne swallowed her pride and made enquiries amongst the neighbours. She was on nodding terms with some of them, but knew few by name. By and large, they were a common lot. The house next door, for instance, was in an even worse state of repair than her own and occupied by a number of villainous-looking families whose children ran wild and who were visited on a regular basis by the police. Mrs Baines, however, three doors down, was a respectable woman and recommended a girl called Daphne. Apparently, Daphne had been in service for some years with a family in Tooley Street who had recently moved away, and she was now looking for a position.

Daphne, it transpired, was a middle-aged woman of forbidding appearance. Her demeanour implied that it was she who was doing the favour. Eithne refused to be intimidated but in fact surrendered to the woman's demands for five pounds a month and two days off a week. The creature, sensing Eithne's desperation, was taking advantage of the situation and Eithne was powerless to resist. *Oh Winnie*, she wailed, *come back to me!*

After their interview, Eithne showed the woman her living quarters. She found herself apologising for the state of Winnie's room. She hadn't inspected it for some time. It looked decidedly shabby, with its stained walls and smell of mould. Seeing things from an outsider's eyes was always something of a shock.

'It could do with a lick of paint, couldn't it?' she said brightly. 'My husband has plans for the whole house, in fact. Putting in the electricity was just a start. He wants to run the plumbing into the front bedrooms, which will save you a lot of trouble. No more jugs of water, no more slops!' She smiled encouragingly, but there was no response. 'He's going to smarten up the place. Oh yes, he has a lot of ideas up his sleeve.'

She still didn't know the nature of these plans, but Neville would no doubt tell her in due course. *You're sitting on a gold mine*, he had said, that first day in the kitchen. A sudden thought struck Eithne: did he marry her just to get his hands on the house?

This wasn't true, of course. Their passion wasn't based on bricks and mortar. If Neville had wanted a woman of property he could have found one with more substantial assets. Eithne had been in society with him often enough to notice the galvanising effect he had upon members of the opposite sex, most of them wealthier than Eithne's wildest dreams. He had hinted, too, about such conquests in the past.

Besides, he had enough money himself. The source of this remained a mystery to her, but she suspected some wise investments. Her husband had a canny head on his shoulders.

What a contrast he made to her dear, departed Paul! Eithne could hardly remember the beaky-nosed type-setter, with his sloping shoulders and general air of bemusement. It was hard to believe that only two years had passed since his death. Her marriage seemed to have happened to another woman, in another life. She remembered him with fondness but sometimes, if truth be told, a week could pass without her thinking about him at all.

*

Daphne was to start work in the morning. She emerged on the dot of seven, dressed smartly in black, with white apron and cap. For some reason this filled Eithne with misgiving. She helped her with the breakfasts, and then prepared to leave the house.

'The vacuum cleaner's a blessing,' she told Daphne. 'It'll cut the work by half.'

Hurrying out of the door, she made her escape.

*

Ralph was walking back with the shopping. He took his time. His reluctance was caused by the presence of that alien woman in the house. They had only exchanged a few words but already he had taken a dislike to the new maid. She smelt of mothballs; tall and gaunt, she felt like an invader in his home. He longed for Winnie. What was happening to her? Would he ever see her again?

It was a drizzly day. He took the long way back, past the pickle factory in Mercer Street. The cobblestones were greasy; another horse had fallen. It lay across the street, blocking the traffic, its head resting on the pavement. Its eyes were glazed; only its nostrils, opening and closing, flaring crimson, betrayed its distress.

Ralph thought of the tender-hearted Winnie; the way she sat on the stairs, crying, when she talked about the horses being led away. Men were spreading sacks on the road, to help the animal up.

Ralph walked on. Now they had engaged a maid he would have to start work at the butcher's shop. The thought filled him with dread. Didn't they know he was a vegetarian? That his abhorrence of meat extended to an abhorrence of Mr Turk? In fact, was caused by it? It seemed the cruellest of punishments.

Not that his mother minded. She was too blinded by passion to see the pain this inflicted on her son. Ralph realised he was muttering to himself, like the cripples who sold matches in the street. He too had a grievance. Now he had talked to Alwyne, the whole thing had taken on a deeper importance. How could Ralph take orders from a criminal? A man who had not only evaded the war but was profiting from it? Him and his Wolseley!

Ralph turned the corner and saw Lettie, stationed in her usual position outside the pub. She beckoned him over.

Stepping nearer, Ralph noticed her pigtails. They looked as if they had been rubbed in dung. Did nobody care for the girl? He knew he should feel sorry for her. The little girl's life had been a hard one. For some reason, however, he had always felt wary of her; even more so now, since the incident in his bedroom.

'I've been thinking,' Lettie said.

'What about?'

Her sharp little eyes glinted at him. 'You give me sixpence a week, and I promise not to tell.'

The dog nuzzled against her. Lettie, her eyes fixed on Ralph's face, gave Brutus her hand to lick.

'I'll give it to the Crutch Fund,' she said.

'The Crutch Fund?'

'For the limbless men. I danced for them and they liked me.'

She held his gaze. Behind her the door opened. Voices roared and two men staggered out. Lettie moved aside. They stumbled down the street.

Lettie waited. Her peaky face was too adult for her child's body. She reminded him of Jenny Wren, old before her time.

'I bet you won't give it to them,' said Ralph.

Lettie wiped her nose with the back of her hand. She didn't care. There was no way he could argue with that. Ralph knew he was beaten.

*

Alwyne said: 'Some hatched-faced harridan's been banging around in here.'

'She's called Daphne,' said Ralph. 'She's the new maid.'

'Felt like lifting up her skirt with my stick, to see her armour-plated combinations.' Alwyne chuckled. 'No man would breach *those* fortifications and survive.'

Ralph sat down in a chair. Its rush seat had broken. 'I've just seen Lettie,' he said. 'We've got to pay her sixpence a week or she'll tell people you're not blind.'

A moment passed. Alwyne rubbed the back of his hand across his beard. 'Well I never,' he said. 'That girl's got an interesting future ahead of her.'

'I said yes. I think we can trust her. I know the type.'

'You do, do you?'

Ralph nodded. In fact he did trust the child. He was still so close to childhood himself that he remembered its

247

cast-iron bargains. How uncomplicated life had been then!

'We're going to seal it in blood,' Ralph said. 'She's coming to my room this afternoon. We're going to cut ourselves with Mother's nail scissors.'

'And who's going to pay the sixpence?'

'You are, of course,' said Ralph. 'This whole thing's your fault.'

How strange it was, Ralph thought, to be cowed by a little girl and yet boss about a grown man! Truly these were curious times.

Alwyne scratched his hair. Black and greasy, it hung to his shoulders. With no Winnie to cut it, sooner or later it would reach his waist. His beard, too. Time would pass, his hair would grow and he would still be stuck at page fifteen of his *magnum opus*. Lettie would dance around him as he toiled, draping him with cobwebs. Ralph felt queasy; he was living in a fairy story – the hairy man, the cunning elf, the magic sixpence. In a moment he would open his eyes and his father would be smiling down at him. *Wake up, little lad. You'll be late for school.*

Ralph was stuck in his seat. His bottom seemed to be wedged in the hole. Alwyne was shaking his head.

'Things have come to a pretty pass when a man of forty finds himself blackmailed by a ten-year-old.'

'Not just her,' said Ralph.

Alwyne looked at him, his eyebrows raised.

Ralph said: 'I want you to get proof that Mr Turk's a criminal.'

'And why should I do that?'

'You owe it to us.'

'I do, do I?'

'For everything we've done for you,' said Ralph. 'That *I've* done for you. For all the times I've fetched you things. The way I've been nice to you even though you weren't nice back. For the way you've cheated.'

'Goodness me.' Alwyne felt for his cigarettes. 'And how do you propose I do this?'

'Find out things. Look at things. You can do it because people think you can't. You can pay me back for pretending to be blind.' Ralph's voice rose. 'It's better than killing him. We can send him to prison! Everybody will see what a bad man he is. We can destroy him.'

Ralph sat there, wedged in his chair. A moment passed.

Alwyne shook his head. 'I can't do that.'

'Why not?'

'They'll find me out and all hell'll break loose.'

'They won't. I'll protect you.'

'What about your mother? She'll be destroyed too. Don't you care about her?'

'She's better off without him.'

'I wonder if *she'd* agree with that,' said Alwyne.

'He'll go to prison and it'll all be like it was before.'

Alwyne gazed at him through the smoke. 'Dear boy, do you really think it's that easy?'

'All right then. I'll tell.'

'Don't do that,' said Alwyne. 'I need to write my book.'

'Your book!'

'I need to stay here, in peace and quiet, and get on with my work. It'll be a great deal more important than telling tales on a common little shopkeeper. I promise you that.'

Alwyne said no more. He sat there, sallow-faced and stubborn, sucking on his cigarette.

249

Ralph extricated himself from his chair. 'Blast you to hell!' he said, and left the room.

How could Alwyne let him down like that? His only ally had revealed himself to be a thoroughgoing coward. Anything for a quiet life. How could the man live with his conscience?

Still, what could be expected from a fellow who lied to save his own skin? Who let others go to war and be butchered on his behalf? In a way Alwyne was as bad as Mr Turk. Worse, in fact, because he had poisoned Ralph's mind with images which burned into it like acid.

Soldiers lay dead in the mud, their guts spilt. Limbs were scattered around. Amongst them stepped a man. It was Mr Turk. He moved from corpse to corpse, bending down and stealing their watches.

He, Ralph, would kill them both – Mr Turk and Alwyne. The world would be well rid of the two of them. So he'd be caught – who cared? He had nothing to live for any more. And at least nobody could call *him* a coward.

In the hallway Ralph came face to face with a figure. It took him a moment to recollect who she was.

It was Daphne, the new maid. She was dressed in her hat and coat.

'Where's your mother?' she snapped.

*

When Eithne came home Daphne was waiting in the parlour. She wore her outdoor clothes. Her suitcase sat on the floor.

'Mrs Turk,' she said, 'I wish to terminate my employment.'

Eithne put down her hatbox. She had been shopping at

Swan and Edgars. 'You can't,' she said. 'It's laundry day tomorrow.'

'I started at the top,' said Daphne. 'I always start at the top, of course, and work down. I found a man there, in bed, in a state of indescribable filth. A child was with him, playing on the floor.'

'That's Mr Spooner. He's not too well.'

'On the floor below I found an old lady who suffers from incontinence.'

'That's only happened recently.' This was true. Eithne had only discovered it in the past week or so, after the departure of Winnie. It was Winnie who had dealt with all that.

'Not just the sheets and the mattress. That would be bad enough. The whole room was permeated. I've never smelt anything like it. Even the armchair.'

Daphne's hard, virgin's face glared at Eithne. She didn't even have the decency to call her *madam*.

'There was no way I could attempt to clean the back room. A sort of tramp seemed to be living there –'

'That's Mr Flyte –'

'– in a room I can only describe as a pigsty. I've never seen anything so disgusting.'

'That's because he's blind.'

'The insolence of the man! I won't repeat what he called me, I'm a respectable woman. Suffice it to say that nothing would induce me to stay here a moment longer. I'm only surprised you didn't see fit to warn me.' She stood up, clutching her collar around her throat as if she might catch germs. 'Good-day.'

*

Neville hadn't gone home for dinner. The new maid needed to find her feet. She was going to have her work cut out, as it was, without cooking a midday meal. He sat in the bar of the Waterloo Hotel, one of the local establishments with which he did business. He was eating a sandwich and reading the newspaper. The day before, a major battle had taken place.

A BRILLIANT SUCCESS read the headline. *ENEMY TAKEN BY SURPRISE. TANKS' GREAT AID. Troubles are multiplying for the Germans. Today, with French co-operation we launched the first offensive on a large scale that we have made this year, recalling the great attacks of the Somme, the Battle of Arras, or that of Flanders. It was admirable in its organization and execution, taking the enemy completely by surprise . . .*

This was the turning-point; Neville felt it in his bones. August the eighth, 1918, would go down in history. The British were heading for victory. With the Yankee muscle behind them, they were finally beating back the Boche. The Germans were mortally weakened; at last the Allies had the strength to push ahead with their advantage. It was just a matter of time.

Neville sensed these things; he had a nose for which way the wind was blowing. *Trust your instincts* was his motto, whether it was the feel of a carcass or the offer of shares in the *Titanic* – an offer which, heeding his inner prompting, he had wisely turned down. His mother had recognised this, bless her soul. She knew that business thrived on anticipation, not reaction. And now was the time to get moving.

At three o'clock, Neville had a meeting arranged with his bank manager. Harold Smyllie and he went back a long way; they had undergone their Initiation together and their relationship was based on the deepest trust. If the end of the war was indeed in sight Neville had some important matters to discuss. A large loan would be needed, but Neville had every confidence that Harold would see his way to oblige him. The fellow knew that matters could be arranged to their mutual advantage, with substantial benefits all round. It just required boldness of vision.

It was Eithne's possible reaction that made him hesitate. She was a stubborn woman, and surprisingly resistant to change. He had noticed this, in the weaker sex. Though Eithne chafed at her present circumstances she dug in her heels at any prospect of progress. It could be damned annoying.

To be fair, it wasn't just the women who had succumbed to the general paralysis. These four years had drained people of vim. He could understand this in the case of those who had lost loved ones – he, too, had shed a tear when his mother died. With nobody to bring home the bacon, families were suffering hardship, there was no question about that. He saw this every day: customers pleading for credit and feeding a family of ten on a sixpenny wrap.The sense of stagnation, however, was all-pervading. It was as if everyone had fallen into a coma for the duration. Perhaps they believed that if the war were lost, what would be the point?

This left a lot of scope for a man like himself, of course. There was no denying that the war had been the making of him, but a man had to capitalise on his assets. When peace came he would have all the cards in his hand. See Eithne's face then!

When Neville arrived home that evening, however, Eithne was in no state for discussion.

'She's gone,' she said. 'She didn't even last the day.' His proud and beautiful wife sat slumped at the kitchen table, her head in her hands. 'Oh, I miss Winnie! How could she leave me?'

Chapter Ten

Every time a horse is unbridled, the bit should be carefully washed and dried, and the leather wiped, to keep them sweet, as well as the girths and saddle, the latter being carefully dried and beaten with a switch before it is again put on. In washing a horse's feet after a day's work, the master should insist upon the legs and feet being washed thoroughly with a sponge until the water flows over them, and then rubbed with a brush until quite dry.

Mrs Beeton's Book of Household Management

Winnie had fled back to Kent. When she arrived at Swaffley, however, she found the village deep in mourning. Lord Elbourne had been killed in action three months earlier, leading his unit into battle at Ypres. The big house was closed up and nearly all the servants gone. His wife and little boys had moved away, and nobody knew if they would ever come back. Most of the villagers were out of a job.

Winnie had moved back into her old bedroom above the stables, a screened-off portion of the bigger room where her brothers used to sleep. Her father had remained living there; he had nowhere else to go. Down in the yard the weeds were already pushing through the cobblestones – fat hen, thistles. A few weeks of neglect, and nature was taking over. The flowerbeds of the great house were choked with nettles. With nobody to tend it, life reverted to chaos. Only servants could keep it at bay. Winnie thought of the dust gathering in the house she had left behind. The *home* she had left behind. That she would still be living in if that thing hadn't happened.

Swaffley was no longer her home; she had lived in fear of her father and had escaped into service at the earliest opportunity. Where else, however, could she go? She was utterly alone in the world. At night she lay in bed, pining for the sound of the trains.

She could still hardly believe what Alwyne had done. It was beyond her poor brain. Why had the man pretended to be blind? As some sort of horrible joke? Again and again she went over the times she had spent with Alwyne. There were some things she couldn't bear to think about. Never, *ever* could she think about them. They made her want to die.

Other events, however, swam to the surface. All those books she had read to him, stumbling over the words when she should have been polishing the cutlery. Alwyne could have read them himself! Why hadn't he told her his secret? She would have kept mum; she was utterly to be trusted. They had a bond together – she'd *thought* they had a bond together. She had even grown fond of him. He had told her he loved her! And all the time he had been taking advantage of her in the cruellest way imaginable.

Could Ralph have been wrong? Yet there *had* been something odd about Alwyne, something furtive. Now she remembered, there had been moments when he had seemed to look at her – to actually look at her – from behind his spectacles. Oh, she wanted to crawl under a stone!

For at times Winnie felt she was going mad – she who was the sane one, who had held her family together after her mother died, and looked after her brothers. Her father noticed nothing. He didn't ask her why she had come home; he had no interest. He drank, and this took up all his time. He sat slumped in his chair, drinking all day, and then he went to the pub and drank all night. His condition had shocked her; she hadn't seen him since Christmas. It was hard to believe she had ever been frightened of him. Once he had been a powerful man but now he seemed to have shrunk. The loss of the hunters had broken his heart and Winnie should have felt sorry for him but she just thought: why don't my brothers come and look after him? Why does it always have to be me?

A new hardness had entered Winnie's soul. Men were all the same; they bullied and tricked you, they humiliated you. And if they weren't doing that they were drinking themselves into a stupor. They deserved the war.

Winnie took refuge in the stables. Her father hadn't set foot in them since the requisitions officer had arrived. The floor was littered with the dust of the horses' droppings. She sat in Dulcie's stall, its basket still stuffed with mouldy hay. She sat there and tried not to blame Alwyne. God was punishing her for her sin. It wasn't Alwyne's fault; it was her own for goading him on. He had simply taken advantage of her need to be wanted and now she had lost her true family, Ralph and his mother, who had meant the world to her. She missed them deeply – the other lodgers too, despite their funny ways. What were they doing now? How were they coping after she had left them in the lurch? Did anybody cook Mrs O'Malley's bloater? Come to think of it, did bloaters *need* to be cooked?

Those hot August days, Winnie moved around in a daze. She couldn't think about the future, not yet. She cleaned her father's rooms and helped him home from the pub; she cooked him meals. The stable yard was silent. Beyond it the house loomed through the trees, its shutters closed. What was going to happen to it? Would it be sold? Only Mrs Maitland, the housekeeper, remained, with her son, and the lame groundsman who had nowhere else to go. Winnie had presumed that the aristocracy led a charmed life, that nothing could touch them. The war, however, proved that they were flesh and blood like everybody else. A shell had no respect for a title. Perhaps Alwyne was right: an era had come to an end. One way or another, this war would destroy the ruling class, and like Lord Elbourne they would be gone for ever. '*We have to seize the moment, Winnie, when the enemy is weak, to sweep the capitalist class system out of existence!*'

Winnie remembered the ash flying as Alwyne waved his arms. In the twilight she sat at the window, watching the darkness thicken. She gazed at the black clots of the yew trees, the black bulk of the unlit house. A barn owl flew out, like the last, departing ghost. When she was a child the estate was filled with people and animals. Now they were all gone – all but her father, racked with coughing, mourning his horses.

Winnie sat there, waiting. Days turned into weeks, and

nothing happened. As the fox barked, she remembered her blushes when Mr Turk cooked steak for dinner and she sat on the best chair, the wetness seeping through. Out in the fields the full moon came and went.

Winnie waited for the blood to appear. The corn was harvested with the help of Bismarck, the one remaining farm horse. She collected her father from the King's Head, holding his arm as they made their way home across the pasture that had been ploughed up for potatoes. 'Don't ever leave me,' he said, in his piteous drunkard's voice. 'You'll always be my little girl.'

She waited, but by September Winnie could pretend to herself no longer. She was expecting a child.

Chapter Eleven

*Up the road we staggered, shells bursting around us. A man
stopped dead in front of me, and exasperated I cursed him and
butted him with my knee. Very gently he said 'I'm blind, sir',
and turned to show me his eyes and nose torn away by a piece
of shell. 'Oh God, I'm sorry sonny' I said. 'Keep going on the
hard part', and left him staggering back in his darkness.*

Lieutenant Edwin Campion Vaughan, 8th Royal Warwicks

'A hotel?' Eithne stared up at her husband. She was
midway through pulling off his boot; it was a nightly ritual
between them.'You want to turn our house into a hotel?'

Neville, sitting on the bed, nodded.

'And next door,' he said.

'Next door? What have you done with next door?'

'Bought it.'

Eithne sat back on her heels. Neville wriggled his boot,
to remind her, but she was too stunned to move.

'When did you do that?' she asked.

'Last week.'

'You bought the freehold?'

Neville nodded. 'They were glad to get shot of it.
Tenants been causing them nothing but trouble.'

'And I suppose that surveyor of yours said it was
riddled with rot.'

Neville grinned. 'Riddled.' He put his foot in front of her face and moved it from side to side like a metronome.

Eithne pulled off his boot. 'Well I never,' she said.

'Best investment we'll ever make, my sweet. This war'll be over by Christmas, you mark my words. Property like that'll be worth a fortune.'

'But what's this about a hotel?'

'Remember that Yankee boy?' said Neville. 'My thinking entirely. The old ways are dead and gone. You won't get the servants any more, not now those girls have got out and about, driving buses and whatnot. Not now they've got a taste for it. They're going to be typists and suchlike. Got the bit between their teeth. Look at those suffragette ladies – catch them mopping up Ada O'Malley's wee-wee.'

Eithne unlaced his other boot. He was right, of course. A month had passed since the Daphne episode. Another maid had been engaged but she had lasted only three days before marching out of the house.

'They want the independence, see,' said Neville. 'There's going to be a lot of women around with no men to marry 'em, so they won't be setting up a home. But they'll be needing a place to stay. A residential hotel – respectable establishment, nice décor, piped hot water to every room, handy for connections to the Continent because these are career ladies, they'll be off in their motor cars, they'll be catching the train, they'll be gadding about all over the place. Gentlemen, too – business types, professionals. No riff-raff.' His voice throbbed with excitement. 'I'm getting an architect to draw up the plans. We'll knock through the wall next door and that'll be twelve bedrooms, we'll fit a modern kitchen and put a dining room on the ground floor, the big margin's in the consumables, three hundred per cent mark-up, there's a lot of profit to be made out of food.'

'You'd know about that,' said Eithne, pulling off his boot.

'Been talking to my customers, hotels and restaurants around here, been getting a few tips. Nothing that I didn't know already, of course, I got the know-how here.' He tapped his nose. 'It's instincts, see? There's a whole new class of customer being born, and I plan to get my foot in the door. We're looking at a return of twenty per cent per year, we're sitting on a bloody gold mine!' His voice softened. 'Come here.'

Eithne was kneeling on the floor. He took her shoulders and pulled her towards him.

'Come here, my love.'

Eithne shifted, reluctantly.

'We'll call it the Continental Hotel,' he said. 'Like it? Gay Paree, a touch of sophistication.'

'You've worked all this out?'

'And that's just the start.'

'The start?'

'You set up a brand, then people know where they are. Guaranteed quality. Look at Lipton's. Sixty grocery shops they got, all over London, and more opening. Look at the Lyons Corner House. Start small and think big!' He moved Eithne up, so her head rested against his chest. 'I'm thinking, in ten years' time there'll be a Continental Hotel in every major town.' She felt his hand fiddling with his trouser buttons. 'So what do you think of your husband now?' he murmured.

His hand grasped her hair. His member sprang up, red

262

and raw. Gently he lowered her head, guiding her down on to him. Her mouth closed over his flesh.

He gasped. 'That's the sort of man you married,' he muttered.

Steadying her between his legs, he moved her head up and down. He gripped her hair so tightly it hurt.

'Oh yes . . .' he muttered. 'Oh dear God.'

As she sucked, Eithne heard a voice within her head. It came from far away, from another era – her son's croaking voice, just broken.

> *'When the war is over and the sword at last we sheathe*
> *I'm going to keep a jelly-fish and listen to it breathe.'*

She squeezed her eyes shut.

*

Eithne wiped her mouth with the flannel. She said: 'You could have told me before. It's my money too.'

'Don't come all sarky with me.' Neville paused in his undressing.'Where's your spirit, woman?'

'When are you thinking to start?' she asked.

'When the plans are drawn up.'

'What about my lodgers?'

'What about them?'

'I can't just throw them out on the street.'

Neville pulled off his vest. 'Ask yourself this, my pumpkin. Would *they* show *you* the same consideration? Eh?'

Eithne didn't reply. She moved away from the wash-stand and stood at the mantelpiece.

'It's dog eat dog in this world,' said Neville. 'Not realised that yet?'

She looked at her husband in the mirror. 'Think that, do you?'

'You owe them bugger all,' he said. 'They're a bunch of blooming parasites. Had it soft for too long.'

The marble mantel was dusted with soot. Eithne touched it with her finger. All this dirt, who was ever going to clean it away?

'Can't get a maid, they scare them off,' said Neville. 'And is it any wonder?'

Eithne wiped her finger on her skirt. Where would they go? Mr Spooner was just starting to improve – very slowly, but he was showing signs of recovery. And how could Alwyne cope, a blind man alone in the world? He appeared to have no family. Neville had no idea what those two men had been through, fighting for their country. Then, nor had she.

Love me, love my lodgers. They were more than just her livelihood.

'Anyway, they don't like me,' said Neville.

'That's not true.'

'Your son said so.'

'He didn't mean it. He's just . . .' She couldn't explain.

'That boy needs to do a good day's work.'

'He helps me here. I couldn't do without him.'

'Needs to get out from under your apron strings. Too bloody mollycoddled, if you want my opinion.'

Her husband sat there, a big man on her bed. The room, with its wallpaper of cabbage roses, seemed to press in around her. Neville had a point, of course – about Ralph, about the lodgers – but she didn't like his tone. He sat there as if he owned the place. He *did* own the place.

Tonight, he looked like a cuckoo in the nest, sitting there with his great hairy thighs planted on her eiderdown. She wanted him to kiss her and tell her how beautiful she was. She wanted him to take her dancing. There was something presumptuous in his manner nowadays. And it still hurt, where he had pulled her hair.

Chapter Twelve

The flowers left thick at nightfall in the wood
This Eastertide call into mind the men,
Now far from home, who, with their sweethearts, should
Have gathered them and will do never again.

Philip Edward Thomas

The German army was in retreat. By mid-October their lines had been broken along a twenty-mile front; the newspapers were optimistic that peace was in sight.

In Palmerston Road, too, an era was ending. Next door, the tenants were evicted. A ragged bunch, they emerged like refugees from their own war of attrition. Though they had caused trouble in the past, Ralph was sorry to see them go, pushing their handcarts along the street and spitting at the enforcement officer. It was the beginning of the end.

'Our turn next,' said Alwyne. The lodgers had been told the news, and given their notice. Mrs Turk, however, was allowing them to stay on until Christmas, out of the goodness of her heart.

For this, no doubt, they were grateful. Nobody spoke about it, though, as if by keeping quiet they hoped it might never happen. As far as Ralph knew, they had made no alternative arrangements. A listless air hung over the house. Fog rolled in from the river; it permeated the rooms and chilled their bones. Ralph and his mother had given up their battle against the soot; it was hard enough work keeping people fed and the fires going, now the nights were drawing in. Besides, in two months the place would be torn apart. What was the point?

Ralph tried to goad Alwyne into action. 'Now's our last chance!' he said. 'If you tell the police they'll put him in prison and you can stay here, everyone can stay here. Don't you understand?'

'Why don't *you* do it, if you're so keen?'

'You know I can't. My mother will never speak to me again.'

'And if *I* do it they'll ask me for proof, and then they'll find out I can see and put *me* into prison. You really want that on your conscience?'

'You should think of the greater good.'

Alwyne smiled. 'Grow up, dear boy.'

Ralph seethed, in a fury of frustration. How the man irritated him – the stink of his cigarettes, the stained clothes, the sloth! The lisp, as if his tongue were too thick for his mouth. His championing of the working class was a charade. Winnie had slaved away and Alwyne had never lifted a finger to help. In fact, his attitude towards his fellow men seemed to be one of thoroughgoing contempt. Being blind, Alwyne admitted quite freely, was an enjoyable experience. People did things for him and saved him the trouble of doing them himself. Worse than that, he seemed to despise them for it. 'Having a secret's most gratifying,' he said. 'A feeling of completely unearned power. You should try it yourself.'

No wonder his wife had left him. Ralph had

discovered this during one of their talks. Back in Bolton, apparently, Alwyne had been a married man, with a wife and children. His wife, however, had finally lost patience with him and walked out; there had been no contact between them for years.

What made it aggravating was Alwyne's openness about it all. The man had no shame; it was like kicking against a brick wall. He even offered perfectly reasonable explanations for his behaviour, as if he were talking about a laboratory specimen.

'Our friend Sigmund would no doubt trace it back to my mother,' he said. 'She doted on me, you see. My brother had died and I was her darling, we adored each other.' One day, however, his father had sent him away to boarding school. Alwyne called it the Expulsion from Eden. He said he could never forgive them, as long as he lived.

That Alwyne came from a wealthy background was something of a surprise. He also admitted to being bullied at school. 'I looked different, you understand – swarthy complexion, something of the johnny foreigner about me. They used to taunt me – *Dago, Jew-boy* – witless little nincompoops.'

'*I've* been nice to you,' said Ralph. 'I've even kept mum. So has Lettie.'

'That extortioness. Sixpence a week, my foot.'

'But you'll have to agree she's been playing fair.'

'So have you, old chap. Don't think I'm not grateful.'

'Do something, then,' said Ralph.

Alwyne shrugged. He seemed to have lost interest. Ralph was exasperated. The fellow was sitting on a bombshell. All he had to do was light the fuse and stand back. It wasn't a lot to ask. He was just a snivelling little coward.

And in two months' time this life would be over. Nobody had bothered to ask Ralph's opinion, of course. It had been presented to him as a decision already made; he had no choice in the matter. He, his mother and stepfather were going to move into rented rooms while the building works took place. Mr Turk would then start his progress towards world domination. There was nobody for Ralph to talk to; no Winnie to tut-tut and give him a hug. It was beneath his dignity to confide in Alwyne; he was too angry with the man. Angry and disappointed. Chaps had laid down their lives! Their futures had been rubbed out; nothing remained of their hopes and dreams. Not for them, any thought of the consequences.

Foggy days passed into foggy nights. Ralph walked the dog through the sulphurous streets. Hoofs echoed on the cobblestones. He brooded and seethed. If he had a bomb he would blow Mr Turk to smithereens. The man was worse than any German. He had invaded a place more precious than some unknown country called France. And Ralph, with no allies to support him, was powerless.

Chapter Thirteen

We were still fighting hard and losing men. We knew nothing of the proposed Armistice, we didn't know until a quarter to ten on that day. As we advanced on the village of Guiry a runner came up and told us that the Armistice would be signed at 11 o'clock that day, the 11th of November. That was the first we knew of it.

We were lined up on a railway bank nearby, the same railway bank that the Manchesters had lined up on in 1914. They had fought at the battle of Mons in August that year. Some of us went down to a wood in a little valley and found the skeletons of some of the Manchesters still lying there. Lying there with their boots on, very still, no helmets, no rusty rifles or equipment, just their boots.

Marine Hubert Trotman, Royal Marine Light Infantry

And lo, there was much drunkenness and rejoicing. And in the streets, from John o'Groats to Land's End, the bunting went up and the maidens dressed themselves in their best frocks and tied ribbons in their hair, and the children waved flags to welcome their daddies home, and laughter rang through the air and church bells pealed and joy was unconfined.

'Cheer up,' said Alwyne. 'You're a gloomy little

bugger, aren't you? How about packing up your troubles in that old kitbag and looking on the bright side for once?'

Ralph ignored this. 'So what are you going to do now? Suddenly get your sight back?'

'I don't think that would be advisable.'

'The war's over. They can't put you in prison for avoiding it now.'

'Oh yes they can. I shall go abroad.'

'Where?'

'Where I'm needed by the comrades,' said Alwyne. 'Now peace has been declared, the real war begins.'

'You'd know about war, wouldn't you?'

Alwyne looked at him. 'I like this burgeoning cynicism. You're developing well.'

'You might as well go,' said Ralph. 'Fat lot of use you've been here.'

'My dear boy, Mr Turk will be the architect of his own destruction. He doesn't need me to do it for him.'

'Why?'

'Because a man who's got where he has, using the methods he's used, makes a lot of enemies.'

'Seems to have a lot of friends, to me. All those Masons and whatnots, with their handshakes.'

Alwyne shook his head. 'Don't trust any of them. They've all got their noses in the trough. Bunch of hyenas. Give them the chance and they'll tear each other to pieces.'

Ralph considered this. It was an attractive image. 'And if not,' Ralph said, 'maybe he'll catch the flu and die.' The epidemic had been sweeping through London. In the last month alone, two thousand people had died. 'If that happened,' said Ralph, 'I'd start believing in God again.'

Alwyne raised his eyebrows. 'Steady on, old chap.'

He passed Ralph a Player's, and lit them. Smoking seemed to be doing the trick, so far. Mr Spooner was doing his bit, too, upstairs. The rest of the household should be grateful to them, for waging the battle on their behalf.

Ralph had to admit that Alwyne was generous with his cigarettes. He knew that Ralph, now an enthusiastic smoker, had no money to buy them himself. In some ways Ralph would miss him when he was gone. Oh the man was weak, and unpleasant and a thoroughgoing cowardy-custard, but at least he talked to him.

Ralph got to his feet. 'It's twelve o'clock,' he said. 'I'll lead you to the pub.'

*

A celebration was taking place in the King's Head, Swaffley. Tom Spinks, the road-mender, had returned from the Front. The man sat, as bashful as a bridegroom, as people plied him with drink. It was the end of November. Men had been returning to the village in dribs and drabs – five so far. Demobilisation wasn't happening as swiftly as people had expected. Families had presumed that their boys would be home within the week but it wasn't turning out that way; letters had arrived saying that they might be delayed for months. It was a cruel disappointment. For many families, no letter had been received except an official one of condolence, and there would be nobody coming home. The war had taken a terrible toll on the village: fifteen dead, four of them brothers. Twelve children had lost their fathers.

Winnie's father needed no excuse for ordering another

glass of beer. He was singing along to the piano. *'Shirley, Shirley, why's your hair so curly?'* Winnie sat beside him, waiting to take him home. Her arm rested casually across her lap. Nobody could tell, by her expression, what her forearm was feeling as it lay pressed against her belly. A nudge. The baby was kicking, there was no doubt about it. A nudge to remind her, as if she needed reminding, that it was growing bigger and would soon emerge into the world. When had its life begun – that May evening, the evening of the wedding? That day the man shot himself with his revolver? When did a baby begin to kick? There was nobody she could ask.

Nor had anybody noticed that she had become fatter. She knew everybody in the village, she had grown up with them. A mild surprise had greeted her return but then people had carried on as before; she was just one of the fixtures and fittings, as they were to her. Swaffley folk were not noted for their curiosity. And nobody ever looked at her anyway, they never had. It was a blessing, really.

Winnie had no plans. She lived in the present. She'd had no intention of getting rid of it and now it was too late. The funny thing was that her shame seemed to have disappeared. What had happened, had happened. At some point a baby would be born. *Her* baby. She pictured herself lying in the straw in Dulcie's stable and giving birth like the Virgin Mary. See the vicar's face then!

She knew she was a sinner but she didn't feel it, not any more. She had been brought up to fear the wrath of God but He had other things on His mind. The world was all at sixes and sevens. Mrs Powers's son, Timmy, had returned home with both his arms blown off. God must be busy working out how Timmy was going to pick the apple harvest next year. How could He have time to worry about a little baby? A child born out of wedlock, to be sure, but then how many children were fatherless now? And what had God done to stop *that* happening?

Maybe Alwyne's words were turning her into an atheist. Winnie hadn't listened at the time but perhaps his ideas had soaked through, like stewed fruit dripping through muslin. For all his treachery he was a clever man, and events seemed to be proving him right.

The voices rose around her. *'If you were the only girl in the world, and I were the only boy . . .'* Winnie sat there, thinking about Alwyne. Though she was still upset, her anger had long since subsided. It was a terrible thing, to trick her, but then he had tricked everybody else too. Perhaps he had been suffering from some sort of mental disorder; the gas had poisoned his brain.

And sometimes, just sometimes, when she realised that Alwyne had been able to see her all the time, she thought: I can't be that ugly after all.

Winnie felt herself reddening. She put the glass to her lips, so nobody could see. How confusing it all was! For sometimes she even felt grateful to Alwyne, for taking the trouble to talk to her, for telling her things that had gone into her head and stuck there and changed the way she looked at the world. Nobody else had ever bothered to do that. And sometimes, she even felt pity. For she was going to have a baby, and he had nothing.

'They hadn't been married but a month or more when under her thumb goes he . . .'

Everyone was joining in, even the publican, one of Swaffley's more morose inhabitants. So loud were the voices that Winnie didn't hear the sound of horses clopping past, down South Street.

'Isn't it a pity that the likes of her should put upon the likes of him . . . .'

Her father always sang with his eyes shut. Above him, in its case, hung Swaffley's champion trout, fished out of the river in 1893. Its glass eye was the only one that gazed directly at Winnie, and she could rely on the fish to keep quiet. This couldn't last for ever, of course. Sooner or later she would have to tell Dr Allender. Sooner or later, her father would find out the truth. She couldn't bear to think about this, not yet. Maybe a bomb would blow them all to bits before it happened. This was how they thought, during the war. Live for the moment, because they might all be dead tomorrow. No wonder people gallivanted about. Even people like her.

At half-past two Winnie led her father home. It was bitterly cold, the ground frozen. He stumbled over the ruts as they crossed the field.

'Look,' she said. They were nearing the big house. 'There's more tiles blown off. The rain'll be getting in.' They walked round the back, towards the stable yard. 'And the pigeons.'

Her father stopped dead.

He had heard something. So had Winnie. At first they thought they had imagined it.

The two of them stood rooted to the spot, their breath pumping into the frosty air. Then they heard it again. It was a horse, neighing.

Her father was the first to move. He pulled away from Winnie's arm and stumbled towards the stable yard. Winnie followed.

The housekeeper, Mrs Maitland, stood in the yard, bundled up against the cold.

'There you are, Crooke,' she said, to Winnie's father. 'The fellows were looking for you but they've gone now. I've signed the papers but goodness knows what we're going to do with them. Lady Elbourne's been informed, of course.'

Neither Winnie nor her father heard her. They were heading for the stables.

Winnie could almost sense them before she saw them – the warmth of their bodies, the smell of them. She went inside. It took a moment for her eyes to adjust to the gloom.

Two of the horses had come home.

Dulcie was back in her stall. The old grey mare turned her head and gazed at Winnie. Her ears pricked up in recognition; she made a soft, whickering sound in her nostrils.

'She walked in there all by herself.'

Winnie turned round. Joe, the housekeeper's son, was sitting on a bale of straw.

'Bertie's back too.' He pointed to the big bay gelding, standing in a stall further down the row. Bertie was one of the hunters. 'They walked back in like they'd never been away. They knew their stalls and everything.' He turned to Winnie's father who stood there, unable to move. 'I gave them some oats.'

Chapter Fourteen

Cover him, cover him soon!
And with thick-set
Masses of memoried flowers –
Hide that red wet
Thing I must somehow forget.

Ivor Gurney

At first Neville didn't recognise the boy. The butcher was wrapping up half a pound of kidneys for Mrs Phelps. There were several other customers in the shop but the boy stood a little apart. He wore a greatcoat that was too big for him and carried a bag. There was a growth of stubble on his chin.

'Clear off,' said Neville. 'You can beg in the street.'

'It's Archie,' said the boy. 'D-d-don't you remember me?'

Neville lifted up the counter-flap and led the boy through to his office. Archie sat down.

'Well well,' said Neville. 'Turned up like a bad penny, eh?'

Archie didn't smile. Neville looked at him with curiosity. It was hard to believe that two years earlier this had been the little monkey who had worked for him, who had whistled at the ladies and kicked his football through a plate-glass window. The fellow seemed to have aged twenty years.

'I've c-c-c-c . . .' said Archie.

'Spit it out, boy.'

'I've c-c-come back,' said Archie.

'I can see that.' The chap seemed to have developed a stammer.

'W-when shall I start?'

Neville lit a cheroot. He had forgotten all about his young delivery boy. In fact, now he remembered it, Archie had just started his apprenticeship before he went to the war.

'You want your job back?' he asked.

Archie nodded.

Neville blew out a cloud of smoke. In truth he was short-staffed at present – three counter assistants, one trainee and an unreliable delivery-man of fifty-five, with so-called gas damage to his lungs. Neville had his suspicions about the fellow. Nor had Ralph taken up the position offered him, due to the burden of housework at home. Though his stepson's qualities left a great deal to be desired – not least, his vegetarianism – at least the boy could have made himself useful in one way or another.

Neville looked at Archie. The chap's carroty stubble made him look seedy. He'd made an attempt to grow a moustache but it was a pathetic affair. Still, beggars couldn't be choosers.

'You'll have to smarten yourself up,' he said. 'Get yourself a shave, for a start. I run a top-class estab-lishment, if you recollect.'

Archie stayed sitting there, like an idiot. Didn't he

realise that the interview was over? The fellow seemed to be affected by some sort of tic. His leg jiggled up and down and his hand trembled. Perhaps he was nervous about throwing himself on Neville's mercy. How lucky for him, then, that the butcher had a soft heart.

*

Eithne replaced the telephone receiver. She had been speaking to the receptionist at the Ship Hotel. Clarence hadn't yet returned to claim his photograph.

Of course, the young American could still turn up. Soldiers weren't returning in a rush; it was more like a trickle. He could still be alive. He could, of course, have simply returned to America. She felt a strong attachment to the boy, who had been bathed in her honeymoon glow, who could have been her son.

It could have been Ralph out there in the trenches. The thought of her darling boy cowering under enemy fire didn't bear thinking about. How could mothers so blithely let their sons disappear, perhaps for ever? Victory had not had the desired effect. Strangely enough, it was only now the war had ended that the enormity of it hit her. She felt like a horse that had been trudging along, step by step, only seeing its little patch of road, and now the blinkers had been removed.

That patriotic frenzy, four years earlier, seemed idiotic to Eithne now. She had sent her own husband packing. *Your Country Needs You*. That her country had won seemed strangely irrelevant. She joined in the rejoicing, but with a heavy heart. Paul would never return, to pick snail shells off the South Downs. She hadn't even bothered to accompany him and share his Thermos. He had become frozen in time, knapsack on his back, and this image tormented her. She should have loved him more. She should have known how fragile life was, how her husband's was soon to be extinguished, with all his modest hopes and dreams. Instead of putting her arms around him she had run downstairs to check on her mutton bones.

And what had she done? Slapped Ralph's face when he had reminded her of the fact.

Eithne leaned against the wall. The dog padded past. She heard him walk into the drawing room and settle down. Brutus seemed quite happy with his new life but what did dogs know?

Something had happened that night when Neville tugged her hair. *We're sitting on a bloody gold mine!* Neville didn't care. He didn't give a fig what had been happening to other people, that Mr Fawcett, the draper, had lost both his sons and was closing up his shop. Eithne had a horrible suspicion that the war, for her husband, was a means to an end. She would never dare ask him, because she couldn't bear to hear the answer. Anyway, he would lie. *She* had lied, to herself. She was guilty too.

Eithne realised she was still standing in the hall. She rallied. Enough of this gloom! After all, it was Neville's bullish energy that had attracted her in the first place. And he might not have fought in the trenches but he had behaved decently to her own little household. He had his plans, he was trying to survive in difficult times, trying to do her best for the two of them. The *three* of them. She was simply filled with dread at the upheaval that lay ahead. Packing up was a huge undertaking. Ten years of her life had been spent in this house; they had arrived, from their lodgings in Bow, when Ralph was barely seven. How full of hope they had been! Paul was going to get on in life. A world war, with millions dead, was unimaginable. Those particular dreams were gone; new ones lay ahead of her.

While the building work was in progress Neville planned to show her around the various hotels that were run by customers of his. *You can pick up some tips, my love.* For she was to become manageress of the Continental Hotel. *No point in paying somebody else a salary.* He would be on hand, while still running the butchery business. Eithne had rather expected to become a lady of leisure but Neville said that would come later, when the business was up and running, and in fact, once she became used to the idea, Eithne had started to look forward to it. It was the new thing for women to have careers; indeed, it was on this philosophy that their hotel would be built. Neville had promised her a full complement of staff. Already, he said, he had been making discreet enquiries amongst the disaffected waiters and housekeepers of the local establishments. Poaching was par for the course, apparently, in this sort of thing.

Ralph's role was already decided. He would pass his exams and help with the accounts. Not run them, of course; Neville had an accountant already, a Mr Postlethwaite, who was experienced in these matters. But her son would be trained up to become an essential member of their team. Eithne had every confidence in Ralph. After this minor hiccup he would knuckle under. And they would all live happily ever after, with potted palms in the lounge.

Eithne's spirits were restored. At supper Neville, too, was in high good humour. A Victory Banquet was being planned at the Lodge. Weeks of preparation were going into it and the chef of the Athenaeum club, a famous Frenchman, had been hired at considerable expense to prepare the dishes.

'Cheese soufflé followed by truffles with *foie gras*,' said Neville. 'Followed by salmon *aux fines herbes*, and Aberdeen Angus beef supplied by yours truly.'

Mayors from all the London boroughs would be attending, and local dignitaries – Neville amongst them, of course – with their lady wives. There would be speeches and celebrations.

'It'll beat the other ones into a cocked hat,' said Neville.

'Shouldn't you be inviting the soldiers?' asked Ralph.

Neville turned. 'What was that?'

Ralph flushed. 'Shouldn't it be the soldiers having the dinner, not you?'

'Ralph!' hissed Eithne.

They were sitting at the little table in the drawing room. Neville wiped his moustache with his napkin. 'Plenty's being done for them, my lad. In fact, I took back one of them myself only this week.'

'Who's that?' asked Eithne.

'Gingery little chap called Archie.'

'I remember him,' said Eithne. 'Always whistling. He used to deliver the meat.'

Neville chuckled. 'Couldn't deliver it now.'

'Why?'

'He's got this jerky arm. It'd end up half-way down the street.' Neville pushed back his chair. 'Like this.' He shook his arm, as if shaking water off himself. The dog barked. 'I said to him this morning, *you got a wasp up your sleeve?*'

'Perhaps he's taking the mickey,' said Eithne, laughing. 'He was a little devil, if I remember.'

*

Neville had exaggerated, to make his wife laugh. But there was definitely something wrong with the boy. Butchery was out of the question. How could the fellow bone a shoulder of mutton with a hand that shook like a drunkard's? He shouldn't even be picking up a knife.

Archie stammered his excuses. 'It's only in the one h-hand, sir, and I can feel when it's coming on. Give me another chance, p-please.'

Neville shook his head. 'You should see a doctor.' The boy was obviously suffering from some nervous disorder; he was as jumpy as a jack-rabbit.

A week had passed. He had given Archie the more menial jobs – taking down the shutters in the morning, sweeping the floor and scattering fresh sawdust, fetching and carrying. He had even sent him on the occasional errand but the fellow took forever. Once Neville had spotted him standing under the railway bridge, trembling, as a train thundered overhead.

Neville might have persevered because he was, indeed, short-staffed. However, there was something about the boy that made him uncomfortable. More to the point, his customers were made uncomfortable too. The chap hung around like a spectre at a feast. He always seemed to be standing in the wrong place, getting in the way. There was a gormless look to him – shifty eyes, sweaty pale face. All in all, he made folk uneasy. Neville ran a popular

283

shop, filled with banter and flirtation; the ladies liked it. Archie was bad for business and would have to go.

Neville broke the news when the shop was opening for the day. No customers had yet arrived. Archie stood there, blank-faced. Above him, legs and shoulders hung from their S-hooks.

'You can collect your wages for the week,' said Neville.

Archie's lip trembled. 'W-what did you say?'

'I said, you can take your wages. Nobody can say I'm not a generous man.'

'You w-want me to go?'

'Sorry, lad.' Neville put his hand on his shoulder.

Archie jumped, as if he had been hit. He shrank back and, pulling off his apron, stumbled out into the fog.

Will and Ted, behind the counter, looked at each other and raised their eyebrows.

*

For the umpteenth time, Ralph was mulling over his initiation into manhood on Jenny Wren's bed. Four months had passed since the event but it still had the power to thrill him. In fact it had grown more thrilling in retrospect – more intense, more gratifying for both parties and by now of a much longer duration. It had mutated into something on an epic scale. He wondered if he dared tell Alwyne about it, before the man left. The fellow would look at Ralph with quite different eyes.

The fog was thick, a real pea-souper. Ralph was walking the dog back from the park. It was only five o'clock and already dark – raw and clammy, the street lamps the faintest glow, as if muffled in cotton wool. Vehicles crawled past, their headlights feeling their way through the fog.

The old resentment flared up again. Ralph tried to work out how much money Jenny Wren must have made since his visit. Three men a night, say, at two pounds each. Ralph had reached Stage Three in his bookkeeping course; he ought to be able to do the sums.

He was almost upon Archie before he saw him. Bundled up in a coat, the chap stood under a lamp. He was staring into space.

'Hello there,' said Ralph. He hadn't seen Archie for two years, not since the delivery boy had enlisted and disappeared to the war. Archie didn't notice him. He stood there, trembling in the cold.

Ralph walked on. Maybe Jenny Wren had seen the light and forsworn her wicked ways. Perhaps his own visit had been a turning-point. His outburst of weeping, though embarrassing at the time, had affected her powerfully and she had put her life of shame behind her.

Ralph let himself into the house. Upstairs, he found his mother all in a fluster. It was the night of the big dinner and her bedroom was strewn with clothes.

'My moiré's got a stain down the bust! Oh Winnie, I need you!'

'I'll help,' said Ralph. He loved helping her dress.

'You've got to do the suppers. There's pickled herrings and some beetroot. Check on the bread. I couldn't see any when I looked in the kitchen, Mrs O'Malley's been on the prowl again.'

'I saw Archie just now.'

'Who?' She pulled another dress out of the wardrobe.

'Archie, the delivery boy. I don't think he recognised me.'

'Oh, yes.' She stood in front of the mirror, holding the dress against herself. 'Neville gave him the sack today.'

'The sack?'

'He said he shook all the time.' She tilted her head sideways. 'Could I wear my jet with this? Would it look as if I were going to a funeral?'

Ralph went downstairs and started laying the table in the parlour. The front door opened and Alwyne arrived home.

'Ah, it's only you.' Alwyne came into the room and took off his spectacles. 'Couldn't see a blind thing in that fog.'

Ralph said: 'I suppose it'll be a relief, that you can stop that soon.' He laid out the place-mats. 'Except then you'll have to start doing things for yourself.'

Alwyne showed him a paper bag. 'Bought myself some Chivers's Old English Marmalade. Won't have that, where I'm going.'

This was to be Alwyne's last supper. His belongings were packed. In the morning he was taking the train to the Continent. He still hadn't told Ralph where he was going.

Ralph fetched the cutlery from the sideboard. It was tarnished; nobody had polished it for weeks.

He wanted to tell Alwyne that he would miss him, that nobody else seemed to listen to anything he said. His mother was too busy primping and preening; she hadn't shown the slightest interest in Archie.

Alwyne at least gave him his attention. Ralph told him about the delivery boy. 'Cheeky bastard, wasn't he,' said Alwyne. 'I remember seeing him bicycling down the street, staring at that mongol fellow. You remember him, lived with his mother and walked around holding her hand? Archie was laughing at him so hard he ran straight

286

into a lamppost.' Alwyne lit a cigarette. 'Just like Charlie Chaplin. I had to try not to laugh too.'

'*That* would have given the game away.'

'It would, wouldn't it,' said Alwyne. 'So he's been fired, has he?'

'They said he shook too much.'

Alwyne nodded. 'I saw him in the shop last week. Bugger's suffering from the shell-shock. Could tell it a mile off.'

'Shell-shock?'

'Those poor boys,' said Alwyne. 'Somebody should be looking after them. Nobody gives a monkey's.'

Footsteps pattered down the stairs. Alwyne put on his spectacles. But it was only Lettie, coming for her final payment.

Alwyne thanked her for playing fair. 'At least one person's honest,' he said.

*

The Victory Dinner was over. Eithne was so stuffed with food she could hardly move. She took one last look at the banqueting hall – the crystal chandeliers, wreathed in cigar smoke; the milling mayors, their chains glinting.

A flunkey gave them their coats. Eithne linked arms with Neville and they stepped out, into the night. Headlamps loomed through the fog as the motor cars arrived. Chauffeurs, as dim as ghosts, opened the doors.

'We'll have one of those fellows soon,' said Neville. 'Only a matter of time, my love.'

Eithne thought: how could I have doubted him? How could I have doubted our life together? A little drunk, she clung to her husband's arm as they walked towards their car.

*

Ralph and Alwyne were down at the Albion, having a farewell glass of beer. The regulars knew Alwyne was leaving and stood him and Ralph drinks. 'Crying shame, isn't it?' said one of them, leaning towards Ralph. 'War's over for the likes of us, but he's got to live with that for ever.'

Ralph looked at Alwyne as he sat there, feeling for his matchbox. Somebody put it into his hand. The man had missed his vocation; he should have been an actor. He *was* an actor. He'd made a good living out of it too, thought Ralph as he watched Alwyne drain yet another free pint of mild. For a year he had been trading on people's goodwill and gratitude; the whole business was shabby beyond words. There was just one way he could have made amends and he hadn't the spunk for it.

On the way home Ralph said: 'You've still got time. You could get up early and put some rat poison in his tea and by the time they find out you'll be gone. Nobody even knows your name.'

Alwyne chuckled. 'Any other bright ideas?'

'I relied on you,' said Ralph. 'You've been a great disappointment.'

'I've told you, dear boy. Violence will get you nowhere. That's one lesson we can learn from this terrible war.'

'But we've won it.'

'You think so?' Alwyne sighed. 'Oh, Ralph.'

'Stop treating me like a child!'

'Then stop behaving like one.' Alwyne stopped and turned to him. 'Take my advice and get out of here.'

'What do you mean?'

'Get away from that man. It's eating you up. You'll never grow up if you're consumed with hatred.' The muffled church clock struck eleven. 'Trust me,' said Alwyne. 'I know what I'm talking about. Only too well, as it happens. It corrodes you like bloody acid.'

They walked on through the fog, the blind leading the blind. It was eerily quiet. Far off, on the river, they heard the foghorns.

'Where shall I go?' asked Ralph.

'Anywhere. Just get out. It's a question of self-preservation.' Alwyne spoke with passion. 'Don't work for them in that hotel! The place will be the death of you.'

'The death?'

'I'm talking metaphorically, of course. You must have nothing to do with it. It'll be built on blood, you and I know that only too well. It's just a shame your mother can't see it too.'

'Huh,' said Ralph. '*She's* the blind one.'

'It's understandable. She's in love. Wait till it happens to you.'

They walked along Back Lane. A bundled-up figure loomed out of the fog, muttering to itself, and disappeared. They arrived at Palmerston Road. Ralph took a breath; it was now or never. 'It has, in fact.'

'What?'

'It has happened to me,' said Ralph.

'You've fallen in love?'

289

'Well, not exactly love –'

A loud *bang* shattered the silence. They froze.

Alwyne clutched Ralph's arm. 'My God! Is that a bomb?'

Ralph cocked his head, listening. 'No,' he said. 'It's a car, backfiring.'

Sure enough, they heard the *putter-putter* of an engine approaching. Alwyne disengaged his arm. 'Silly me,' he said, with a little laugh.

They crossed the road, towards the house. Up above them an unseen train rattled over the bridge. Smoke swirled down.

'You despise me, don't you,' said Alwyne, his voice flat. 'I've tried to help you, believe me, but not in the way you want and now we'll never see each other again. I'll just be another grown-up who's let you down.'

'It's all right,' muttered Ralph.

'I can only talk, you see,' said Alwyne. 'It's all I'm good at.'

Later, Ralph remembered these words. At the time he just felt a dismal sort of impatience with the man, as they walked towards the front door.

'It's all right,' he said again.

'It's not, is it,' said Alwyne. 'It's not at all.'

Ralph tried to think of a reply. The noise of the motor car grew louder. Two headlights appeared. The Wolseley materialised out of the fog. Ralph's mother and Mr Turk were returning home from the dinner.

It all happened in a flash. The motor car pulled up in front of the house. With a final splutter, the engine stopped. Ralph's mother saw them and waved.

A figure stepped out, from behind the street lamp – a

small, slight figure, dressed in a greatcoat. It was Archie. He lifted a revolver and fired.

A *crack*. In the car Mr Turk folded over, as if inspecting something on the floor. Archie melted back into the fog.

Ralph's mother screamed.

Chapter Fifteen

Shall they return to beating of great bells
In wild train-loads?
A few, a few, too few for drums and yells,
May creep back, silent, to still village wells
Up half-known roads.

Wilfred Owen

The back room was filled with people; Ralph had had to bring in chairs from the parlour. All the lodgers were there – even Mr Spooner – coats and shawls over their nightclothes. They sat bundled up like tramps at the scene of a traffic collision. It was freezing cold; nobody had thought to light a fire. His mother sat hunched and shuddering in an armchair. Ralph had tried to put his arm around her, awkwardly, but she hadn't responded. Her face, when she raised it, looked quite undone, as if her features had been shaken up and rearranged. It had chilled his blood. Where had her old face gone? He wondered if his own death would create such a reaction. A glass of brandy sat untouched on the table beside her.

Out in the street the crowd would have got bigger. It would be the talk of the neighbourhood; the talk of *London*. It would be reported in the newspaper! Perhaps a barrier had been erected; perhaps an ambulance had arrived, to take the body away – the body that a few hours ago had been Mr Turk, living and breathing. Ralph had no idea of the procedure in a situation like this. He hadn't been in a situation like this before.

The whole thing seemed to be happening to someone else, in a dream. No doubt the shock would hit him, but it hadn't caught up with him yet. He listened to the two policemen who were trying to question his mother, but there was something unreal about them too, as if they had just put on their uniforms for the night. They seemed too big for the room, too official. People like that didn't come into his house.

It had all been staged, like a theatre show. A show he had imagined for months. *The Death of Mr Turk!* They were putting it on for his benefit – the performance, the audience of shivering boarders, the weeping woman who sat there in her finery, in the glaring electric light, impersonating his mother. They knew he had longed for this, that he had brooded and seethed for nine months, willing it to happen, so they had decided to oblige him. At this very moment Mr Turk was stepping out of the motor car and dusting himself down. Archie was shaking his hand. They grinned at each other, sharing the joke.

And in a moment the front door would open and in would step Mr Turk. His eye, and the side of his face, would be back in place. He would look at Ralph and chuckle. *Think you can get rid of me that easily, eh, my boy?* Everyone would turn to look at Ralph, because they all knew, of course. They were in on it together. *Nobody kills me*, Mr Turk would say. *I'm the one that does the killing, if you remember*. Ralph's mother would cease her weeping; her face would blaze with love. Mr Turk would sit on the

293

arm of her chair, as Ralph used to do, and stroke her hair. She would turn briefly to her son. *You're disgusting*, she would say, and then she would turn back to her husband, and Ralph would be forgotten.

'Ralph!' said his mother. 'He's talking to you.'

The policeman, a big man, was sitting on the flimsiest chair. He had shifted around, to face Ralph. He held his pencil like a schoolboy. 'This must be a big shock for you, young lad,' he said.

Ralph nodded. His mother was still wearing her dark-green dress. It was only now that Ralph noticed a darker stain on her lap, where she had cradled Mr Turk's head. It had taken the butcher some time to die.

'We'll take it slowly,' said the policeman. 'I want you to think very carefully.' *Could I wear my jet with this? Would it look as if I were going to a funeral?*

'You must have seen something!' blurted out his mother. 'You were right beside us.'

'Thank you, Mrs Turk,' said the policeman. 'Let me ask the boy.' He turned back to Ralph. 'Now, let's get this straight. You and Mr . . .' He peered at his notebook.

'Mr Flyte,' said Ralph.

'Who is, I believe . . . er, blind, am I right?'

Ralph nodded. Alwyne sat beneath the cabinet of boxing trophies. He could barely be seen through the cigarette smoke. Mrs O'Malley, holding her shawl against her mouth, coughed discreetly.

'You were making your way home from the public house at the time of the incident, I believe,' said the policeman. 'Can you tell us what happened?'

'We were walking up the street,' said Ralph. 'The fog was very thick. You couldn't even see the houses.'

'And did you pass anybody? Did you see anything suspicious?'

Ralph shook his head. 'There was nobody about. Just us.'

The policeman wrote it down, slowly. 'If people had been looking out of their windows, would they have been able to see anything?'

'No. The fog was too thick.'

The grandfather clock struck. They all jumped. It chimed three times and was silent.

'Now, somebody shot Mr Turk,' said the policeman. 'That's quite clear. From close range too. Did you see that person?'

Ralph didn't reply. They were all looking at him.

'You must have seen him!' said his mother.

'Please, Mrs Turk –' said the policeman.

'There was somebody!' she cried. 'I saw somebody moving, but I couldn't see who it was.'

'Please. Let the boy think.'

Ralph *was* thinking, fast. His paralysis had lifted. It was obvious he had seen somebody. It would look very curious if he denied it. They would think he was hiding something. But if he said he saw the person he would have to admit it was Archie, and then Archie would go to prison. He would be *hanged*. Even if he didn't say it was Archie, people would put two and two together. Archie had been sacked that morning; there had probably been a row in the shop. He would be the obvious suspect – out for revenge, his wits shattered by the war. It all made sense. Indeed, so it should, seeing as that's what had happened.

'Ralph,' said the other policeman. 'You saw someone, didn't you?'

Ralph nodded.

'Did you recognise them?' The second policeman had pale, penetrating eyes. 'Come along, lad. There's no point in protecting anybody, we'll find out soon enough.'

'I saw somebody but I don't know who it was,' said Ralph.

'Can you give us a description?'

Ralph's head span. What could he say?

'Not really,' he muttered.

He tried to gather his wits. Archie would be caught; they were bound to ask questions and then he would be caught and hanged. For doing the very thing Ralph had been dreaming of doing but hadn't the guts to do himself.

Ralph knew that he sounded unconvincing. The policemen exchanged glances. The one with the pale eyes cleared his throat. He was just about to speak when Alwyne leaned forward and stubbed out his cigarette.

'I saw who did it,' he said.

The lodgers froze.

'What did you say?' someone whispered.

'I saw who shot him,' said Alwyne.

There was a silence. A silence so profound that the grandfather clock could be heard ticking in the next room. Fearfully, one by one, the lodgers stole a look at Alwyne. His face was empty of expression.

Ralph's mother was the first to speak. 'But you're blind,' she said.

Alwyne shook his head and took off his spectacles.

Mrs O'Malley made a whimpering sound. Mrs Spooner grabbed Lettie, as if she had seen a rat.

Alwyne took no notice. He addressed the policemen. 'I saw the man quite clearly. He was a stout gentleman of middle age, in a frock coat, wearing a top hat.'

The policeman, his mouth open, stared at Alwyne.

'Go on, write it down,' said Alwyne.

The policeman rallied, and started writing in his notebook. Alwyne's eyes flickered to Ralph, then away again.

'Did you recognise him, sir?' asked the policeman.

Alwyne shook his head. 'Didn't get a good look at his face.' He shrugged. 'To be perfectly honest, I'm surprised it didn't happen sooner.'

'What do you mean by that, sir?'

'Mr Turk had a lot of enemies,' said Alwyne. 'Oh yes, plenty of people with a grudge against *him*. He'd been engaged in some very dubious activities.'

Ralph's mother stared at him. 'What activities?'

The others weren't interested. They were still staring at Alwyne.

'Did he say he wasn't blind?' whispered Mrs O'Malley.

'I knew it all the time,' said Lettie, detaching herself from her mother's grasp.

Alwyne sat there impassively. Only Ralph noticed the beads of sweat on his forehead.

Mrs Spooner summoned up her courage and looked directly at Alwyne. 'Excuse me, but why did you pretend you were blind?'

'Dear lady, can't you guess?'

'Why?'

'So I wasn't called up.'

Mrs Spooner stared at him. 'You did it to avoid going to war?'

Alwyne nodded. 'Strangely enough, I didn't care to be blown to pieces.'

Ralph sat there in a turmoil. The man had saved Archie!

What on earth had made him do it? He longed to say something to Alwyne – to thank him, to apologise, to say *anything*, but he couldn't with all the people there. He tried to meet Alwyne's eye but the fellow had dropped his gaze and was looking at the dog, his eyebrows raised conspiratorially, as if Brutus had been in on the secret all the time. His composure didn't fool Ralph, however, who saw that Alwyne was now sweating heavily.

The policeman said: 'You realise that evading conscription is a criminal offence?'

Alwyne nodded.

For a moment nobody knew what to do. Events had taken such a startling turn that it had caught them on the hop. The policemen caught each other's eye. Finally one of them turned to Alwyne.

'We'll have to ask you to come down to the station, sir.'

The two policemen stood up. Alwyne, too, got to his feet. He picked up his overcoat and stood there for a moment inspecting it on his arm, as if searching for stains. Ralph willed him to look up.

The policeman put away his notebook and turned to Ralph's mother. 'That'll be all for now, Mrs Turk. I wish you every sympathy in your loss.'

'What are you going to do with him?' she asked.

'We'll be back in the morning,' said the policeman. 'In the meantime, I suggest you all try to get some sleep.'

They moved to the door. Alwyne turned to Ralph's mother. 'I'm truly sorry,' he said. Then he touched Ralph on the shoulder, glanced at him, and was gone.

All that remained were his spectacles, lying on the arm of the chair.

Ralph never saw Alwyne again. A few days later a man arrived and removed his belongings, which were already packed up. He gave Ralph a note.

Dear Ralph, look after your mother. If you ever see Winnie again, please tell her I'm sorry. All best wishes, dear boy, Alwyne.

Chapter Sixteen

'My love!' one moaned. Love-languid seemed his mood,
Till, slowly lowered, his whole face kissed the mud.
And the bayonets' long teeth grinned;
Rabbles of shells hooted and groaned;
And the Gas hissed.

Wilfred Owen

Ralph and his mother sat in the parlour. Papers were strewn over the tablecloth. Flossie lay sleeping on Mr Turk's bank statements.

The accountant, Mr Postlethwaite, had long since gone. In the grate, the coals shifted and settled. Ralph's mother raised her head and gazed at her son.

'I used to sit here,' she said. 'I used to sit here and worry myself sick, you'd no idea.'

'Yes I did,' said Ralph.

She reached out and stroked his finger. 'My only boy,' she said.

Her face was parchment pale above the black dress. She hadn't worn mourning for Ralph's father, it was considered bad for morale. The war was over now, however, and sorrow could be acknowledged.

'We're rich,' she said in a flat voice. 'We can do anything, we can do whatever we please. We can go anywhere.' She paused. 'The further away the better.' She lowered her head and scratched at a scab of food on the tablecloth. 'Not that there's anything irregular, of course. Mr Postlethwaite made that quite clear. But it might be advisable.'

Ralph looked at her lowered head. 'We can't keep it all,' he said.

He expected his mother to snap back, but she remained silent.

'You know we can't,' he said.

'And why not?'

'It wouldn't be right.'

She looked up. 'Since when has right got to do with anything?'

'Since all sorts of things,' said Ralph. Emboldened, he met his mother's eyes. She sat there, fiddling with the loops of jet around her throat. He took a breath and said: 'I think you should listen to me, for once.'

Chapter Seventeen

We gentle-nurtured, timid sex did not want the war. It is no pleasure to us to have our homes made desolate and the apple of our eye taken away. We would sooner our loveable, promising, rollicking boy stayed at school. We would have much preferred to have gone on in a light-hearted way with our amusements and our hobbies. But the bugle-call came, and we have hung up the tennis racquet, we've fetched our laddie from school, we've put his cap away, and we've glanced lovingly over his last report which said 'Excellent' – we've wrapped them all in a Union Jack and locked them up, to be taken out only after the war to be looked at . . . We are proud of our men, and they in turn are proud of us . . . Women are created for the purpose of giving life, and men to take it.

Yours etc, 'A Little Mother'.

The Morning Post

Elsie's funeral took place at the end of March. Winnie travelled to London to pay her last respects to her friend, who had turned as yellow as a canary and died in the process. It was a damp, raw day. Winnie kept her baby bundled up in a shawl, warm against her chest.

The funeral was in Kennington. After it was over, she took the tram to Southwark and made her way to

Palmerston Road. She hadn't been back since the day she had fled, the previous summer. Curiosity drew her to it. Her fear had long since gone; having a baby had made it disappear. Nobody had told her how becoming a mother would change everything. Anxieties flew away, like a flock of starlings, and landed somewhere else; around her child, the only creature that mattered in the world, the hot, beating heart of her worries and her love.

Winnie entered the railway tunnel. The brickwork rumbled as a train passed overhead. She had forgotten how dank it was; drips falling from the ceiling, slime gleaming on the walls. The chalk-marks of Archie's goalpost had disappeared.

She emerged into the daylight. The side of the house loomed up, plastered with posters. 'Our Miss Gibbs' was playing at the Duke of York's. She would walk past, on the other side of the street, and see if she could glimpse a sign of life. Maybe Ralph would come out, to walk the dog. She missed him very much. He was such a sensitive boy; she worried about him. How had he been keeping? In her head, circumstances stayed the same as she had left them but she knew things would have changed. Ralph would be working in Mr Turk's shop by now. There would be a new maid in residence; how had she been coping with the lodgers' rooms? Could she support Mrs Turk through her emotional ups and downs? Did Mrs Turk like her better?

Winnie's heart beat faster. What if Alwyne came out of the front door? In her imagination she walked up to him, with a pitying smile, and showed him his child. No word of blame would pass her lips. The poor man had been unhinged by the war, and by now she had forgiven him.

In fact, she felt sorry for him. She would tell him this; she had prepared a little speech. She would tell him that *she* had a baby, and this was all that mattered. The poor man had no inkling of how it felt. *He* wouldn't see his daughter growing up.

Besides, he had been replaced by her dead fiancé. In the end, it had been surprisingly easy. As her time approached Winnie had simply told people that her baby's father had been killed in action. He was called Harold. Everyone in the village had believed in Harold and as time passed she had started to believe in him herself. Even her father seemed to think that in some funny way she had been doing her duty. War, it seemed, had its advantages. The world forgave a girl who had anticipated her marriage vows and given herself to a man who was leaving for the Front.

And she wasn't alone; several of the Swaffley girls had found themselves in the same predicament. One or two had bought themselves a wedding ring but that fooled nobody. Morals had been relaxed in these special circumstances and the odd thing was that Harold had become as real to Winnie as if he had really existed. It was Alwyne who had become irrelevant. That's what she would tell the man if he walked out of the door.

Actually, she would scarper.

Winnie had been standing for some time on the pavement opposite the house. Only now did it sink in that the building was empty. The shutters were closed. The parlour window pane was cracked. Nobody was home. In fact, it appeared as if nobody had been at home for some time. The house looked as neglected as Lord Elbourne's had been. Winnie, familiar with every inch, could almost feel the damp rising, the rot setting in.

Where was everybody? What had happened? Winnie hurried off. She cut down Mercer Street and emerged into the Southwark High Road. And there she met her second shock.

The butcher's shop was still there, but its sign had gone. TURK QUALITY BUTCHERS had been replaced by red gilt lettering: BROWN AND SONS. TOP-CLASS MEAT AND POULTRY. Winnie peered through the window. She recognised some of the men but none of them was Mr Turk, or indeed Ralph.

She went into the greengrocer's shop next door. To her relief Mr Bunting was still there, his neck still swollen with the goitre. He was cutting the outer leaves off a cabbage.

He nodded to her as if she had never been away. Nor did he notice the baby in her shawl. Perhaps he thought it was shopping.

'Where's Mr Turk gone?' Winnie asked.

'You not heard?' He paused, knife in mid-air.

Winnie shook her head.

'Dead, isn't he.'

'Dead?'

'Shot dead. Never found the man who did it.' He threw the cabbage on a heap. A customer appeared and he turned away to serve her.

Winnie's head reeled. She made her way out of the shop. How could Mr Turk be dead? Why would anyone do such a thing?

What had happened to Mrs Turk and Ralph? In a daze, she walked back to Palmerston Road. The house looked sinister now; it looked like a crime scene, like a place in which she had never lived. She averted her eyes. Hurrying past, she knocked on the door of number 39. Mrs Baines would know what had happened. She and Mrs Turk had always been on cordial terms.

An unknown man opened the door. He rubbed his eyes, as if he had been woken from sleep.

'Can I speak to Mrs Baines?' asked Winnie.

He shook his head. 'Passed away.'

Winnie asked when it had happened. The man spoke with enthusiasm.

'December. Caught the influenza. Went through the house like wildfire, six of 'em dead by morning.'

He was new to the area and knew nothing about number 45.

Clutching her baby, Winnie walked away. Perhaps they had all died of the flu, Mrs Turk and Ralph and the lodgers; perhaps it had ripped through their house like wildfire too. Murder, influenza . . . London seemed a more dangerous place than it had ever been in wartime.

Dusk was falling. Winnie walked towards the railway station. Suddenly she wanted to be home, safe in the stable yard. Things had improved there in the past three months. Lord Elbourne's house had been sold; the new owners were turning it into a boarding-school and had promised to keep on her father. He had taken the pledge and was learning motor car mechanics. The stables were to be converted into garages. And the two horses, who had been through four years of battle, who had seen things Winnie could never start to imagine, had been put out to grass.

Mr Turk, murdered. Who would do such a thing?

A dog padded up, wagging its tail.

306

'Brutus!' said Winnie, with surprise. 'What are you doing here?'

He looked older; she noticed grey hairs around his muzzle. Then she saw Lettie. The little girl was waiting outside the pub. Some things, at least, hadn't changed. Her matted pigtails hung down over her pinafore.

'Lettie, love!' Winnie kissed her. 'I'm that glad to see you. Where is everybody?'

'Gone.'

'They're not dead?'

Lettie shook her head. 'When Mr Turk was shot, Mrs Turk and Ralph went away.'

'Where did they go?'

'They gave us some money,' said Lettie. 'We've got lodgings in Mercer Street, I've got a bedroom all to myself.' She jerked her head at the frosted glass. 'My daddy's ever so pleased because he can spend it all in there. Mrs O'Malley took the cat. She's gone to live in Whitstable.'

'Does anyone know where they've gone? What about your mother, does she know?'

Lettie shook her head. She was gazing at the baby. 'What's it called?'

'Matilda.'

'I never knew you had a baby. Is that why you went away?'

Winnie nodded.

'Can I hold it?'

Winnie carefully passed the bundle over. Lettie looked into the baby's face. 'Its eyebrows are the same as his.'

'Whose?'

'Its daddy's.'

Winnie paused. 'Who's he, then?'

'Mr Flyte, of course.'

A coal lorry rumbled past. Winnie said: 'You knew?'

'Of course.' Lettie shrugged. 'I was going to ask for sixpence a week, not to tell.' She looked at Winnie. 'From both of you. But then you went away.'

Winnie paused for a moment, digesting this. 'And where's Mr Flyte gone?'

'The police took him.'

Winnie stared. 'The police? Why?'

'When they found out he wasn't blind,' said Lettie.

'Why would they do that?'

Lettie shrugged again.

'How did they find out?' asked Winnie.

'He told them.'

'Why?'

'I don't know,' Lettie said, suddenly bored. 'I don't know *everything*.'

Epilogue

1919

Emily Bild was alone in the house when the doorbell rang. For this she was grateful. Her mother had taken the tram-car into Manhattan, to go window-shopping; her father was at work, and it was Grace's day off.

Emily sat on the piano stool, revolving round and round. It was a breezy spring day; the nets billowed at the window. Outside, the cherry tree was in blossom. She pushed herself round with her foot. Sooner or later she should be tackling the Scarlatti. How lucky, then, that she prevaricated, for if she had been playing she wouldn't have heard the bell.

Emily went downstairs and opened the door. A woman stood there, accompanied by a young man. The woman stared at her.

'Goodness,' she said. 'We've found you.'

She was English – a tall, alluring woman, fashionably dressed in lilac.

The boy nudged her. 'Mother,' he murmured.

'I beg your pardon.' She put out her hand. 'I'm Mrs Turk, this is my son Ralph. We've been looking for you for weeks now.'

'Don't worry,' said her son. 'Not all the time.'

'I knew we'd find you in the end.'

Emily led them into the parlour.

'Would you like some tea?' she asked.

Mrs Turk shook her head and sat down. 'I'm sorry to barge in like this,' she said. 'All I knew was that your name was Emily and you lived in Brooklyn Heights and your father was a furrier. So I showed the photograph to people in the shops and in the end it was the grocer who recognised you. The grocer in Atlantic Avenue.'

'What photograph?' asked Emily.

Mrs Turk opened her handbag and took out an envelope. 'It's of you and Clarence,' she said.

There was a silence. Outside, the bells of the Episcopalian church chimed the hour.

Mrs Turk cleared her throat. 'May I ask – did he come back?'

Emily shook her head.

Mrs Turk gave her the envelope. Emily took out the photograph and looked at it.

'I'm so sorry,' said Mrs Turk.

Emily gazed at the faded image: herself and Clarence, standing outside the Astoria Hotel. Nobody spoke for a while.

'I thought you might want it,' said Mrs Turk.

'Yes,' said Emily. 'I do.'

'Seeing as it's got the two of you in it.'

Emily said: 'This is the only copy. I thought I'd never see it again.'

'I met Clarence in Brighton. He was ever such a nice young man. He told me wonderful things about New York, it made me want to see it. But mostly he talked about you. He loved you a great deal.'

Ralph turned to his mother. 'I think we should go.'

'No, wait.' Emily pulled out a handkerchief. 'I'll be all right in a minute.'

Ralph sat down.

Emily blew her nose. 'You came all this way to give me back my photograph?'

Ralph shook his head. 'We've come to live here.'

'My husband died, you see,' said Mrs Turk.

'I'm real sorry,' said Emily. 'What regiment was he in? I've been reading the papers, I've been learning them all. I knew so little, you see.'

'No regiment,' said Mrs Turk. 'He didn't serve in the war.' She stood up. 'Well, we mustn't be keeping you.'

She put out her hand, to shake Emily's. Then, on impulse, she put her arms around her and kissed her on the cheek.

Ralph smiled at Emily – a quick, shy smile – and then they were gone. Emily heard their footsteps crossing the parquet, and the click of the door. She couldn't even gather her wits to show them out.

The sun shone; upstairs, the canary sang in its cage. Emily sat there, her hands clasped together, looking at the photograph of her dead fiancé.

Acknowledgements

I'd like to thank Max Arthur, military historian, for his extraordinarily helpful reading of the manuscript which went beyond the bounds of friendship. Amongst the many books I read for research, his *Forgotten Voices of the Great War: A New History of WWI in the Words of the Men and Women Who Were There* (Ebury Press, 2003) was particularly inspirational, too, as was Richard Holmes's *Tommy: The British Soldier on the Western Front* (HarperPerennial, 2005), from which I've quoted for epigraphs to a couple of chapters and for which many thanks. Verses from 'From a Full Heart', from *The Sunny Side* by A. A. Milne © A. A. Milne 1921 reproduced with permission of Curtis Brown Group Ltd, London. Lines from 'To His love' from *Collected Poems* by Ivor Gurney, are reproduced with kind permission of Carcanet Press Limited. Lines from 'The Last Laugh' and from 'The Send-Off' by Wilfred Owen are reproduced by kind permission of the Random House Group. Others who have helped with their comments or by giving me information include The Imperial War Museum, Genista McIntosh, Tom and Lottie Moggach, Patricia Brent, Ruth Cowen, Alexandra Hough, Judy Taylor Hough, Geraldine Willson-Fraser, Sarah Garland, Simon Booker, Christopher Hampton and Sathnam Sanghera. Thanks also to my editor Alison Samuel, and my agents Rochelle Stevens and Jonathan Lloyd for their useful comments. Special thanks, too, to Matt Whitticase who bought Emily Bild her cameo role in the novel on behalf of Free Tibet. And finally, thanks to Nina Jaglom for the strange and wonderful conversation that started the whole thing off.

www.deborahmoggach.com
